I0613294

DEAD SILENT

Book Two, Marshall House Mysteries

By Tracy L. Ward

Willow Hill House

Ontario, Canada

DEAD SILENT

First Edition
ISBN-978-0-9881334-2-6
Copyright © 2013 by Tracy L. Ward

Cover Art Copyright © 2013
by Claudia McKinney
@ phatpuppyart.com

Edited by Lourdes Venard

Chapter Headings are linear excerpts from the poem "All Things Will Die" by Alfred Lord Tennyson (1809-1892)

DEAD SILENT

For my children,
without whom I would have nothing

DEAD SILENT

Chapter 1

Clearly the blue river chimes in its flowing
Under my eye;

December 1867

Peter Ainsley was anxious to get home, which only made the marathon train journey back to London all the more excruciating. He hadn't been able to think clearly since receiving news that his mother was reported missing. The telegraph said very little, which threatened Ainsley's sanity while his mind conjured all manner of possible scenarios.

Margaret, his sister, was very quiet. She spent the majority of the train ride suppressing tears and licking her lips, like she always did when she was nervous. Ainsley ventured to say very little, not wanting to cause her to lose her composure. However, when the telegraph had first arrived he could hardly stop talking. He must have examined the telegraph a hundred times, rereading each word carefully, trying to pull out any further information hidden within the letters. He used the same scrutiny he employed when performing autopsies, his own stubbornness refusing to accept there was no further clue. With bodies, there were always clues, but in this regard he was completely helpless.

Once at King's Cross, Ainsley hailed a hansom carriage, which proceeded unhurriedly through the congested streets of London to their family home in Belgravia. Ainsley shifted in his seat, half of his body practically hanging out of the carriage as they rolled along.

"Peter, please. You make me fret even more when you behave so." Beside him, Margaret gave a look of displeasure though he doubted she was displeased with him. Ainsley slipped into the middle of the bench seat, well enough away from the sides where he would be tempted to crane his neck to see if traffic was moving more swiftly.

"We have almost arrived," he said, as reassuringly as he could muster. He clasped his hands tightly in front of him, his grip so pronounced his knuckles turned white.

"Peter!" Margaret reproved him once more, drawing his attention to his tightly wrung hands.

He quickly loosened his grip and allowed his hands to slip to his sides. He had been fighting the urge to empty the contents of his flask the entire journey. Margaret would most assuredly disapprove. He fidgeted partly out of fear for his mother and partly because of the absence of drink.

"I'd wager he did it," Ainsley said all of a sudden, breaking the pattern of their near-silent journey.

"Who?"

Ainsley raised an eyebrow. "Father."

Margaret's shoulders sank. "You don't know that," she said, her voice lacking conviction.

Ainsley almost laughed at the suggestion. In his mind, his father, the one and only enemy their mother could have had, was the primary suspect. "Is it not odd that Mother takes a lover and then suddenly she goes missing?"

"We cannot think like that, Peter. Father could never do such a thing."

Ainsley slipped deeper into the cushioned seat. Any energy he would have normally had to argue was depleted thanks to their long journey. "Your faith in him astounds me," he muttered.

☙ ❧

The house looked like it always did, ramrod straight and daintily kept. The stone steps that led from the street were flanked by a wrought iron fence that was synonymous with their Belgravia neighbourhood. Two large iron urn planters framed the door but the bushes they held were lackluster in appearance, thanks to the increasingly absent December sun.

Despite his eagerness to get inside, Ainsley was careful to assist his sister from the carriage, offering a hand as she stepped down, and waiting while she climbed the four steps to their front door. The hansom driver clamoured from his perch and set about to dislodge their trunks and Margaret's valise from the rear of the carriage.

Billis, the family butler, appeared at the door within moments of their arrival and summoned the footman, Cutter, to assist the driver with the luggage.

"Oh, I have missed you, Billis," Margaret said as she stepped into the warmth of the house. She unclasped her cloak and turned slightly so he could take it from her shoulders.

Cloak draped over his arm, Billis gave the siblings a flourished bow. "Your absence has been hard on Lord Marshall."

Ainsley and Margaret exchanged knowing glances as they unburdened themselves from the heavy outer clothing required during the long journey from the northern townships. Margaret had been absent without permission and, as a matter of fact, so had Ainsley, but a young man of independent means was more or less free to explore as he wished. A young lady, however, a young *unmarried* lady, had no such leeway. She had not given much thought to her transgression, or its repercussions, not when their mother was missing.

"Is he severely cross?" Margaret ventured to ask.

Billis accepted Ainsley's jacket and held it by the inside collar. "No, Miss Margaret. He has other worries at present."

"Haven't they located her?" Ainsley asked, knowing Billis could be trusted above all others.

"No, my lord."

The last threads of hope slipped from Ainsley and Margaret's faces.

"His lordship is in a meeting with an inspector at present. I shall have your belongings laundered," he said, gesturing to their trunks, which flowed like a toy train into the foyer. "Shall I bring you tea in the drawing room?" he asked.

Ainsley nodded. "Thank you, Billis."

The pair, Margaret and Ainsley, made their way to the empty drawing room and stationed themselves in front of the fire to warm their tingling toes and fingers.

"I expect Father will be more cross with me than you,"

Ainsley said.

"How so?"

"You are one of the favourites."

"That's not true. He is very proud of you," Margaret answered. "I once heard him and Billis talking about all the work you do at the hospital."

"Oh truly? Why are such conversations hidden among the servants? He is ashamed of me. He'd rather I wasn't a surgeon. He wishes I were a man of business, or law or, God forbid, the clergy. A proud father would not forbid the hired help from admitting knowledge of my position." Ainsley could not hide his distaste.

Lord Marshall had been so disapproving of his second son's career choice that Peter had taken his mother's maiden name, Ainsley, to attend school and in effect assume another life. While working, he was Doctor Peter Ainsley, morgue surgeon. While among family and London's elite, he was Peter Marshall, second son to one of the wealthiest men in the English Empire, the Earl of Montcliff.

"Oh, that's just politics." Margaret waved her hand.

"Is that so—?" Ainsley's words were cut short when the door opposite them opened, and their father, Lord Abraham Marshall, entered from his study escorting a stocky gentleman. Ainsley watched as his normally composed father stopped suddenly, seeing the pair of them warming themselves by the fire. He bore a pained look accented by fatigue and resignation. It was not a side of his father that Ainsley had seen before.

"Father!" Margaret rose suddenly and greeted him. "Have they found her?"

Lord Marshall clasped her softly on her upper arms and gave a slight smile. "No," he said, in a defeated tone. He turned to the detective who stood behind him. "This gentleman has promised to do all he can."

Margaret turned to him and gave a slight curtsey in greeting.

"These are my two younger children, Peter, my second son," Lord Marshall gestured to Ainsley, who turned to look at his father but remained before the fire, his hands deep in his pockets. Before his father turned to introduce Margaret, Ainsley saw a sneer directed at him. He had been right. The old man harboured contempt and had not fully forgiven him for leaving on assignment with the hospital. No doubt he blamed Ainsley for Margaret's sudden and unauthorized departure as well.

"This is Detective Inspector Simms of Scotland Yard," Lord Marshall said by way of introduction.

Ainsley finally stepped forward, offering a hand of greeting.

"I appreciate your continued cooperation," Inspector Simms said, throwing a hand out to Ainsley in greeting. Inspector Simms shook Peter's hand firmly while looking him in the eye.

"Good evening, Inspector," Ainsley said, purposely avoiding his father's gaze. "We are most anxious to help, if we may." Margaret gave an emphatic nod of agreement when Ainsley looked to her.

"I have just been relaying your mother's and my last conversation," Lord Marshall explained.

Ainsley saw Margaret's eyes drop to the floor. He too remembered hearing of his parents' explosive episode. Inspector Simms saw her reaction as well.

"Have you travelled to The Briar in Tunbridge Wells?" Ainsley ventured to ask, hoping to save his sister closer scrutiny. Their mother spent the majority of her time at their country home, avoiding contact with her domineering husband and, from what Ainsley and Margaret had recently discovered, entertaining her lover away from the prying eyes of London society.

"I will go once I have exhausted all leads here," Inspector Simms explained.

"But she had been there this past week," Margaret said in protest. "She left the city the day before I left. If she has gone missing, the trail certainly starts there."

Lord Marshall gave a long exhale of breath. "No, my dear, the trail does not start there. Your mother was here for three days before leaving yesterday for Tunbridge Wells. She never arrived."

"She was here?" Margaret's voice cracked slightly as she spoke.

"Yes, and yesterday we quarreled." Lord Marshall sounded abashed while Ainsley felt somewhat vindicated.

Their family secret was finally out. "She left and I have not heard from her."

Ainsley and Margaret exchanged knowing glances. Inspector Simms raised an eyebrow at the exchange and jotted something down, an act that made Ainsley regret his unguarded reaction.

Lord Marshall must have seen it as well because suddenly he clasped his hands together loudly. "Well, Inspector, unless you have any more questions, my children have been away for some time and I'd like to spend some time with them before my meeting this evening."

"Actually, sir, I'd like to interview Margaret, if I may, seeing as she was one of the last family members to see Lady Marshall," Inspector Simms answered, indicating Margaret with a point of his pencil.

Ainsley saw Margaret's jaw clench. Lord Marshall pulled back his shoulders and slipped his hands into his trouser pockets. "Is that necessary? She has just returned from a long journey." Lord Marshall looked to his daughter sympathetically.

"Yes, sir. The sooner the better, else our trail goes cold."

Lord Marshall nodded reluctantly. "Margaret, my dear," he said, gesturing to the door he had just brought them through. "You may use my study for your interview." He forced a smile. "Peter and I will remain here, if you need us."

Margaret nodded, straightened her stance and led the way into her father's private room. The detective followed her as Lord Marshall and Ainsley looked on. They watched as Inspector Simms pulled the double doors closed.

"So Mother was here after I left?" Ainsley asked almost as soon as the door had closed. He stared at his father, giving no means of escape from his line of questioning.

"Yes," Lord Marshall breathed. "Her sudden arrival put our staff in a right tizzy as well. We had no idea we should expect her."

"Does she not send word ahead of her?" Ainsley asked, unsure of the protocol that ruled his parents' marriage.

"No, but I could always count on Violetta to send a note announcing their departure from The Briar," he explained. "This instance her note never arrived."

Next to Billis, Violetta was the only other servant the Marshall family employed since before Ainsley was born. Her loyalty, though strong, extended to Lady Charlotte Marshall alone, only being given to the children as needed and rarely ever to Lord Marshall himself. If she was known to send word it would be for the betterment of Lady Marshall, not the Belgravia staff.

Lord Marshall turned to a chair set before the fire and took a seat, exhaling loudly as if finally able to relax after a long day.

"Violetta is with her then?" Ainsley asked, seeing a glimmer of hope.

Lord Marshall shrugged. "Knowing your mother's character, anything is possible."

"But if Violetta is with her she may contact us, assure us of their safety."

Lord Marshall nodded. "That is my hope as well."

Ainsley took a seat across from his father, and was grateful for the aura of heat radiating from the fire in the fireplace. "Tell me about your last conversation," he pressed while sitting on the edge of his seat.

"Why must—?"

"Because it's important, Father!" Ainsley bellowed. As soon as he spoke he looked to the closed door where Margaret was with Inspector Simms. He turned back to his father with an internal note to keep his voice low. "I need to know what you argued about," he whispered. "There may be clues."

Lord Marshall shook his head and turned his gaze from his son. "I will not be scrutinized by my child on the particulars of my marriage," he said firmly.

"I will find the truth, Father. I always do."

"Then do so without compromising my dignity." Lord Marshall's tone was quiet and almost pleading. It was not a side of his father that Ainsley was used to seeing. Perhaps he was afraid of what Ainsley would uncover if given free rein to investigate. Ainsley smiled slightly at the thought. His father knew him well enough to know how resourceful and stubborn he was. He would know that Ainsley would not rest until answers were found, especially where his mother was concerned.

After a few moments of silence had passed between them, Lord Marshall looked to the closed doors of his study and shook his head. "Good God." He stood and walked to the armoire on the opposite wall to the fireplace.

Lord Marshall was almost Ainsley's height, tall and slim with a slight muscular bulk to his frame. His hair was nearly all grey, cut short and neat, and his complexion showed many years of ageing thanks to his preference for tobacco and drink. Despite all of the outward signs of age, Lord Marshall possessed a youthful dignity, distinguishing him from many of his peers in the House of Lords.

"Nervous?" Ainsley charged, watching from his chair as his father opened the glass doors of the armoire and took down his box of cigars.

"You know how women are," Lord Marshall said, snipping the end from his cigar. "Storytellers." Pulling a slender wooden stick from a porcelain vase on the mantel, he held it above the flames of the fire in the hearth and waited for it to light. He used the tiny flame to kindle the tobacco in his cigar before snuffing out the flame and replacing the stick, charred side up, among the others.

Ainsley shook his head as he watched the smoke spill from his father's mouth while he sucked in air through the cigar repeatedly to ensure it was lit. "Margaret is not a storyteller," Ainsley answered plainly, remembering how hard it had been for him and his brother Daniel to convince her to lie to their governess when they wanted her to believe they were sick. She could never do it. Her conscience was too strong.

Lord Marshall resumed his seat close to the fire, and propped his elbow on the arm of the chair to hold his cigar. "You have a lot to learn about the opposite sex, my boy." He pulled air through the cigar and then released the smoke into the room. "They are all storytellers. They will tell you it is raining when you clearly see the sun. They will tell you sad stories to crack open your heart before pouring acid in your veins and running the other way. They are deceptive with their stories. That is the way of the woman."

Lord Marshall's bitter words hit Ainsley like a sucker punch to the stomach. Until a few days ago, Ainsley would have dismissed his father's words of warning as the drink-induced ramblings of a shrewd businessman, but now Ainsley pondered his father's words, carefully. Ainsley had believed a woman, Lillian, and her tale of woe, and had been ready to commit himself to erroneous action had he not clued in, eventually, to her devious ways. She had nearly bewitched him, allowing him to abandon all scientific reason in favour of blind belief. She would forever be a reminder of how close he had come to his complete undoing.

"Ah, I can see by the pain in your face that I am right and you agree with me." Lord Marshall pointed his cigar toward his son.

Ainsley shrugged, forcing a frown. "I cannot say I disagree with you entirely."

Lord Marshall nodded, and allowed a smug smile to touch his lips.

Ainsley could not think of anything to say. His father had always been the bitter ogre in the family. Hollering when the children played too loudly. Barking orders when the servants neglected a minor detail. Bringing a dark gloom over any room he entered. Lord Marshall was feared by everyone but the family butler, Billis.

Ainsley crossed one leg over the other and leaned back into his seat, willing the conversation to continue so he could forget Lillian all together. His wish went ignored.

 Both men sat for a long time in silence, watching the flames lick the wood, twisting and turning as it searched for more fuel. The young doctor was not able to subdue the myriad of thoughts that rushed through his mind the way the flames rushed through the air and wood in front of him. A woman he nearly came to love was slowly dying in agony many miles away while his mother was missing, and could be dead as well.

Lord Marshall must have been thinking along the same lines because their silence was a strained one. After a time Lord Marshall spoke up in an inquisitive yet reprimanding tone. "I do not know how you live with yourself," he said, not bothering to look at his son. "Placing your hands inside the bodies of the recently dead."

Ainsley watched, expecting his father to shudder in repulsion, but he did not. The man was too dignified for that.

"Your profession exists because people die," Lord Marshall continued.

"Your profession exists because your great-grandfather gained favour with the King," Ainsley answered with a laugh. "Your wealth grew in the fields of Barbados under the shadows of hardworking slaves before you were a glimmer in Grandmother's eye. Indentured men work your fields now while you sit smugly in your chair smoking their spoils. I dare say my profession is a worthy profession, born of my own willing hands, whereas yours is one in which you hardly need to lift a finger." Ainsley shook his head and turned his attention back to the fire. "I would examine a hundred bodies before I considered making my living as you do."

Ainsley steeled himself for a rebuke. His father was not known for allowing his children, or anyone else, to express their opinion without his approval. It took a moment before Ainsley realized it would not come. Lord Marshall sat quietly, drawing from his cigar on one side of his mouth and then venting the smoke from the other side.

"And I suppose I should count my lucky stars that you are only the second born. Your brother Daniel does not see things as you do." Lord Marshall looked to his son, allowing what Ainsley thought to be a slight smile. "Grant me this wish, however," Lord Marshall began, straightening himself in his chair, "I ask you to keep up the ruse. While it pains me to not have you seek a proper living, one that I can boast about to my colleagues, I remind you that in this house, and while you are in the company of this family, you are Peter Marshall and nothing more. You can be Peter Ainsley to all others."

Ainsley smiled. "You mean, Doctor Peter Ainsley."

Chapter 2

*Warmly and broadly the south winds are blowing
Over the sky.*

Margaret led the detective into the study, unnerved by the thought of him watching her as she went ahead of him. She took a seat in her father's chair and was thankful for the large mahogany desk that separated her from her inquisitor. Inspector Simms walked to the window, notepad poised in his hand, and looked beyond the long velvet curtains to the street.

"This 'ere is a quiet street, Miss," he said. "Your family has lived here a long time." He did not ask. It was as if he already knew.

"Yes," she said. She swallowed hard as she crossed her ankles and interlaced her fingers on her lap. "We moved here when I was a little girl."

The detective nodded. "And you have all lived here. Together?"

"What do you mean?" Margaret asked, wondering if he heard the crack in her voice.

"Your parents. They live separately," Inspector Simms pressed. Sensing her hesitation, he turned to her squarely and explained. "It will help me understand the dynamic of the family. Everything you tell me will be held with the greatest of confidence."

Margaret saw Inspector Simms twist his mouth to the side. He looked as if the words meant less to him than they should have. She hesitated, not willing to confess just how strained her parents' marriage had been of late. The fact that her mother entertained a lover weighed heavily on her mind and the possibility of his involvement in her disappearance was ever present. "My parents spend the majority of their time apart," she confessed. "My father prefers the city house, my mother the country estate."

Inspector Simms nodded and walked from the window. He crossed the room and stood in front of a bookcase. With his hands clasped behind his back he leaned in close as though to read the spines.

"They love each other still," Margaret added quickly. "In their own way."

"Of course they do, Lady Marshall," Inspector Simms said with a slight smile. "Of course they do."

Margaret licked her lips.

"Your father mentioned that you left the city a few days ago to visit her in Tunbridge Wells," Inspector Simms said.

"Yes, I did."

"You went with a young man?" Again he spoke as if he already knew the answer.

"Yes."

"Can you give us his name. Lady Marshall?"

"His name is Dr. Davies, Jonas Davies. He is a dear friend... of my brother's."

The detective began scribbling something on his paper, an action which startled Margaret somewhat. "What is it, Lady Marshall? Would you like to change your response?" he asked, his pencil poised above the paper.

Margaret shook her head. "For what reason?" She shrugged in a vain attempt to show nonchalance. "He can verify my whereabouts."

"Why did you visit your family's country estate?" he asked, walking toward the desk. He loomed over her for a moment, before half sitting on the desk's edge.

Margaret's eyes fell involuntarily to the floor for a moment before she forced them back up. She didn't want anything in her words or actions to reveal she was hiding something. She would refuse to acknowledge her mother's affair. She had no wish to see the entire account in the society pages the next day. Detectives or not, there was no way she was going to reveal her family's darkest secrets unless necessary.

The thought made her stomach churn and she saw them then, in her mind, the memory rushing back in flashes and waves of recollection. Her mother naked in the fire light and that man's body on hers. Margaret tried to shake the thought from her mind but it would not go away. Once again, she heard her mother's laughter that next morning, and her complete denial of any indiscretion. Margaret could still feel the sting of her singsong dismissal and harsh teasing. And then Margaret remembered Jonas' arms about her, consoling her as she cried into his sweetly scented shirt.

"Miss Marshall?"

Margaret's attention was brought back to the present abruptly. "Yes, sir?" she asked meekly, aware that Inspector Simms stared at her unrelentingly.

"You looked ill for a moment. Are you all right?" he asked, with a genuine look of concern on his face.

"Yes, quite all right. Just tired. It's been a long day Are we almost done?"

"Just a few more questions if you don't mind," Inspector Simms said. "What made you visit the Briar?"

Margaret swallowed. "Am I not allowed to visit my mother?"

Dissatisfied with her answer, Simms pressed his lips together and moved on.

"How long did you stay in Tunbridge Wells?"

"One night."

"Why did you leave so suddenly?"

"I wanted to visit my brother, Peter, north of the city. He was... conducting business on behalf of Father. I had never been to any of the mill towns and wanted to see what they were like." Margaret shrugged and pouted slightly, as if it were no big deal. She wondered if he believed her.

"Did"—he scanned his notepad—"Dr. Davies accompany you there as well?"

"Yes."

"Was your mother not happy to see you?" he pressed.

"No... I mean yes, she was happy to see me...us, I mean." She saw his smile of amusement.

"Did your father give you permission to travel in Jonas Davies' company?"

Margaret fidgeted slightly in her chair "No, not exactly."

"Then why did you go with him? You are a young lady of good breeding. Why associate yourself with a doctor, of all trades." A smirk spread over his face. "There must be something you are not telling me. Something between you and this doctor?"

"I beg your pardon! What are you implying?" Margaret sat up straighter and flashed wide eyes at the inquisitive detective, who raised his hands defensively while releasing a slight laugh.

"Nothing, Lady Margaret, nothing. I am only asking questions."

Margaret swallowed hard and looked away briefly before turning back to the detective. "I asked him to accompany me because he is a dear family friend and—" Margaret stopped. She could scarcely reveal the true depth of her feelings.

"What is it?"

"And he had business with my brother as well," she lied.

Inspector Simms nodded and scribbled something on his notepad. "Your brother and this doctor had business dealings? Were you privy to what those might entail?"

"No," she replied. "I am only a woman." She nearly choked at her own words, as if betraying her entire sex. She needed to lie to cover the lie. She knew she needed to play the part.

"Quite right," the detective answered, folding his notepad with one quick movement.

"Is that all, *sir*?" She hated to say the word but courtesy required it of her. Margaret slipped from her chair and stood up in one graceful motion. Her hands still clasped in front of her, she looked at the detective standing on the other side of her father's desk.

"Just one more thing," Inspector Simms started, "When you saw your mother, was she behaving strangely?"

"What do you mean, Inspector?" Margaret worked hard to feign an air of ignorance.

"Was she acting like herself? Did anything happen out of the ordinary?"

Margaret let the room fall into silence as she pondered the detective's question. If he meant, did she see her mother coupling with a man not her husband, then yes, it was quite out of the ordinary.

"No, Inspector, I cannot recall anything strange at all."

She could feel his eyes burning into her as she stood in

front of him. She wondered if he could sense her falsehoods, her blatant lies. She did her best to remain stoic and unchanged but secretly feared she bore her betrayal on her face. The pair of them stood silent for a moment, Inspector Simms poking the inside of his mouth with his tongue, and Margaret twisting her fingers together behind her back to suppress her urge to have another outburst.

"Now, if you will excuse me, it's been a long day of travel and I am weary." She motioned for the door. "I suspect you wish to speak with Peter?"

Simms shook his head. "No ma'am, just you and Lord Marshall since you were the last family members to see her alive."

Margaret nodded, the gravity of his words sending a quiver to her lips. "Our butler will show you to the door," she managed to say. With two steps, she was able to pull the cord for the bell, summoning Billis to the study.

Simms nodded slightly just as Billis appeared at the door that led into the main floor hallway. "Thank you for your time and patience, Miss," Inspector Simms said before turning to the door.

Left alone at last, Margaret let out a deep exhale of breath and clutched her chest. Then suddenly she began to cry. Leaning into her father's desk for strength she gasped for breath and let the tears stream down her cheeks uncontrollably. Her mother was missing, most likely dead, and there was nothing she could do to help them find her. She wished she could tell them. She wished that her mother's transgressions did not have such a stain on every member of her family. Margaret knew she did not lie for her own sake, but for that of her brothers, Peter and Daniel, and most importantly for her father, who did not deserve the stigma of a wayward wife.

She cried for some time, holding her wrist to her mouth and nose to muffle her audible cries. She was not sure how long she stood there like that, but eventually the tears dried up and her gasps for breath subsided. She sniffled slightly as she straightened, dabbing her cheeks dry with the back of her hand. She pushed some loose strands of hair from her face and adjusted her skirt. Blinking, Margaret waited for her composure to return before leaving the room.

Chapter 3

One after another the white clouds are fleeting;

Ainsley climbed the main staircase, his legs weary from their long day of travel. As much as he wanted to retreat to his room, and the bottled comfort he had hidden there, he knew there was still much work to be done. He walked past his own door and marched instead for his mother's suite of rooms, situated at the back of the house. There was one entrance to her rooms, a single door framed with intricately carved molding, which opened into her sitting room. Ainsley stood in the doorway for a moment, his hands shoved in his pockets as he looked around.

It looked as it always did, impeccably tidy without a pillow or vase out of place. A gold striped sofa and settee took up the main portion of the room, a low table between them. A writing table was placed near the window, a collection of pens and ink silhouetted by the light coming in through the window. The rest of the room was adorned with mirrors, paintings and imported pottery from France. There were fresh arrangements of flowers and Ainsley could smell the lavender and rose oils the maids used to keep the linens smelling fresh.

Aside from the occasional visit by the household staff, his mother's chamber was scarcely visited and, even though he had been told she visited recently, her set of rooms gave no clue that anyone had walked across the threshold in weeks. Ainsley remembered his mother often describing how she felt like a stranger in her apartment, segregated from the rest of the house and hidden at the back. She had said her room and its darkness unnerved her like no other room. Even so, Ainsley could not recall a time when she had visited his father's room at the other end of the hall.

Ainsley walked in but stopped suddenly when he caught

sight of his reflection in one of the large, ornate mirrors. He looked tired and haggard, almost a decade older than when he left London the week before. He ran a hand through his dark hair in an attempt to tame it but the locks just fell back into their haphazard places. He hardly looked the part of an earl's son, barely resembling the man of fortune he had been raised to be. His clothes, though hand-tailored and fitted snugly to his broad shoulders and slender form, bore an unkempt look synonymous with extensive travel. He looked more like his colleagues at the hospital than he did a gentleman in London's high society. His profession was taking its toll, ageing him before he was ready and causing stress he had never known existed.

His mother's bedchamber was accessed by a door to the right and from there he could see her deep roll top bateau bathtub set against the window. No pipes, faucets or taps protruded from the bath and so it sat independently on the floor, swathed in the sun from the window.

His mother was particularly fond of warm baths in the evenings. Lord Marshall had spent a pretty penny procuring this model for her from Paris so now he refused to install the new gas-burning ones that many of their friends were rushing to buy. Such an inclusion would require a full renovation of Lady Marshall's rooms and since the countess scarcely lived there, he saw no need to see to her comfort in that regard. The housemaids were the ones required to fetch bucketful after bucketful of water from the kitchens and so it did not inconvenience Lord Marshall in the least.

Above the bath was an arched stained glass window installed a number of years before the Marshalls moved in. With red and green geometric shapes, the window was dominated by a large white lotus flower in the middle of the arch. Ainsley had often found Margaret in their mother's room, sitting cross-legged on the floor staring up at the colours and the way they sparkled in the light. It was such a pity the room was not used very much.

Ainsley heard someone walk into the sitting room and he turned abruptly. Margaret gave a forced smile as she peered at him from the doorway.

"Has the inspector gone?" he asked, walking back toward her with his hands shoved deep into his pockets.

"Yes," Margaret answered quietly. "He is gone."

"What did you tell him? Everything?"

Margaret shook her head. "No." She looked as if she would cry and Ainsley wondered, seeing the redness around her eyes, if she had already been crying. "How could I? It's too disgraceful," she explained.

Ainsley moved toward her but she dodged him, slipping further into Lady Marshall's bedchamber as she passed. When he rounded he saw Margaret opening the bureau drawers and shifting their mother's belongings from side to side.

"I do not trust him, Peter," she said as she rummaged. "He seemed so... condemnable." She spoke through gritted teeth, her choppy movements punctuating her anger.

Ainsley let out a breath and looked around the room. "He is only doing his job, nothing more." Enough detectives and police officers had come through the hospital that Ainsley felt at ease around them. Most of them seemed like amiable folk, though some appeared rougher than others.

"But Peter, it's just so invasive." Margaret did not stop taking her inventory as she spoke. She pulled each drawer out, one by one, and shuffled through everything inside before throwing it all back in and slamming the drawer shut.

"What do you expect to find?" Ainsley finally asked.

"Something, anything to tell me where she could be." Margaret marched into the bedchamber and began stripping down the quilts, blankets, and sheets from the mattress. With a few quick motions the once untouched room became a housekeeper's nightmare.

"I'll be damned if those policemen are going to find her with that man, doing God knows what." Margaret paused, wiping her forehead with the back of her hand. She surveyed the bedclothes before pulling them back up, not caring that they did not fall as neatly as before she had attacked them.

She turned to her mother's wardrobe and opened the double doors in one swift movement. "She has subjected this family to disgrace for long enough. I will find her and drag her back home by force if I have to." Margaret pulled two hatboxes down from the highest shelf and held them out to her brother. "Peter, take these."

Reluctantly, Ainsley walked toward her and accepted the parcels she presented to him. He laid them out on the bed and then Margaret was at his side with two more.

"I doubt she will have left a hidden note stating, *'I have run away with my lover and we are hidden here'*," he said.

Margaret acted as if she had not heard him. She flipped the lid of the hatbox closest to her. It was filled with embroidered handkerchiefs and an empty bottle of perfume from Paris. There was a tiny leather-bound book at the bottom of the box. Ainsley watched Margaret flip through the pages. From his spot, he could see it was a journal of some sort. For a moment, Margaret looked elated but her joy fell flat when the pages turned blank.

"She stopped writing in this two years ago," Margaret said, tossing the book back into the box. When her attention had turned to the next box Ainsley reached over and grabbed the journal, tucking it neatly into his inside breast pocket without his sister noticing. What he expected to find within its pages he did not know, but he wondered if something could be gleaned from the handwritten words of his mother, even if they were from two years before.

He turned his attention to Margaret just as she was pulling a green glass bottle from beneath a mound of lace gloves. There was no label on the bottle. Margaret held it delicately, and looked up at Ainsley.

Taking the bottle, he removed the cork stopper and raised it to his nose. "Laudanum," he said without a moment of hesitation. "Enough of my classmates were dependent on this stuff by the time we graduated. I can distinguish it at a distance."

"Dependent?"

Ainsley nodded. "Physicians prescribe it for a number of ailments; rheumatism, female complaints, and diarrhoea. It's quite common, though many are starting to see negative drawbacks. Some people can't stop using it once they've started. It's as if they can't function without it." He examined the bottle, which was smaller than the palm of his hand. "Remember when she fell down the stairs a few years back? Her ankle swelled up like a potato. She always complained her foot never felt the same."

Margaret unearthed three more bottles, slightly bigger than the first, from the same hatbox. They remained quiet while the bottles clinked daintily in Margaret's palms.

"Do you think Mother may be dependent?"

Ainsley shrugged, through his expression remained somber. "I suppose anything is possible. Suppose a physician recommended this to her, for the pain. Not only does it take away her pain but it makes her feel good, perhaps really good. Perhaps she won't stop, not for anything."

"You could make her stop. Tell her the pain is in her head. You could—" Her voice trailed away when Ainsley shook his head vehemently.

"Not if it takes her pain away. Pain cannot be measured. What could be excruciating to you may be a walk in the park for me. I could no more tell you that your pain is an illusion than you could tell me. Pain is very individual. Whatever ails Mother, I have to believe she needs this."

Margaret closed her eyes, as if trying to banish the thought. "I don't want to believe it."

Ainsley shook his head. "Do not rummage through other people's things if you don't want to find anything.' He began replacing all the box lids. He could feel Margaret's eyes on him, intensely staring, as if he held all the answers to the questions she had. As the older brother, he had always been expected to guide her, to tell her what she needed to know, but in this case he was just as lost as she. Never had he suspected their mother of being a regular laudanum user and he refused to believe it now.

"Where could she be, Peter?"

Ainsley could not meet his sister's gaze. "If what you say is true, if Mother has taken a lover—" Margaret's lips thinned into a defiant grimace. Ainsley raised a hand to calm her anger. "And I understand you saw what you saw, then she probably ran off with him and is still in the city somewhere."

"Doesn't she understand the pain she is causing?" Margaret asked.

Ainsley shrugged.

"Still think Father has something to do with it?" Margaret asked, her tone suggesting she had been vindicated.

Ainsley nearly laughed. "I wouldn't put it past him, if that's what you mean. Suppose he found out about Mother's affair, what do you imagine he would do?"

Margaret's shoulders slumped. "Peter, you can't mean that." Margaret's defiance faded away and her gaze shifted. "But Father would never—" her voice trailed off, her conviction lost.

"I hope I am wrong, but I have to entertain the possibility that I could be right." Ainsley stood then, and walked to Margaret. He planted a kiss on her forehead and squeezed her shoulder as he continued past.

"Peter?"

He turned at the door and looked to his sister, who sat on the edge of the bed.

"What are we supposed to do?" she asked quietly.

"We wait. Something will turn up. She will come to her senses or someone will find them out. But for now, we wait."

Margaret nodded, knowing his words to be true.

"Get some sleep, Margaret. And we will tackle this in the morning."

Ainsley left her, silent and staring at nothing in particular, and retreated to his room down the hall. The staff had brought his trunk to his room and everything had been unpacked, either sent to the laundry or placed in its proper location. His room, like his mother's, looked like it hadn't been inhabited in weeks. Everything was crisp and clean, nothing out of place.

He went straight to his bedside table, and opened the top drawer. He pulled out a glass tumbler and the small bottle of whiskey he had stored inside. Gulp after gulp he drank, only stopping to refill his empty glass. Soon his bottle was empty and his glass as well, but it did not matter. His task was accomplished. He did not shed one tear that night.

Chapter 4

Every heart this May morning in joyance is beating
Full merrily;

Breakfast was somber with only the occasional clinking of silverware on porcelain shattering the silence. Ainsley watched as Margaret picked at her food, eating very little, but chose not to say anything. His father too, usually so assured and arrogant, seemed humbled by his wife's disappearance. He didn't even touch the morning's paper that had been positioned beside his place setting at the table.

When Lord Marshall cleared his throat he startled both Ainsley and Margaret. "Peter, do you intend to head to the hospital this morning?" he asked.

Ainsley gave a quick glance to Margaret, unsure of what exactly their father wanted to hear. It was no secret that his father despised his chosen profession. Ainsley was not in a mood to argue yet again. "Yes, Father," Ainsley answered, somewhat defensively. "I will walk over after breakfast."

Ainsley saw Margaret pull her hands from the table and place them on her lap. She looked to her plate. It seemed she too was preparing for a fierce argument.

"Won't you take a carriage?" Lord Marshall asked. He reached for his teacup with one hand, and pulled his paper closer to him with the other.

No argument? No appeal to remain with family on such a day? Both men had fought relentlessly for months regarding Ainsley's new position at the hospital. Had Lord Marshall finally conceded? Dumbfounded, Ainsley hesitated and stared at his father, who simply raised his eyebrows as he looked at him over the raised teacup.

"No, I prefer the walk," was all Ainsley could muster.

Lord Marshall shrugged. "Very well." He placed his teacup on its saucer and finally opened his newspaper.

Ainsley looked to his sister across the table. Swallowing, she shook her head bewildered. She hadn't expected that response either.

"Your brother Daniel has bought a house in town," Lord Marshall continued, oblivious to his children's confusion. "You should stop by before you come home. Let him give you the grand tour. It's a lovely spot."

"I had not realized he was surveying the market," Ainsley answered.

"You've had other worries." Lord Marshall gave a forced smile.

Billis approached the breakfast table and began taking away the dishes, passing them to the footman, Cutter, who waited behind him with a trolley. Cutter looked like a pickpocket in comparison to Billis' refined aura of dignity. "Thank you, Billis."

"Of course, my lord." The butler gave a slight bow, and walked behind his master's chair to retrieve Ainsley's plate. Ainsley nodded in thanks.

"Your brother has been working hard," Lord Marshall continued.

Ainsley saw a slight smile tickle the corner of his father's lips as he spoke.

"He has much to tell you."

"Very well," Ainsley agreed. "I will stop by this afternoon. What is the address?"

"Oh," Lord Marshall snapped his fingers toward Billis and Cutter, who had nearly exited the room. "Billis, give Peter the address of Daniel's new house."

Billis bowed at the waist again. "Right away, sir."

Lord Marshall smiled, as if basking in the command he held over the household. "A good man, Billis is."

Margaret nodded, giving Ainsley a smirk across the table. "Yes, Father, he is."

Their father said this often and none of the Marshall children had ever been allowed to disagree with him. Once, when Ainsley was young, he tried to have the butler fired for laughing at him. He was playing a very silly game of some sort and when Billis entered the room he chuckled at the boy's antics. Indignant as young, privileged children often are, Ainsley called for his immediate dismissal. Lord

Marshall would not hear a word of it, and instructed Ainsley's nanny to give him a few switches once she had removed him to the nursery.

No one was allowed to disrespect Billis, at least not in front of Lord Marshall. The two men had been in each other's lives since they were young adults. Over the years Billis had become less of a servant and more of a confidant. He had known all of the children since birth and watched over them as if they were his own. There was a genuine camaraderie there, between Billis and Lord Marshall. Of all the servants, Lord Marshall trusted Billis the most.

"Absolutely, Father," Ainsley agreed warmly. "We are lucky he has stayed with us all these years."

In the hallway, as Ainsley put on his coat, Billis appeared with a folded piece of paper in his hand. "The address, sir."

Ainsley smiled, taking the paper and placing it in his jacket pocket. "Thank you, Billis."

"And where are you off to today, young Mister Marshall?" Billis asked as he straightened Peter's coat.

"Why the hospital, of course."

"The hospital? You are not ill are you, sir?"

Ainsley smiled. This had become a standard jest between the young man and family servant. Although not allowed to refer to Ainsley's occupation directly, they flirted with the idea and played it as an inside joke. "Not in the slightest."

Billis opened the door and Ainsley walked through to the cold London street. Momentarily pausing on the stoop, he pulled his jacket in tighter around his torso and buttoned his collar against the December cold. A thin layer of snow dusted the scenery and trace amounts still cascaded from the clouds.

His usual walk to work was short and that day it felt even shorter. Each female with chestnut hair reminded him of his mother. A governess holding the hand of a small child. The wife of a cobbler sweeping the front pavement to their storefront. A genteel lady walking arm in arm with a man in a beaver top hat. None of them was her, of course. Ainsley doubted his mother would remain so close to home, knowing everyone would be looking for her. If she had run away he knew she'd be far away in Brighton or Bristol, and not flaunting her new life for all of London to see. She was reckless, childish even, but not stupid. Knowing this did not stop his mind from filling in the details, and conjuring her everywhere he went.

Truth be told, he was worried for her. Worried for their family as a whole. His father was behaving strangely, far too accommodating and far less confrontational than Ainsley was used to. It felt as if a lot had changed during the time that he was away and as much as Ainsley complained about the way his father lorded over everyone and the way his parents always seemed to be at odds, he missed the predictability of it.

St. Thomas Hospital was brisk with activity by the time he arrived. He slipped by a huddle of nurses at the main doors who were no doubt taking the chance to imbibe a hidden drink or smoke a communal cigarette before heading out to mop up vomit or redress festering wounds. He did not envy their jobs and it was clear why no respectable girl stepped forward to fill them. They were often reformed prostitutes and showgirls. Very rarely did he meet one whom he did not suspect to have some sordid past.

Some watched him as he passed. He could sense their eyes following him and when he tipped his hat in greeting one seemed to swoon.

"What do ya t'ink?" he heard another sneer. "Ya t'ink he's gonna pay any mind ta ye?"

Ainsley did not turn to see who it was who had spoken but he heard nothing more as he walked through the hospital doors.

He was met by the unmistakable smell of decay and rot. In a distant room he could hear a man wailing, no doubt in agony over losing a limb or a finger or perhaps two. Or it might be gangrene seeping through his appendages, and oozing from a wound. Ainsley wondered how long it would take before someone doused the patient with laudanum just so the other patients could rest in relative peace. He headed for the main stairwell and stopped when he saw his school chum, Jonas Davies, walking toward him. Jonas was a surgeon as well, but the last thing Ainsley had heard was that Jonas had been relieved of his position at the university.

"Jonas?" Ainsley said as soon as he saw him.

Jonas was heading his way, surveying a stack of papers he held in his hands. When he looked up, he seemed much less surprised to see Ainsley than Ainsley had been to see him. "Good morning, Peter," he said, a smile touching the corners of his lips.

"What are you doing here?" Ainsley asked.

"I'm working under Dr. Lehmann, assisting him in surgery." Jonas seemed to beam as he spoke.

In the few days since he had last seen him, Jonas had secured a job with one of the hospital's most celebrated surgeons, and Ainsley had no doubt Jonas would quickly be one himself.

"Dr. Lehmann?" Ainsley could not hide his surprise.

Dr. Lehmann was a revered surgeon, nearly the top in London, which was amusing since he was an immigrant from Germany. Despite living in England for more than twenty years, he still held a thick German accent, a condition that annoyed doctors and patients who could not understand some of the things he said. His talent redeemed him, though, and had rapidly elevated him to his spot as head of surgery.

Ainsley had once envisioned himself as the surgeon's assistant and then full-fledged surgeon but his own methodology was far too slow. A surgeon needed to be quick, even at the cost of accuracy, both things Ainsley could not do. He was accurate to a fault and painfully slow, and that was why the morgue suited him best.

"We happened upon each other yesterday," Jonas explained, "when he was signaling a cab and I offered him mine. He remembered me from the reception at the Royal College of Physicians and Surgeons held a few months back."

Ainsley nodded, remembering the night and how he glowed arrogantly among his fellow graduates, who had yet to secure such a stable position as he. Perhaps he had always felt it would be that way, him rising to the top so easily, his parents' money and the confidence it gave him opening doors that would forever be closed to the other boys raised to be tradesmen.

Ainsley was unable to hide his discomfort at the idea

that Jonas' career could one day eclipse his own, and he scowled at the sheer luck that had found his friend. Jonas, on the other hand, seemed to relish the thought that he could be in a far superior position to Ainsley's before long. Their friendly competition from school had followed them into adulthood, only perhaps it wasn't so friendly anymore.

"And so he hired you?" Ainsley's mind was reeling and he could not hide his shock. "Hiring an assistant sight unseen?"

"Don't be so arrogant," Jonas said sharply. "You are not the only one who comes highly recommended."

Ainsley shrugged, preparing to apologize but nothing came. He opened his mouth and closed it again.

"Apology accepted," Jonas said, presuming the words that failed his friend. "Your mother, has she returned yet?" he asked, wisely changing the subject.

"No," Ainsley answered. "How did you know she was missing?"

"An inspector showed up at my door last night. He asked about my affiliations with your family." Jonas' face turned solemn. "Wondered how someone in my trade could associate with an earl's family." Jonas slipped a hand into his pocket, coyly touching the corner of his mouth with his tongue. He was trying to make it seem like he was unaffected by the insinuation, Ainsley realized. "He wanted to know the circumstances by which we met."

Ainsley swallowed nervously. He had been successful in keeping his two lives separate for nearly four years, acting the part of gentleman's son or acclaimed morgue surgeon as circumstances dictated. Jonas was his only bridge between the two lives he led and he realized for the first time that his mother's disappearance could be the undoing of it all.

Ainsley looked about the hospital hall, noticing a porter at the farthest end sitting at a small desk and one nurse just beside him. Neither one was close enough to hear their conversation. "And what did you tell him?" he asked, turning his attention back to Jonas.

"I told him it was doctor-patient privilege and left it at that."

"Did he ask anything else?" Ainsley could feel his mouth

go dry.

"He asked about Margaret, and I said she had come to me, knowing I was your friend, and asked for my help—"

"Which you were more than happy to oblige," Ainsley inserted.

Jonas pressed his lips together and tilted his head slightly to the side. "I did it out of concern for your family, Peter. My feelings for Margaret came after."

Ainsley nodded. "Of course," he said.

"I am only telling you this so you are aware. He is suspicious of your family. He said he believed Margaret to be holding back something and—"

"Jonas, you did not tell him what happened in Tunbridge Wells, about mother...did you?" Ainsley pointed a ridged finger at his friend. His temper surprising even him.

"No, of course not," Jonas hissed in return.

Ainsley lowered his hand and glanced around them again. The hall was becoming busy with people and they would need to be more guarded.

"Peter, I am well aware of the possible scandal," Jonas whispered. "I may be a commoner but I know what this would do to you, to all of you."

"We are counting on your discretion," Ainsley said, with a forced smiled. He waved to a porter who worked in the morgue with him as he passed them. As he turned back to Jonas, he saw Dr. Crawford, with his disapproving superior walk, come through the double doors. Ainsley gave Jonas a reassuring pat on the upper arm. "Thank you, my friend. I knew we could." Ainsley began to walk away, heading away from Dr. Crawford.

"Peter, we should talk," Jonas called to his friend as he walked away.

Ainsley turned but continued to walk backward. "We will. Come by the morgue sometime."

Ainsley slipped down the back stairs, hoping Crawford had not seen him. He could not avoid him for the rest of the day but he certainly did not want his friend to be witness to the inevitable reprimand.

The stairway grew dark as he descended, and there was a marked chill in the air though the smell remained the same. The morgue and accompanying offices were tucked away at the back of the hospital, making sure to be far enough removed from visiting family members and female nurses. Only surgeons, medical students, male porters, and families of the deceased were allowed so far back.

Ainsley passed the porter's reception table that regulated admittance, tapping a knuckle on the desk as he passed. The porter, Frisker, looked up and his gaze followed Ainsley as he walked by.

"Good day, Dr. Ainsley," he called after him.

"Good morning, Frisker." Ainsley had heard the scraping of the dry wooden chair on the floor and knew the porter had stood and was now shadowing him down the hall.

"Anyone wake up while I was gone?" Ainsley asked, knowing Frisker to be a serious fellow and not at all inclined to jovial speech.

"No, sir," he answered with due seriousness. Frisker was a coloured man who spoke in an indistinguishable accent that Ainsley imagined to be from Barbados or somewhere else in the West Indies. He walked one pace behind Ainsley as he made his way toward the morgue examination room.

Ainsley paused at the doors, turning slightly to face him. "Can you tell Dr. Crawford that I do not wish to be disturbed?"

Frisker nodded. "If you think he will listen, sir."

"It's worth a shot."

"Shall I take your jacket and hat, sir?" Frisker asked, offering both hands.

Ainsley nodded. He slipped his arms from his jacket sleeves and allowed Frisker to take it by the collar before he tipped his hat from his head. "You are a fine dresser, if you don't mind me saying, sir."

Ainsley nodded his thanks and pushed through the extra wide door into his work area.

The bodies laid out on the tables were different than the ones there when he left. Those bodies had by now been processed and released by other surgeons in his absence. This new stock of corpses, covered by thin sheets of off-white and stained cloth, was lined up systematically, parallel to each other in a specific order. A single sheet of paper sat beneath the heel of each dead body, identifying it.

Ainsley sighed as he walked down the aisle between the

bodies. London never seemed to have a shortage of them and he could rest assured that he would always have employment. He went straight for his workspace at the back wall, where large windows, though slightly grimy from the soot and dust of the city, illuminated his space. He stopped briefly to examine his tools, saws, forceps, clamps and scalpels, seeing they were clean and placed where they should be. Being there made him eager to return to work, to busy himself so he didn't have to think about home or his mother.

He reached for his leather apron, hanging from a hook next to the window, and turned just as the door in the adjoining room opened. He craned his neck and his eyes strained to see past the bright light above him to the dim light beyond. He saw Frisker and another porter bringing in a stretcher. They weaved, almost effortlessly, through the maze of bodies and stopped in front of him. Two others entered the room but Ainsley did not notice. He saw the stretcher, a thin sheet over another body, and an unmistakable, fresh bloodstain on the sheet just above what would be the midsection of the body.

The two porters hoisted the stretcher onto the table. Frisker gave Ainsley an apologetic look and retreated with the other porter without a word. Ainsley saw Crawford then, and he understood Frisker's silent apology.

"Dr. Ainsley, this is an important case," Dr. Crawford said authoritatively.

"Aren't they all, Dr. Crawford?" Ainsley asked, his tone showing he was more annoyed than usual. Ainsley was not at all interested in getting into details about his trip to the north and the murders he had witnessed there. Ainsley looked to the dark figure behind the senior doctor and recognized Inspector Simms instantly. Ainsley's mouth immediately grew dry and his hands began to shake. Ainsley shifted slightly away in an effort to compose himself and worried that Inspector Simms had recognized him as Peter Marshall.

Dr. Crawford either did not notice, or he decided to ignore Ainsley's strange behaviour. "This here is believed to be Lady Charlotte Marshall, wife to house representative Lord Abraham Marshall."

Ainsley turned, not caring whether the inspector recognized him. He stared at the sheet-covered body and the reddish-brown blotch that stained its midsection.

"It cannot be," Ainsley said quietly.

"Oh, yeah?" Dr. Crawford sneered, "And how would you know?" He slapped some sheets of papers onto Ainsley's chest.

Ainsley grasped for them before they all cascaded to the floor but his grip was loose.

"Take care with her, Ainsley, and tell this man, Inspector Simms, all you find."

Ainsley swallowed hard and tried to hide a shiver that traced up his spine.

Dr. Crawford glanced to the body in front of them and crossed himself with his hand. When he turned to leave the room he called out over his shoulder. "Dr. Ainsley is my best man, Inspector. She is in good hands."

Ainsley struggled for air and used the edge of the examination table to hold himself up.

"Are you going to be all right, doctor?" Inspector Simms asked, stepping forward. He held his hands together in front of him.

Ainsley nodded. "Just give me a moment," he said, unsure. Even in that dim light Simms should have recognized him.

"Perhaps we should arrange for another doctor to examine the body," Inspector Simms continued, "considering your relationship to the deceased."

Ainsley looked up slowly.

"I had wondered why Dr. Jonas was described as a good friend. Now I see." Inspector Simms walked around the examination table and surveyed the arrangement of tools with a self-satisfied grin. "What an odd profession for someone of your station."

Ainsley did not move as Inspector Simms took in his array of tools and workspace. Ainsley simply stared at the covered body in front of him, not willing to believe it could be the body of his mother. "Where did you find her?" Ainsley asked, almost choking on his words.

"In a rooming house. The matron said she had arrived with a man a few days before and no one had seen her go in or out of her room for a couple of days." Inspector Simms spoke matter-of-factly, but then, as if suddenly remembering who he was speaking to, he softened his tone. "They checked in the day your mother was supposed to be travelling back to Tunbridge Wells."

Ainsley nodded at all of this. "How did she die?"

Inspector Simms came to the foot of the table and locked to Ainsley. "Stab wound to the stomach."

It took a moment for Ainsley to steel himself against the horror that struck him. The image of his mother dying alone in a letted room, no doubt bleeding for some time, writhing in pain, before finally succumbing, seemed almost too much to bear. His sorrow was diluted by his love for his profession and his ability to shut off all emotion as he worked on body after body throughout his daily life. Ainsley reached for the cloth, preparing to pull it down.

Inspector Simms grabbed his wrist and stopped him. "Perhaps we should have someone else do this," he said, looking Ainsley squarely in the eye.

"Who better to do it?" Ainsley asked.

Once Simms released his wrist, Ainsley pulled down the sheet to the woman's shoulders. He bowed his head and once again braced himself on the edge of the table. The silent tears came like waves, uncontrolled and unending as he hid his face from view. With the back of his hand to his mouth, Ainsley cried all the tears he had held back the night before and all the tears he had wanted to cry while on his way home. He did not care that Inspector Simms saw him. He wept for his mother and the fact that this woman who lay dead in front of him was not her.

Inspector Simms moved to cover the body but Ainsley raised a hand to stop him.

"It's not her," Ainsley said in a gasp. "It's not her." He breathed in deeply, pushing the tears back and composing himself.

Inspector Simms looked to the body, almost in doubt of what Ainsley had told him. "She fits the description," he said, reaching for his notepad in his inside pocket.

"I agree, but it is not her." Ainsley looked over the woman's features once more. The woman in front of him did have brown hair, though it was not as thick and wavy as his mother's was. Her skin was not nearly as pale, and he also noticed, now that he was able to see without fear, that this woman was much shorter, slimmer, and younger than his mother. In all other respects, it did indeed look like Charlotte Marshall. He knew it was not his mother but anyone who did not know her would not see those differences as easily.

Inspector Simms let out a long breath and replaced his notepad to his inside pocket. "Your being here has saved me the embarrassment of contacting your family."

Ainsley said nothing at this. His torment had saved his family from the same.

The detective looked at the dead woman contemplatively. "If you don't mind making her a priority, I would be much obliged. We have no idea who this woman is."

Ainsley nodded. "Absolutely."

Simms shook his head, as if in disbelief. "Such a shame."

He turned to leave but Ainsley called him back. "Inspector Simms, you won't tell anyone, will you?"

Ainsley watched as the detective stared. "We should share drinks," he said, neither confirming nor allaying Ainsley's biggest fear. The detective was gone a few moments later, the door closing loudly as he left.

ᘏ ᘋ

Her body was not quite as bloody as he was used to. When Ainsley opened her, she was pink but not red, as she ought to have been. He examined her wound first, noting the depth and type of cut that was made. It was a single thrust, he determined, and he imagined, as he looked over her, that the assailant had pulled away suddenly. He either wanted to watch her flail or he was surprised at his actions.

When Ainsley cut into her skin and then pulled back the layers of muscle he saw that her stomach was punctured and had bled out slowly. Ainsley silently wished he could have visited her at the site of death. He could have seen where she fell and how. He could have judged, by the amount of blood on the floor, how long she had lingered before dying.

She was cold, and no longer stiff. She would have died

the evening before, or perhaps prior, given those clues. Ainsley could not help identify who she was, though; that was Simms' job. He would tell the detective that the woman was over twenty, perhaps twenty-five. Within a few moments he could determine if she had ever bore a child, but not whether that child was still living, or in her care.

When his examination was done, he replaced all of her organs and sewed her up as best he could, using a thick, black thread. Just as he tied off the last stitch Frisker walked in, his arms loaded with folded, cleaned sheets. They were still near grey with yellow circular blotches showing on the folds. Frisker nodded slightly, acknowledging the doctor before walking past him and placing the sheets in a nearby cupboard.

"I am just about done," Ainsley said over his shoulder to the porter.

Ainsley stood at the white porcelain sink near the cupboard and turned on the water. He washed his hands, scrubbing up and down his arms all the way to his elbows. Then he grabbed the small square of soap, made by one of the nurses upstairs looking for some extra money to her regular wages.

"Would you rather I washed the body, sir?" Frisker asked, his head bent low as he spoke. "Save you the trouble."

Ainsley smiled. "Thank you, Frisker. You can help me bring over another one. Let's see if I can make Dr. Crawford not hate me so much."

Ainsley walked back toward the body and pulled the sheet from her feet to just below her chin.

"Oh no, sir," Frisker said approaching the examination table. "He does not hate you sir. Every day while you were gone he asked if you had returned."

Ainsley let out a slight laugh. "Angered with me, no doubt."

"No, anxious for you to return. He said you are his best surgeon."

Ainsley stopped and stared at the old porter. "He said that?"

Frisker nodded.

"Well, I'll be...." Ainsley's mouth contorted into a smile.

"Thank you, Frisker. You have made my day."

Chapter 5

Yet all things must die.

Margaret began to fidget, her needlepoint lay on her lap neglected, and soon the grandfather clock grew to annoy her immensely. She had changed her seat innumerable times that morning, and found no break from her anxiety. She desperately wanted to leave the house and search for her mother. She would have liked to knock on every door in the city, and would be doing so had her father not forbade her. She had thought to visit close friends and family but when she suggested it he scowled and grew angry.

"Would you like to take out an advertisement as well?" he yelled, "Tell everyone I cannot suppress my own wife?" He was right in his own way, though Margaret hated to admit it.

It simply was not fair that Peter had a vocation with which to occupy himself whilst she sat in wait with her nails bitten to the quick and loose strands of thread picked from her clothing.

Her last change of seat brought her next to the window in the drawing room, which overlooked the back garden. In her quest to forget that her mother was gone and she was helpless to find her, Margaret had already traced the perimeter of every stone in the walkway and counted each plank of wood that made up the stout fence. There were no flowers or foliage to see, though the holly bush stood out crisply against its grey surroundings. Christmas was in a few weeks' time and she would have to gather some sprigs soon from that bush, though it pained her every time she did it. She'd make a wreath for the front door and perhaps use some laurel and other greenery to make a centerpiece for the holidays.

Oh please, Margaret, she chided herself, as if your projects matter in comparison! She knew it to be true. If her mother turned up dead she'd be even more angered with herself. But then again what else was there for her to do?

Perhaps her mother was at a friend's house, stopped there to break her journey or for company. The country house could be rather lonely, especially at that time of year. But which friends remained, she wondered, when the parties and gatherings ended months ago? Who would stay in the city?

Margaret stood suddenly, remembering her mother's dearest friend, Lady Gemma Brant, who made her home in Chelsea. Margaret was at the door and nearly through when her father walked in from the other side of the room.

"Where can you be off too?" he asked.

Margaret turned, twisting her hands in front of her. His voice was brash, and it reminded Margaret of when her father had been drinking. She glanced to the clock and saw that it was barely dinnertime.

"Come sit a while with your Papa."

"I was otherwise engaged in a task," she said, hoping he would not press further.

"I imagine it can wait." He patted the back cushion of a chair while he stood behind it.

Margaret hesitated for a moment, pondering an argument they would have if she disobeyed him. She would need to leave the house at some point and angering him would not serve her well then. She relented, crossed back toward him and took a seat in the chair that he indicated. He sat opposite her.

She could smell his whiskey-tainted breath from a few feet away and saw how his mood had changed since she had last seen him at breakfast. He had been tucked away in his study all morning, not seeing to business as she had supposed, but drinking.

"What is it, Father?" she asked lightly.

He raised an eyebrow in her direction and she knew he meant it as a warning. "What did you tell the inspector?" he asked in a monotone.

His question surprised her, as he had been the one to encourage her to speak with him in the first place, and had allowed her to do so alone.

"I don't know what you mean," she answered, unsure

whether it would anger him or not.

"You should take care, daughter, for your reputation," he said. "It will do no one any good to have your honour tarnished publicly."

"My honour?"

"Yes, Margaret, I have not forgotten that you left without my blessing, with the last man whom I'd approve as your escort."

Margaret bowed her head, accepting her part in the misadventure. "Jonas is a good man." Her voice was quiet and queer, lacking the conviction she displayed when speaking with her brother about Jonas. She heard her father laugh slightly but chose to ignore it. It would do no good to anger him further, not when she could smell the whiskey as if he had bathed in it.

They sat in silence for a long while, Margaret letting her eyes move over the room and Lord Marshall trailing his fingers along the fabric of the arm of the chair. When Margaret finally looked at him she saw his jaw clenched.

"You find yourself attached to him to spite me?" he asked.

Margaret shook her head. "Of course not. I was thinking rashly. I knew you would not allow me to leave."

"What kind of father do you believe I am?" he hollered.

Margaret swallowed, her heart rate quickening. "Father, you have been drinking," she dared to say. "Perhaps we should have this conversation another time?" She winced slightly against a forthcoming rebuke.

Instead, her father let out a long breath, suddenly relaxing his shoulders, and then nodded. "Tell Billis I am in my rooms." He left with a defeated air, taking slow steps across the room and into the hall.

With him gone, Margaret allowed herself a full breath and closed her eyes. It was a long while before her heart rate returned to normal.

∽ ∽

Margaret was shown to a room that would have been the parlour in any ordinary house, but she was quickly reminded that she was not in an ordinary house. The parlour of Lady Gemma Brant's house was more of a museum of sorts, a laboratory of human remains and embalmed body parts on display. As Margaret walked in she was struck by the collection of various-sized jars, each holding preserved items in cloudy green liquid. There were foetuses and severed hands, a dissected ear canal and a cross-sectioned skull with the brain perfectly intact.

Margaret saw how quickly the housekeeper, who had led her in, retreated to the foyer, saying her mistress would meet her shortly. The tall slender door was closed, confining Margaret to the room of medical horrors, marvels to her brother, who had visited there often during their formative years. Lady Gemma Brant was a friend of their mother's and she had brought her children there for tea many times. Peter often credited his interest in science to all he learned and observed while eating jam on crumpets and lacing his Earl Grey with gobs of sugar at Lady Brant's house. He relished the display cases, the jars, and the artwork.

Margaret found an interest in them as well, though she was never quite as comfortable around the specimens as he was. It did not help that the collection always seemed to change between visits. Lady Brant would add new pieces as she discovered and perfected her technique, or rearrange the specimens like a shopkeeper would rearrange their window display. Her laboratory was in another room, hidden from view, but her specimens, her gems of science, were put on display for everyone who dared to visit.

Margaret could hardly look away. Her eyes were drawn to the plumpness of the arteries and the clean white of exposed bone. Lady Brant was meticulous in her work, which blurred the lines between works of science and works of art.

"I've had offers from the czar of Russia, you know," Lady Brant said from behind Margaret as she bent over for a closer look.

"For this piece?" Margaret asked. She was looking at a hand, severed at the mid-forearm. It was not in water or formaldehyde but it was dry in a rectangular display case. The skin, hardened to dark leather, had been slit and pulled back to reveal the pink muscles and lily-white bones beneath. The skin curled and the veins looked plump despite a complete absence of blood or fluid.

"For the whole collection," Lady Brant explained.

Margaret could hear the anxiety in her voice and turned.

"How will I ever part with it?" Lady Brant asked, without expecting a reply.

"Has he offered a large sum?" Margaret asked.

"Oh, yes," Lady Brant chuckled, "not that I have much use for it. But I fear I am running out of room, even after a quarter of it was sent to Denmark last summer. It will be hard to see them go." She laughed as she glanced around the room, her hands folded demurely in front of her. "Listen to me, cooing as if they were my children." She motioned to a settee near the window. "Please sit. I have not seen you in ages, my dear."

Margaret went to where her host indicated and they both sat simultaneously.

"How is your mother?" Lady Brant asked, "I fear it has been too long since we last corresponded. Does she still spend most of her time in the country?"

Margaret saw her smile and winced. She hadn't the fortitude to tell her.

"Margaret dear, what is it? Nothing terrible, I hope?"

"No one knows where she is," Margaret confessed.

"What can you mean, no one know where she is?" Lady Brant leaned forward in her chair and furrowed her brow deeply.

"She and Father quarreled, or at least I think they did, and she left for the country house but never arrived. No one has seen her in three days."

Lady Brant put a hand to her chest. "Oh, Margaret, my dear." And then the look on her face changed from shock to acceptance, a reaction Margaret had not expected.

"What? What is it? Tell me Lady Brant, for I am dying inside. I had hoped she was here with you, knowing how close the two of you are, but I see you had not heard from her in some time. If you know anything, you must tell me."

Lady Brant swallowed and avoided Margaret's gaze.

"I fear she may be dead," Margaret said, unable to control her anxiety.

Lady Brant shook her head and clicked her tongue. "Oh,

I highly doubt that, my dear. A woman like your mother is not one to fall prey so easily. Most likely she is hidden somewhere."

"But why?" Margaret asked.

"I'm sure your mother has good reason, even if we cannot fathom what it is." Their eyes finally met and Lady Brant's face was as solemn as Margaret's was tense.

"I cannot accept that," Margaret said, leaning forward in her seat slightly.

Lady Brant shook her head and shrugged. "I confess I have no more information than you. It is as much a mystery to me."

"Had I not seen your shock with my own eyes I would believe you were assisting her in some way. You would tell me if you had spoken with her, wouldn't you?"

Lady Brant gave a slight smile, as if she were laughing at Margaret in her distraught state. "Of course," she answered softly. The look on Margaret's face must have been doubtful, for Lady Brant spoke again, attempting a more convincing tone. "I may agree with her right to freedom but I do not condone the manner in which she seeks it. Look at how it affects you, my dear." She clicked her tongue in the pitying sort of way one does with a child. "Why, any mother should be ashamed to cause her children such upheaval."

"And my father, does he deserve such treatment?" Margaret asked, knowing already what Lady Brant's answer would be. It was no secret Lord Marshall and Lady Brant had been at odds for as long as Margaret could recall. As a child, their quips and jabs at special dinners and parties had seemed playful and familiar but as she grew Margaret noticed a deep-seated strain in their relationship that tainted the air of any room they were in together and forced everyone to tread lightly.

"Your father does not need sympathy from me. He's such a proud man—"

"But do you think he deserves to be abandoned by his wife?" Margaret pressed.

Lady Brant sat silent for a moment, her eyes still and her shoulders straight. "I cannot tell what I believe he deserves. It would not be charitable." She shifted in her seat, tucking some folds of her dress beneath her thigh before making

DEAD SILENT

eye contact with Margaret again. "Your father is more than capable of feeling sorry for himself."

Margaret wondered what her mother's friend meant but said nothing. The room had grown uncomfortable and it was not something Margaret dared to pursue. In many ways, Margaret was still the child, expected to be seen and not heard, though it vexed her greatly that she did not feel comfortable saying how she truly felt.

"You think I am unfair," Lady Brant said after a long pause.

Margaret shook her head slightly and forced a cordial smile. "No, Lady Brant," Margaret answered quickly. "I think you are a woman who speaks her mind."

Lady Brant smiled and leaned forward to take Margaret's hand. "It was very brave of you to come. Have you visited any others?" Lady Brant patted Margaret's hand soothingly.

Margaret shook her head. "No. I spoke with an inspector from Scotland Yard just last night."

"Scotland Yard!" Lady Brant dropped Margaret's hand. "Oh dear, why did he go and summon them? They are thieves—"

"Reformed thieves," Margaret corrected. She had wanted to say they were not all criminals but stopped short, not seeing the point in the debate it would bring.

Lady Brant shook her finger in disapproval. "No such creature exists. Oh, count on your father to be so selfish. I can just imagine the social pages."

"Father said he would keep it confidential. He has no desire for a scandal any more than you or I."

"So he says."

Margaret watched as Lady Brant rose, clutching her stomach as she paced the room, pushing her hair from her face with her free hand.

"I will pay a visit to my friend at the paper and tell them Charlotte has decided to take a holiday, near the coast—"

"In December?" Margaret looked doubtful. She bit her lower lip.

"Quite right. I shall say her cousin, who lives in Edinburgh, has fallen ill and she has gone to nurse her." Lady Brant smiled, pleased with her creative explanation. "That ought to hold the vultures at bay. And in the meantime, I will hire a private enquiry agent, which is what your father should have done, and go to her to verify she is in good health." Lady Brant gave a short but loud inhale and smiled. "I will not force her to come home, mind you, but I will enquire about her whereabouts, if only to set your minds at ease."

"Do you think it best to concoct such stories?" Margaret asked, trying to resist the knot that grew in the pit of her stomach.

Lady Brant shrugged. "I do not see the harm. They will print what we say or they will create their own version. Besides, it's a more favourable version than running off with her lover."

Margaret started, sitting up straighter and throwing her hands to the cushions beside her. "What did you just say?" she asked, her voice cracking.

Lady Brant paused momentarily before speaking, "That is what they are going to say. Well-to-do women who leave their husbands do so often. If we give them our version they won't dare make up such lies."

"That is not how you said it," Margaret pressed. "You spoke as if you knew she had a lover."

"Did I?"

"Yes." Margaret suddenly grew impatient. "You do not have to hide the fact from me. I saw them, Mother and her lover, in Tunbridge Wells. Nothing you tell me will come as a shock."

Lady Brant smiled and turned away. "I doubt that very much, my dear."

Margaret watched as Lady Brant walked to the farthest end of the room. She held her hand to her stomach again as she fingered a brass balance set up on a desk. Books sat next to it, and an array of weights was nearby.

"How long?" Margaret asked, her voice commanding and defiant.

"What, dear?" Lady Brant feigned ignorance.

Margaret left the sofa and marched the length of the room. Child or not, she was not leaving without satisfactory answers. "How long has she had a lover?"

Lady Brant unfolded a pair of round spectacles and positioned them on her nose. She reached for a book, avoiding Margaret's intense scrutiny. "I apologize, my dear, I am very busy. I have said too much."

"I'm not leaving," Margaret answered. "Not until you tell me who he is and where I may find him."

Book in hand, Lady Brant began to walk away but stopped two paces from Margaret. She turned. "I do not know his name," she answered quietly. "I have never met him. All I know is that he has made your mother happy like no other." Margaret's gaze met hers and she saw the sincerity in Lady Brant's eyes.

"Unlike my father."

Lady Brant did not need to answer.

"How long have you known?" Margaret asked.

"Two years," Lady Brant answered. "Had I known how truly unhappy she was before, I would have encouraged her to do it sooner."

Margaret felt her throat grow dry and she found herself wincing from the pain of it all. Unable to forget the words that Lady Brant had spoken, Margaret suddenly made for the door. "Thank you, Lady Brant," she said quickly, "for your hospitality."

"Margaret!" Lady Brant called after her but Margaret was struggling for air and needed to be outside. The room, nay, the entire house was suffocatingly warm, all of a sudden. Lady Brant's housemaid appeared at the door, Margaret's cloak in her hands.

Lady Brant met them in the foyer. "There is an exhibition at the hospital, a public dissection, in a week. I thought perhaps you would like to go since you have shown interest in my work."

Margaret nodded absentmindedly as she turned to allow the maid to place the cloak over her shoulders.

"You will come?" Lady Brant implored.

Swallowing hard, Margaret looked up, hoping her tears were not so noticeable. "I will come," she choked.

Chapter 6

The stream will cease to flow;
The wind will cease to blow;

Ainsley left the hospital, wondering if the group of nurses he had encountered earlier would be outside the front doors again. His disappointment surprised him and then he saw Inspector Simms a little farther down, seated on a bench placed against the hospital wall. Ainsley slowed his pace as he approached and wondered if the detective was waiting for him in particular. When Inspector Simms looked right at him, Ainsley received his answer.

"I sent a messenger with your report," Ainsley said when he was closer.

"Very good, but I've been out of the office all day." The detective motioned for the public house across the street. "Care to join me?"

The pub, a primitive and rowdy place, was busy thanks to the evening hour but Ainsley and Simms were still able to find seats near the back wall. Within minutes, they both had a pint of ale in front of them. Ainsley watched as Inspector Simms pulled out a small cigarette case from his inside jacket pocket. He offered one to Ainsley, who politely refused with a shake of his head.

"I thought all doctors smoked?" Simms asked between pressed lips, the brown-papered cigarette moving with the words he spoke.

"Most do," Ainsley answered. "It's a great service in school to have at least one or two students smoking during a dissection."

Simms struck a match and lit the end of his cigarette. "But not you."

"Mother would never abide by it. The smell bothers her."

Simms nodded and pulled the cigarette from his mouth and held it between his index and middle finger as his hand rested on the tabletop. "My wife hates the smell too." He blew the smoke from his nose and laughed.

"Why did your family not tell me you were a surgeon?" Simms asked.

"Father would prefer I wasn't in any profession. My work at the hospital is only permissible because I agreed to work under the name Ainsley, mother's maiden name." Ainsley shifted nervously, glancing to the tables around them. "I cannot emphasize enough how important your discretion is with this. My father would love nothing more than for me to be relieved of my position."

Simms raised an eyebrow. "You think it would cost you your position at the hospital?"

"Most certainly. Dr. Crawford constantly reminds us that we are mere labourers, a dime a dozen, as there are so many wishing to enter surgical medicine as a way to advance social status. I doubt he would want me working under him if he knew I outranked him in breeding and society."

"You are unkind," Simms said, drawing his mug of ale to his mouth.

"I am kinder than most, I am afraid."

"And arrogant."

Ainsley contemplated this. "Perhaps." Ainsley took a drink of his ale, muscling it down and willing himself to ignore the musky odour. He decided he much preferred a whiskey or brandy. Even wine would taste better than the watered-down alcohol that filled his mug.

"I have no desire to expose your secret," Simms said at last.

Ainsley smiled but his elation was short-lived.

"I will not protect it, however, especially if it begins to interfere with my investigations."

"Fair enough," Ainsley answered with a nod.

Simms blew smoke into the air above them. "Had I known this secret earlier I would have never brought the girl to St. Thomas."

Ainsley felt a shiver run down his spine, remembering the feeling he had while looking over the shrouded body thought to be his mother. He suddenly was very thankful to have Inspector Simms on his side, someone in the field with whom he could share his secret.

"I will do everything I can," Simms continued, "to help find your mother, but I must admit, my trail has run cold."

Ainsley nodded, suspecting as much. He knew if the detective were not permitted to enquire with friends and extended family, there would be little else he could find. "My father has tied your hands," Ainsley said, eyeing his drink. He loathed taking another sip of the putrid ale, though he had never needed a drink more.

"Your sister, Margaret, does she know of your chosen profession?" Simms asked.

Peter leaned back into his chair and crossed his arms. "Of course."

"I only ask because she seemed rather put out yesterday when I questioned her."

"You'll have to forgive us. We are not often questioned by the police." Ainsley laughed nervously, his arrogance unchecked.

"Of course," Simms conceded. "It's only... I am afraid I rattled her some during my questioning. I would have expected someone of her nature to be more honest and forthcoming."

"Do you suspect my sister was anything but honest?" Ainsley asked incredulously.

Inspector Simms avoided Ainsley's stare while he placed the cigarette to his mouth. "Yes, as a matter of fact, I do," he answered. He lifted his eyes, meeting Ainsley's squarely. "I am going to try to help you, but you and your family need to start being honest with me."

There was a silence between them for some time. Ainsley swallowed, and stared at the liquid in his mug.

"Judging by your silence, I believe I have hit the nail on the head, as they say."

Ainsley shook his head. "Quite the opposite, actually. I believe it is my right to protect the interests of my family. My sister has yet to marry, my brother as well. How do you feel it will reflect on them to have our family so closely scrutinized?"

"How will they feel to learn their mother died because we could not get to her in time?" Simms raised an eyebrow.

Ainsley looked away, his mind caught in a fishnet of

emotions, not knowing which way to turn. His mother was gallivanting, most likely with her lover in some seaside village, not caring for the turmoil she left in her absence. He had pitied her once, while he journeyed back to London, believing she had befallen some horrible end most likely at the hands of his father, but now he saved his pity for no one, and realized both man and wife had a part to play. The real victims would be Daniel and Margaret, whose place in proper society would be tarnished permanently.

The pub was busy given the evening hour and the below-seasonal temperature outside. The barmaid weaved carefully through the crowd, protecting her tray with her free hand. Ainsley watched, unwittingly, as she moved through a cluster of inebriated customers. And then Ainsley noticed one of the women who was a part of the group she served. Was that his mother? She smiled at him and Ainsley meant to call her name but the barmaid blocked his view as she approached them. The young doctor stood up suddenly and walked passed the barmaid, mindful of her tray.

The crowd seemed to swell, filling in his previous line of sight. It was her. He knew it had been. He walked the floor, squeezing between hard-pressed bodies, and surveyed each table in turn. If she had been there he could not see her anymore. He turned in place, searching the room for her.

"What is it, Dr. Ainsley?"

Ainsley turned at the sound of his name and realized he was back at the table where he had left Inspector Simms.

"My apologies, sir," Ainsley said.

"You thought you saw her?"

Ainsley gave him a look of surprise, wondering how the officer could have known what it was he thought he saw. "You said 'Mother'," Simms explained. "Just now."

"Did I?"

Simms nodded.

Ainsley reached into his pocket and pulled out some shillings, laying them on the table for the barmaid. "I must take my leave," Ainsley said, eyeing the mug of ale and wondering if he should bother downing the last mouthful. In the end, he decided against it.

"One last thing, Dr. Ainsley," Simms said, before Ainsley

could turn. "Would you mind meeting me tomorrow morning?" he asked. "I'd like you to see where we found the body of the woman I brought you today." Simms looked at him in earnest, his hand resting on the tabletop, the cigarette letting off a thin ribbon of smoke into the air.

Ainsley raised an eyebrow, impressed at the detective's ability to read his thoughts from earlier. He had to admit this was not his expertise, but the challenge enticed him all the same. It could certainly bring new light to the circumstances leading to the woman's death. He felt a slight smile on his lips as he thought over the prospect.

"Just meet me at the boardinghouse in the morning," Simms said with a slight chuckle.

"All right then. See you in the morning. Have a good evening, sir." Ainsley shook the detective's hand firmly before plucking his hat from the table and turning to leave.

∂‍ ⊰

There was a marked chill in the air that evening, enough to cause clouds of breath to hover in front of Ainsley's face when he exhaled. He pulled his collar higher up on his neck and tied his scarf in an effort to keep out the cold. It was the first night he had considered taking a carriage, if only to cocoon him from the wind and get him to his destination that much quicker. But then the young doctor thought better of it. There would be colder days to come and he would rarely get a chance to walk when they did. His brother's new address was only a few blocks away, once he crossed the bridge.

As he walked he kept his face to the ground and his shoulders hunched against the wind. He did not notice a couple, a man and a woman tightly clinging to each other, crossing the bridge and walking toward him. He finally heard their footsteps as they approached and lifted his gaze. He moved to the side when they were just a few paces from him to let them pass and heard the woman laugh.

Mother.

He stopped to study them as they passed. The woman's happy expression fell when her eyes met his. Recognition perhaps?

"Mother, wait!" he called out. He reached for her shoulder and she turned before he touched her. It was not her. Nor did it look anything like her. This woman's hair was curly and red whereas his mother's was warm brown. Her face was far too freckled as well, enough so that Ainsley wondered how he could have thought there was a resemblance at all.

"My apologies, ma'am," he said humbly.

Thankfully, the couple turned, no doubt laughing at his confusion, and the man did not take offence to Ainsley reaching for his partner. Ainsley saw his mother three more times during his walk, each time believing the face he saw was more real than the last, but of course it was never her. Like the dead child who had appeared to him numerous times while he was in the north, taunting him daily for not having found her killer, Lady Charlotte Marshall appeared briefly each time and then was gone, leaving him to wonder if he had taken complete leave of his senses.

By the time he arrived at his brother's new home, Ainsley was chilled both inside and out, suddenly aware of the foreboding nature of the darkened city at night. He was surprised when his own brother, Lord Daniel Marshall, heir to their father's earldom, opened the door, not a servant or butler in sight.

"Hello, Daniel," Ainsley said, a slight smile on his face. Daniel was taller than Ainsley, though not by much, and his hair was just the slightest touch more brown compared to Ainsley's near-black hair Despite those two close similarities, everything else about them was entirely different. Where Ainsley had a strong, angular jaw and dark blue eyes, Daniel had brown eyes and softer features that he hid behind a precisely trimmed handlebar moustache.

Despite his subtle features, Daniel's demeanor was that much more resolute and defined, a sharp contrast to Ainsley's constant philosophical questioning, as if never convinced he had found the answers he sought. Life seemed so much simpler for Daniel, the eldest son and heir to their family's large fortune. Everything had been laid out for him and so, Ainsley thought, it was only natural that his brother should be so definitive in mood and action. His brother was also more arrogant than the self-assured

51

Ainsley and it pleased him to see Daniel humbled enough to answer his own door.

"Have you added butler to your curriculum vitae?" Ainsley asked.

"Your attempt at humour is duly noted, though I am not amused." Daniel stepped aside, allowing Ainsley to exit the damp, biting cold. Ainsley laughed slightly to himself as he removed his coat and adjusted the collar of his jacket. "I had to let my butler go," Daniel explained. "He...was not to be trusted, it seems. Especially in these times of trial." Daniel gave Ainsley a strained look and Ainsley knew what he meant.

"Any word of Mother?" Ainsley asked, wondering who would receive word first, his brother, who was no longer living in the family home, or Ainsley, who was so often absent from it he might as well be.

Daniel shook his head. "No. I had hoped you would bring news."

"I have been at the hospital all day," Ainsley confessed. "I haven't even stopped home."

Ainsley thought he saw the hint of a sneer on his brother's face at the mention of the hospital where he worked. Both his brother and father saw eye to eye in regard to Ainsley's profession, neither one caring to hide their contempt.

"It would appear that the man I hired caught wind of our family's troubles and I heard him on the stoop at the servant's entrance speaking with the men from the coal company." Ainsley could hear the stress and strain in the way his brother spoke, angered and yet resigned. "I fear it will not be a private family matter for long."

"Father was amiss when he believed he could keep this a secret," Ainsley said. He hung up his own coat, saving his brother the indignity. "My bet is half of London has heard of it, and the other half will have by sunup, and not because of the indiscretion of your hired man."

"Even so," Daniel said with a long, drawn-out exhale, "I could not keep him on if he cannot prove his loyalty."

"Perhaps Father will let you borrow Billis to help you search," Ainsley suggested.

"I doubt Father would part with him any more than I

could see Billis separated from that house. He's just as reliable as the furniture."

Ainsley took a moment to survey the foyer, his gaze rising with the cathedral ceiling and then tracing the curved mahogany bannister back down. The walls, painted canary yellow, were bare except for white mouldings and flourishes. The large crystal chandelier just above their heads looked an entire storey high and half as wide. The marble floor they stood on gleamed with perfection, only a handful of people having walked on its surface since it was laid. It was clear Daniel had just moved in, and had barely a stick of furniture to his name.

"Construction is still being done," Daniel said apologetically. "Upstairs mostly but the lower floors are complete. Evelyn picked the flooring and the wall colour."

"Evelyn?"

"Yes, of course," Daniel looked at him incredulously. "Didn't Father tell you?"

Ainsley surmised what was to be said next and did not wait for his brother to explain. "You are to be married," Ainsley said. "I had not realized you were on the market for a house and now I see you were on the market for a wife as well."

"What better reason to buy a house?" his brother asked with a slight shrug.

"What better reason to run for the hills!" Ainsley said, only half in jest. "And Father approves of this?"

Daniel laughed and began leading his younger brother to one of the rooms off the hall, his hard-heeled boots thudding on the floor with a marked timing. "He was the one who suggested it."

Ainsley followed, his hands clasped behind his back. "Lord help you both," he muttered. He could no more imagine his brother a dutiful husband than he could imagine himself in that role. Thankfully, though, his brother did not hear his disparaging remark.

Daniel had led Ainsley into what would most likely end up as the parlour, the formal room to receive and entertain guests. Though not as spacious as the parlour at the family home in Belgravia, Ainsley could tell that this room, with its gas sconces and marble fireplace, would awe many who entered. There was a single wingback chair and a delicately upholstered sofa, both of matching velvet cloth, arranged in the center of the room. A small table was placed between them in front of the massive fireplace, a gold clock displayed prominently on the mantel. With due time, that room would swell with belongings, wedding gifts, and acquisitions in the first years of marriage, all displayed for visitors as if they were a material representation of the couple's success. Ainsley had to suppress a groan when the thought reached him.

"I have to admit, I wasn't keen at first," Daniel explained, "but—"

A figure appeared at the door from which they had just walked and when Ainsley turned he saw it was a woman, slight and poised, blonde and pale. "Daniel, what colour did I say for the paper in your room—? Oh, my apologies, I did not realize you were entertaining." She raised a hand to her chest and smiled.

As Evelyn walked across the room to greet them formally, Daniel leaned in to Ainsley and whispered in his ear, "She does not know about Mother and I'd like to keep it that way for now." Ainsley nodded, wondering how he had become ensnared in their first marital secret. Ainsley assumed any talk of his true profession was meant to be kept off of the table as well. Keeping an even smile on his face, Ainsley turned to the woman approaching them.

"This is my brother, Peter, and I hardly need to entertain him," Daniel explained. "Peter, this is Evelyn Weatherall."

When Evelyn reached Ainsley she held her hand in front of her, which Ainsley took and raised to his lips.

"My, you resemble your father!" Evelyn said of Ainsley. "It's like looking at a living portrait from his youth. Don't you agree, Daniel?" Evelyn kept her gaze on Ainsley as he gave a sideways glance to Daniel, wondering why he had been spared the curse of such a claim.

"Very much so," Daniel agreed, with a slight laugh, "Though I doubt Peter wishes for such a comparison."

"Oh," Evelyn again raised her hand to her chest, "do forgive me. I meant no harm."

"Of course not," Ainsley answered. "You may come to any conclusions you wish. I hear that you are to become my sister. Allow me to congratulate you both." All of Ainsley's previous disapproval vanished as he spoke. He began to see Evelyn, sweet and demure, as a young woman entitled to a bit of marital fantasy before heading to the church. "I am sure you will both find due happiness."

Evelyn blushed crimson. "The announcement in the papers has resulted in many congratulations. And Mother has been beside herself preparing the engagement dinner."

Ainsley smiled on the outside but inside he wondered at the timing of it all. Had Evelyn known of the lack of success between her fiance's parents, would she be so willing to enter into matrimony with him? Perhaps. If Evelyn was apprised of their mother's disappearance would she be so enthusiastic about entering into the family? Ainsley thought not. Nonetheless, Ainsley dared not say anything, whatever Daniel's reasons were for keeping it from her.

"Sounds lovely," Ainsley said with formality.

He must have looked dubious because Daniel cleared his throat and looked uneasy for the first time since Ainsley had arrived. "Are you heading home then?" Daniel asked.

Evelyn looked to the doorway and that is when Ainsley first noticed her lady's maid standing just beyond the threshold, with what appeared to be her mistress' cape in her hands. "Yes, shortly," Evelyn admitted. "I'm afraid I have worn out Esmie." She gestured to her maid. "She has been rather spoiled in my father's house. She is not used to such late nights."

Daniel sighed. "You pay too much heed to the demands of servants," he said with a slight laugh. "They are employed because of our demands, we should not cater to theirs."

Evelyn laughed, and slapped him playfully. Daniel himself looked quite impressed at his own remark but Ainsley could not help but sneer. No wonder his brother could not garner loyalty from his staff; he showed them none in return.

Ainsley and Daniel walked Evelyn to the hallway.

"There is still much to be done," Evelyn said, turning in place to allow her maid to lay her cape on her shoulders. Evelyn clasped the brass button on the front herself as her maid adjusted the shoulders. "I am meeting the seamstress in the morning to choose draperies and I was wondering which paper colour we had decided on for the master chamber."

Daniel didn't bother to give the question any thought. He simply shrugged. "I cannot say," he answered quickly. "I am sure you will choose well."

Evelyn's smile faded slightly as she took in his indifference. "Very well," she said, "I will simply reorder more if they are the wrong shade."

Ainsley noted a hint of challenge in her voice, but his brother paid no heed.

"If you think it best," he answered absently.

Evelyn stared at Daniel for a few minutes, blinking but otherwise not moving. Ainsley thought perhaps she was realizing the true nature of the man she had agreed to marry. It was as if the vision she held for her future had just changed with those sentences he had uttered.

"Will I see you in the morrow?" she asked, returning to her previous cheerful disposition.

"No, I should think not," Daniel answered. "I have a committee meeting to attend at the House and I shall be gone all day. The housekeeper, Miss Penny, will let you in."

"If she hears my knock," Evelyn said almost under her breath.

"Then you shall have to knock harder," Daniel nearly hissed.

Ainsley felt as if he were witness to some act of indecency. Evelyn's maid looked uneasy as well at the forced exchange between the betrothed pair. It was never a good sign when things began with such stress and strain and yet here they were, fighting as if it weren't a fight at all.

"It was nice to meet you, Peter," Evelyn said, giving him a nod and genuine smile.

"And you as well," Ainsley answered with a deeper bow than he would normally give.

Daniel opened the door for both fiancée and maid, and the two brothers stood in the relative warmth of the uninhabited house while the women stepped out into the misty night to the carriage that waited at the kerb.

With the women gone, Ainsley turned to his brother, who was already quickly retreating to the parlour.

"Is an engagement party wise?" Ainsley asked, hurrying to catch up to Daniel. "Given the circumstances."

"The invitations had already been delivered," Daniel said, his tone markedly angry. "Father wishes to keep things business as usual." Once in the parlour, Daniel headed straight for the liquor cabinet, a decanter of wine and four empty crystal glasses arranged next to it. Without a moment's hesitation, Daniel poured two glasses. Daniel grimaced as he handed one to his brother. "I have never known you to refuse a drink, brother."

Ainsley took it, sipping gingerly while his brother downed the glass in one gulp. He quickly filled his glass again.

"Why do you keep it from her?" Ainsley asked.

"Do you expect me to air all of our family laundry?" Daniel asked. He shook his head. "She will find out when the time comes."

"When she is married and the law is not on her side," Ainsley said with a hint of bitterness. A girl such as Evelyn did not deserve a fate such as his brother. She seemed sweet enough, too sweet to be paired with the likes of him.

"When has the law ever sided with women?" Daniel asked, eyeing his wine. "You will quickly learn, brother, what is not freely given to a man, a man can freely take. If I choose to keep my fiancée in the dark about our mother's deplorable behaviour that is my prerogative. I am sure she has a few skeletons of her own."

Ainsley looked to the door, as if able to see Evelyn there once more. "And if she doesn't? If she is just a pawn in your and Father's grand political scheme?"

"It will be regrettable but not insurmountable. Whose side are you on, Peter?" Daniel asked, refilling his glass once more.

Ainsley paused for a moment, thinking over his brother's question. He had once been feverishly on Mother's side, defending her as if his life depended on it. He felt she had been harshly treated by his father and was given no choice but to remain at the country estate. It did not help that his father was equally harsh on Ainsley, demanding him to give up his medical studies numerous times and threatening to cut him off from any inheritance. Ainsley had scoffed at him then, determined that none of his threats could put a chink in his armour. If his mother could defy their father, then so could he, Ainsley reasoned. And so a fierce battle ensued where the pair would not speak for weeks at a time. Both were determined to win.

And then Margaret discovered that their mother had a lover. She had used the country house as their hideaway until Margaret arrived unannounced, catching them in the very act. It was horrible for Margaret and doubly so for Ainsley, who had once revered their mother as if she were a saint. Confused and bewildered, Ainsley had no firm understanding of who was in the wrong; his father, who berated his mother and drove her from him, or his mother, who sought refuge illegally in the arms of another man.

"I don't take sides," Ainsley said after much thought.

Daniel laughed, heartily and deep. "It is not my fault Mother could not keep chaste for Father's sake. Had she not run off like a harlot I wouldn't need to break trust with Evelyn now, would I?"

Ainsley winced at his brother's choice of words. "No need for mudslinging," he said, aghast. "Mother is not a harlot."

"No?" Daniel seemed surprised at Ainsley's defense of their mother. "What would you call it then?"

"A woman injured and alone, seeking a small measurement of happiness."

"In the arms of another man?"

"How sure are you that Father has not done it to Mother?" Ainsley asked. "In all the years they've spent apart, he never had a mistress? I'm told all in the House of Lords indulge themselves regularly. We have enough whorehouses in London to prove my point." Ainsley took a large gulp of his wine, thankful the taste was a mite bit better than the ale at the pub.

Daniel looked genuinely annoyed. "If he did, and I am not convinced he has, then the law is on his side to do so. A woman is to be loyal and virtuous."

"And a man is to be wanton and a brute?"

"If he needs to be."

Ainsley regarded his brother steadily. He was on his fourth glass and Ainsley could tell he was loosening under its effects. After the day he had had, and the newfound fears he held for the safety of their mother, he was in no mood for contentious debate on any issue, especially if he was to fight with an unreasonable man.

"And if something has happened to Mother?" Ainsley asked, almost against his will. He knew he should leave but could not stop himself from asking this question. "Would Mother deserve such an end?"

"With the way she has behaved, scandalously and with no care for the family name, I say good riddance. Father is better off without worrying about her loyalty."

Ainsley swallowed, biting his tongue to prevent any forthcoming outburst. It was clear his brother saw their mother, and all women for that matter, as objects to be controlled by force and coercion. Any deviation from his expectation cut them off entirely.

"You, brother, need to stop defending her," Daniel continued, pointing one finger at Ainsley while the rest clutched his crystal glass. "Your approval gives her strength to continue her horrific behaviour."

"She doesn't need my strength. She has more than enough of her own," Ainsley said through clenched teeth, willing himself to remain calm though every cell within him wanted to halt his brother's tirade.

"If she were my wife I would have put her in her place a long time—"

"Is that what Evelyn has to look forward to?" Ainsley asked, his voice becoming loud. "Regular beatings by the one who is supposed to protect her?"

Daniel smiled crookedly. "If need be."

"Good God!" Ainsley no longer bothered to hide his disgust. "Father has done an injustice to you, raising you to be—"

"A man! Which is more than I can say for you." Daniel laughed too loudly, the wine making him self-righteous. "Mother has made you soft."

Perhaps Daniel was right, at least in part. Ainsley had noticed a distinct difference between himself and the rest of his medical school classmates, who were all against women in the medical field, saying they were weak and not suited to such tragic work. Ainsley knew better. Margaret had seen him in his morgue, watched him work on the bodies of children even, and never made a peep. She had not vomited, as many of those would-be surgeons did on their first day in the operating theatre. If she were an example of female fortitude then women could be just as tough as men. Daniel, however, had not seen this side of Margaret; in fact, no one else in the family knew and so he still bought into their father's belief that women were inferior.

"Mother has made me human," Ainsley said after a pause.

Daniel sneered and it was in that moment that Ainsley realized why he had chosen to take his mother's maiden name for his profession. He could have easily made up a name, chosen one from a thousand common names in England. It was clear Ainsley identified more with his mother than his father. Perhaps secretly he wished Lord Marshall were just a man his mother had married, and were not his father at all. Maybe that was why he and his brother were so different.

"I can see you are quite busy," Ainsley said at last, glancing over the empty room and the now-empty wine decanter. Ainsley placed his glass on the table next to the decanter.

"Thank you for stopping by, brother," Daniel said, taking another sip from his glass. His tone denoted a marked unease between them.

A few minutes later Ainsley was pulling his collar up over his neck and huddling against the biting night wind. He was sickened by the words exchanged between his brother and himself, and even the long, cold walk home was not enough to shake his feeling of unease.

Chapter 7

The clouds will cease to fleet;
The heart will cease to beat;

By the time Ainsley arrived at Ms. Bell's boardinghouse the next morning, Inspector Simms was already waiting for him on the front stoop. Ainsley noticed his brown tweed jacket was buttoned to his chin and his shoulders were hunched defensively against the cold. The skies were a dark shade of grey, with heavy clouds closing in, a telltale sign of rain, or perhaps snow, making Ainsley wish he had brought his umbrella.

"I thought perhaps you had decided not to indulge me," Simms admitted as Ainsley drew close. He offered his hand in greeting. Shaking it, Ainsley glanced up to the front facade of the four-storey brick building.

"I doubt my presence is required," Ainsley said, scanning the five small windows of each floor. The building could be considered derelict if it weren't for the handful of people loitering on the front stoop.

Simms turned and headed for the entrance, entreating Ainsley to follow him. "I'm afraid Ms. Bell is anxious for us to be finished with the room," Simms explained.

"She's losing revenue, I imagine," Ainsley answered.

The entranceway was decorated with a dingy, worn red carpet, and a rickety side table. In an adjoining room, Ainsley could see a single green velvet chair with its arms stained to nearly black and the gold paint that had once adorned the wooden arms and legs chipped and made dull. The smell of the building hit Ainsley more squarely as they approached the stairway that would take them up to the higher floors. It was a smell of mold and urine, old urine which seemed to have seeped into the carpeting and the wood planks beneath it.

Simms must have noticed the look on Ainsley's face. "Far cry from Belgrave Square, isn't it?"

Ainsley did not know what to say. The smell was too overwhelming.

"It gets better on the second floor."

Ms. Bell approached them from a room in the back, which Ainsley assumed was the kitchen; his assumption was further supported by the towel she held in her hand. "Back again, are ya'?" she asked in a near snarl. "I told ya' I have no patience for investigations."

"A woman died, Ms. Bell," Ainsley retorted in near frustration. He wondered if Simms, and other constables like him, always received such terse receptions.

"Ain't no matter to me," Ms. Bell answered without bothering to look Ainsley in the eye. "I ain't the one who killed 'er."

"We will be out of here by the end of the day," Simms said, cutting off her words. He pointed up the stairs and motioned for Ainsley to follow him.

At the bottom of the stairs they could hear Ms. Bell calling after them. "I need my daughter to get in there to clean."

"She'll need ten daughters to clean what awaits her in there," Simms muttered to Ainsley as they walked up the stairs.

"Is it that bad, Inspector Simms?" Ainsley asked, glancing to the crumbling wallpaper that peeled from the plaster in strips, revealing circles of mildew beneath.

"The boardinghouse, or the room?" Simms asked, only half-jokingly. He stopped at a closed door not far from the top of the stairs. He pulled a set of keys from his trouser pocket and slipped one into the keyhole above the iron doorknob.

"She had enough funds for a private room?" Ainsley asked, knowing boardinghouses such as these rarely housed private accommodations.

Simms nodded. "Aye, most are glad to share a cot with a stranger."

As Simms turned the key, Ainsley glanced down the hall to the faces that peered out from the other doors. He tilted his head in their direction. "Have you questioned them all?" he asked.

Simms followed Ainsley's gaze. "No one saw or heard

anything, but I plan to question them again." Simms pushed the door open.

With the detective propping the door open, Ainsley stepped inside, aware of a quagmire of glass strewn on the dark red carpet.

Once inside, Ainsley realized the glass was actually shards of a mirror, some facing the floor, but most reflecting his own disjointed image back at him. Ainsley looked farther into the room, looking for the source, a broken vanity mirror or standing mirror but saw nothing. Instead, he saw a single narrow metal bed, with scarcely enough room on either side to walk. A single lamp, white and plain, sat on a small table beside the bed, untouched.

A squishing sound came from beneath his boot and when he looked he realized the dark red carpet beneath the shards of glass was actually blood. He followed the trail that led him around the bed to the headboard. As Ainsley drew near he saw the hurricane glass from the lamp had been broken, a large chunk missing from the side while the majority remained intact despite a long crack.

There was no bureau, no wardrobe, only the bed, the small table, and the lamp. An embroidered Bible verse, framed on the wall, dangled by its corner and looked as if it would drop to the floor at any moment. Ainsley turned his attention to the bed, neatly made save for a large stain of blood, now brown, dried and crusty against the gaudy floral pattern of the thin blanket. And then he noticed another, smaller stain on the bedclothes closer to the foot of the bed, but not as dark and not as widespread as the other.

There were wrinkles too in the cloth, though the smooth position of the linens gave no indication of how the bedclothes had been when the girl was stabbed. Simms remained at the door, his hands deep in his pockets, his eyes watching Ainsley as he leaned in to look at the blood.

"Your officers tidied the crime scene," Ainsley said at last, pulling his eyes from the bed and looking squarely at the detective.

"No," Simms answered.

"Where was the body located then?" Ainsley asked, disbelieving the detective's response.

Simms pointed to the middle of the bed. "She was in her

night shift, under the covers, as if she had been sleeping."

Ainsley looked to where Simms pointed and stared. The bloodstain was not where the wound had been. She had been found in the bed but the majority of the blood was on the carpet. Ainsley pulled back the blanket and looked at the underside and spotted another smaller, less noticeable stain close to where the doctor estimated her stomach would have touched the underside.

"Your officers did not touch her?" Ainsley asked, doubtful. "I only ask to be certain," he explained, not wanting to show any doubt for Simms' abilities, since he had just met the man and Simms was still in charge of the investigation of his mother's disappearance.

"She was not moved."

Ainsley pointed to the lamp. "But the lamp was."

Simms raised an eyebrow.

"The lamp was knocked over," Ainsley explained. "It looks intact but the glass has a large piece missing, the kerosene is also spilt." Ainsley ran his hand along the wallpaper behind the bedside table and showed Simms the oil that slid over his fingertips. "The lamp was knocked over."

Following the trail of blood with his eyes, Ainsley pointed to the foot of the bed. "Stabbed there, she stepped around, maybe to get away from someone there." Ainsley pointed to where Simms stood. Ainsley placed himself at the side of the bed. "She collapsed here. Someone moved her into the bed."

Simms smiled and nodded. "What do you think then, Ainsley?" he asked. "What was used to kill her?"

Ainsley turned from him, glancing over the room.

"A knife?" Simms asked.

"Possibly," Ainsley answered, rubbing his hand on his chin, "But doubtful." Ainsley walked to the foot of the bed, back to the shards of mirror that lay on the carpet. A shattered image stared back at him as he leaned over.

"Glass then?"

Ainsley reached for a piece, but said nothing, not wanting to commit to any conclusion. The mirror was a mass of jagged triangles, splintered from one clear point. Crouching, Ainsley held the largest piece in his forefinger and thumb, turning it over. If a piece of a mirror was the murder weapon, how had the murderer not harmed himself? Each piece was broken or exposed on all sides. The force needed to puncture the skin and the stomach would have severely damaged the hand of the person holding it, even if gloves had been worn.

Ainsley glanced around the walls of the room looking for a bare nail or discoloured patch of wallpaper where the mirror might have fallen from.

"What is this from?" he asked, looking up to Simms.

A smudge dotted the edge of the broken shard and Ainsley tilted it toward the light to see what it was. He had hoped it was a drop of blood but it wasn't. Its colour was not much different from that of the mirror but what it was exactly the doctor could not tell.

"Dr. Ainsley?"

Ainsley looked up to Simms. "I'm going to take these," he said. He did not wait for Simms to agree. Pulling his handkerchief from his breast pocket Ainsley laid the white square of fabric out over the carpet. Gingerly, he placed all of the pieces in his handkerchief and folded the edges carefully so he could safely place them in his pocket.

When he stood up he noticed Simms looking at him doubtfully.

"I am going to compare them to her wound," Ainsley explained. "I am not convinced, however. None of these have a speck of blood on them."

"Perhaps he threw that piece away," the inspector offered. "I'll check the laneways."

Simms wrote something on his notepad before tucking it in its usual spot, his inside breast pocket. "I still need to interview her neighbours," he said, indicating the other rooms. "Care to join me?"

Ainsley gave a smirk. "With that, you are on your own. I prefer the dead. Everything becomes much easier that way."

Slipping the wrapped bundle of glass shards into his pocket, Ainsley rose from his crouched position and noticed a bemused smile on the detective's face. The pair met each other's eyes but no one spoke for a moment, not until Ainsley let out a deep exhale of breath. "What?"

Simms shrugged, pouting his lips as he did so. "Seems odd, that's all."

"What's odd?"

The detective hesitated, perhaps wondering how to phrase his observation. "I would have thought a man like you would prefer the living." Simms' offering was carefully phrased, as if expecting the subject to drop shortly thereafter.

"A man like me?" Ainsley could not help but laugh. "What sort of man do you peg me as?"

"You are the son of an earl. You grew up in the upper crust of society, second son and heir to one of the most powerful families in the empire." Simms must have seen the disdain on Ainsley's face as he spoke. "If you don't want that lifestyle, I'd gladly change places with you. I'd rather attend balls, garden parties, and picnics. It's a mite bit better than this."

Ainsley watched Simms glance around the room, before pulling his brown tweed waistcoat together and buttoning it at the front. "You think I'm spoiled," Ainsley finally said, shifting his weight to one leg and placing a hand in his pants pocket.

"No," Simms answered unconvincingly.

"Of course." Ainsley's smile became indignant. "Everyone with money hasn't a care, is that it?" The young doctor wondered if the detective picked up his sarcasm. "You have seen my family, you met my father. You know what he is like. His money gives him reason to believe he can own anything he wants, including his wife and children."

"And how many in this city have no fathers to tell them where to go and what to do? Many an orphan would be blessed to have but one of your parents."

"And I have both?" Ainsley knew he was behaving self-righteously but in that moment he felt justified. His mother was missing, and she was the better half of his parentage. As far as he knew, he might already be an orphan if anything had befallen her. He ran his hand through his hair, pulling it back from his face and let out a long breath in an effort to return his rapid heartbeat back to normal. "I have to ask, Inspector, do you find my father's story suspect? Is he under suspicion?"

Simms hesitated, but before he could speak Ainsley interrupted.

"Because if he isn't, he should be."

"Your sister says they had a loving marriage."

Ainsley laughed. "She is protecting him. I thought you were trained to detect that."

"I am," Simms answered, his smile hardening. "I have no reason to suspect your father is involved. Your family's servants confirm he was at home the day Lady Marshall left and went missing. In fact, he was in his study while she boarded her carriage."

"Was it our family's carriage?" Ainsley asked, suddenly aware of a possible lead.

Simms shook his head and sighed. "No, she hired a coach."

Ainsley curled his hands into fists at his side. He wondered if all of Simms' work was just as frustrating. "There must be hundreds in London. How can we track down one driver?"

Simms nodded. "Impossible."

The change in Ainsley's mood was palpable. It was becoming hard to find hope when every way Ainsley turned he saw a dead end.

After a moment of avoiding Ainsley's gaze, Simms spoke. "We will find her," he said. "I am meeting with your brother this afternoon and I am confident we will find her."

Chapter 8

For all things must die.

Ainsley returned home just in time to hear the dinner gong.

"Impeccable timing, sir," Billis said as he accepted Ainsley's overcoat, brushing off the tiny ice pellets that had gathered on Ainsley's shoulders as he walked home. "Should I tell his lordship that you will be joining them shortly, once you have had a chance to change?"

Ainsley had it in mind to skip dinner altogether, preferring the comfort of his own room.

"I know Lady Margaret was particularly anxious for your return," Billis offered.

At the mention of his sister, Ainsley relented. "Of course, Billis."

"Very good, sir. Shall I send Cutter to assist you?"

Ainsley chuckled at the absurdity. Where his brother and father enjoyed the benefits of wealth, Ainsley deplored them. "Absolutely not. A grown man can dress himself."

"Very well, sir." Billis bowed at the waist and Ainsley went quickly up the stairs to his room.

When he entered the dining room Ainsley found everyone in a somber mood as they sat around the table. With his head bowed, Lord Marshall sat at the head of the table, his arms resting on either side of his place setting and his hands clenched. Margaret, as well, sat quietly, though she held a spoon in her hand, poised over her bowl.

"Forgive me, Father," Ainsley offered as he took his seat opposite Margaret. It was a gesture of formality rather than genuine regret. Ainsley hardly believed in all the pomp and circumstance with which his father gave a simple dinner. There was only the three of them. The large table, with a capacity for twelve, looked rather empty and awkward despite the four elegant candelabras set ablaze with over twenty candles each. At first glance, the room looked light and cheerful but the expressions on the faces of the family and staff gave another story.

Ainsley swallowed. "They have found her then?" he asked, fearing the worst.

"No." Lord Marshall's voice filled the room.

Ainsley glanced to Margaret, who was looking at him apologetically.

"The paper—"

"Hush, girl!"

Ainsley saw his sister recoil from the conversation, turning her gaze to the food in front of her. When he looked back to his father, a seething anger gathering in his jaw, he saw a look of fury in his father's eyes.

"The paper has reported that your mother has retreated to Edinburgh to play nurse maid to some ill cousin I never knew she had." Lord Marshall gave his daughter a sideways glance. "It would appear your sister has conspired with Lady Gemma Brant to contrive a story—"

"It was only to help," Margaret said.

"You should never have gone to that woman, of all people!" Lord Marshall threw a fist to the table, sending a vibration that rattled the dinnerware and shook the candles in their places. Ainsley saw Billis return a candle to its upright place at the far end of the table before retreating back to the perimeter of the room.

"I can't say I see any harm in it," Ainsley said after a moment's pause. "It would explain her absence from both the city and Tunbridge Wells." Ainsley ignored the look of annoyance his father gave him and turned to Margaret. "How is Lady Brant?" he asked.

"Quite well," Margaret answered demurely. "She asked about you and how you found your new position at the hospital."

"Must I be reminded of *all* the shameful shenanigans of my family?" their father bellowed.

"And she said she looks forward to seeing you both at the engagement party," Margaret continued, perhaps wanting to bring the topic of conversation to a more jovial subject.

It was then that Billis and Cutter, the footman, swooped in to retrieve their soup bowls to make way for the fish course.

Ainsley laughed quietly to himself, remembering the exchange he had witnessed between Daniel and Evelyn. Their marriage seemed doomed to failure. It was almost as if he was witnessing the beginning of his own parent's ill-fated union.

"You have met her then?" Lord Marshall scoffed. "I'll admit she is a timid sort, not the type I had pictured for the likes of your brother, but her family is well suited."

"Well suited meaning rich?" Ainsley asked, knowing full well he was treading on thin ice.

Lord Marshall was quiet for a long while. Plates of snapper were placed in front of them and they began eating. "You would do well to look to your brother Daniel for guidance, more so than the likes of Lady Brant. She is an eccentric, without the slightest capacity to understand the honour and wealth that was bestowed upon her. Her repulsive dabbling in anatomy is enough to turn her late husband over in his grave. She has encouraged your interest in science, as has your mother and against my wishes. Now look what they have done to you."

"Yes, it is because of them I am an up-and-coming surgeon with respect and adoration of all in my field," Ainsley boasted. "Who could want more than that?"

"Men should want power," Lord Marshall bellowed without hesitation. "Men should want money, lots of it to keep their wife and children well at home and to enjoy the leisurely pursuits of this great age."

Ainsley wanted to caution his father that he was beginning to sound like an advertisement for the Great Exhibition or some such industry propaganda pamphlet but he stopped himself. He was already pushing the bounds of their strained, tiresome relationship.

"You should think of taking a wife soon, my son." Lord Marshall did not wait for his son to reply. "Your brother has taken my advice, and I am sure it will do him well."

"With all due respect," Ainsley began, a hint of laughter in his voice, "I don't believe I will be taking a wife anytime soon." If his parents' strained ties and his brother's awkward arrangement were any indication, marriage appeared to be nothing more than a business contract to some and pain to others. If it were all the same, Ainsley

70

could never see himself marrying, especially to please his father.

"I have prepared some funds for you, an inheritance that, if properly cared for, would generate an income five times greater than your allowance now, that is *if* you take an approved wife."

Ainsley let out a long breath, and placed his fork down beside his plate. "Then you can keep your money because I have no intention of taking either." Ainsley surveyed the table, while pressing his thumb into each of his fingers in turn. "Besides, I am but the second son and we all know you have no obligation to give me anything. Save your funds for Margaret." Ainsley looked to his sister across the table, who seemed to be doing well now that he was present. She no longer looked slight and abashed. She was the confident Margaret he knew and admired. She smiled at him.

"Do you not approve of Miss Evelyn Weatherall?" Lord Marshall asked the table, signalling for Billis to remove their plates before the meat course.

"I can scarcely say," Margaret admitted. "I met her once. She seems amiable enough. Though I have my doubts as to her suitability for Daniel. Do you suppose he cares for her?"

Ainsley shook his head. "I don't believe he is concerned with suitability as much as he is concerned about dowry."

After a moment of pause, reflecting on the situation, Margaret asked, "Do you suppose she cares for him?"

"If looks are to be believed, then I would say she does," Ainsley admitted.

"Then she is a fool," Lord Marshall said, his tone denoting contempt and annoyance. "Care, and love for that matter, are useless states and should not be entered willingly."

As opposed to unwillingly, Ainsley wondered. It was no secret his father was cantankerous and spiteful, especially against his own marriage, but to be so disapproving against the happiness of another couple seemed bitter. This time Ainsley took care to hide his misgivings.

"Marriage is about power and money, nothing more. Use the state of marriage wisely or you will both find yourselves regretting it as deeply as I."

Struck by their father's words, Ainsley and Margaret watched dumbfounded as Lord Marshall emptied his near-full wine glass and stood up from the table, leaving his lamb untouched. "I have lost my appetite," he said, before walking from the room.

"Father's temperament seems worse today," Ainsley said, after sufficient time had passed since Lord Marshall's departure.

"He is in more pain than he would like us to know," Margaret said.

Ainsley scoffed but before he could say anything more they heard raised voices in the hallway. Billis, who had been standing nearest the door, slipped from the room with a grave look on his face.

"Peter, what is it?" Margaret asked, but Ainsley was already on his feet, throwing his napkin on the table. In a few strides, he was out the door and in the hallway in time to see the form of his mother slipping up the stairs, though he was not entirely sure he hadn't just been seeing things. Violetta, his mother's maid, walked up the stairs behind her, carrying a carpetbag and Lady Marshall's cape.

Lord Marshall stood at the bottom of the stairs with a look of terror that was quickly becoming an expression of anger. "Confound it, woman!"

"Was that Mother?" Ainsley asked, his voice cracking.

"She is the devil!" Lord Marshall pronounced with a finger pointed up the stairs. Margaret appeared at Ainsley's side then.

"Mother?" she asked confused.

Lord Marshall turned from the stairs, throwing up his hands in resignation. "She can burn in hell for all the trouble she has caused."

Not wanting to hear any more of his father's outburst, Ainsley walked past him and tackled the stairs two at a time. Once at the top, he glanced down to see his father walking toward his study and Margaret wiping tears from her cheeks. He raised his hand, and mouthed the word 'wait' to her when their eyes met. He had decided to be the one to question their mother. Given the way her sudden appearance caused such upheaval, he doubted a flurry of questions and accusations would do any good. He intended to behave as he would at work, intent and detached, finding the answers he sought without emotional interference. Only one thing stood in his way; the reality that she was his mother and had been missing for nearly four days.

He reached the door to her room but hesitated before knocking. He knew more about her than he had before. No longer was she simply the devoted victim of a loveless marriage. She had a lover, and a possible penchant for opiates. His understanding of her had dramatically changed and he could no longer feel as sorry for her as he once had.

He knocked determinedly and entered when he heard her singsong voice saying, "Come in."

Her face lit up when she saw him round the threshold between her sitting room and her bedroom. Ainsley was careful not to show his delight in her return. He was elated, naturally, thankful that he would not go to work one day to find her among the corpses.

Violetta stood in a corner of the room and purposely avoided his gaze.

"Hello, dear," Lady Marshall said with a wide smile. "You look so robust, Peter. I believe your new career is agreeing with you."

She was seated on the edge of her settee, her long skirt flowing out around her legs and only the tips of her high boots could be seen beneath her crinoline and lace. Her hands were above her head, pulling out her hatpin.

She laughed at his silence. "Goodness, Peter, what is the matter with you?" she asked, her smile wide and unrelenting. It was as if she hadn't the faintest clue of the pain her absence had caused, and if she was aware, she was very good at pushing it from the surface.

Violetta quickly brushed past Ainsley, her arms loaded with clothing. She darted into the hall and out of sight, all the while keeping her eyes fixed on the floor.

"We missed you, Mother," Peter said at last.

Lady Marshall pursed her lips, touched by Ainsley's compliment. "Oh, hush now," she said, teasingly. "It wasn't as bad as all that." She got up from her seat and walked to her toilette table and began pulling out her hairpins one by one. "I was only at the country house, nothing terribly unusual. You have decided to live in the city with your father. You can't expect to see me all that often from now on." She smiled at him through the mirror as she let her copious brown curls unravel themselves and fall, bouncing to her shoulders.

She must have thought him stupid. She must have thought them *all* to be stupid to lie so blatantly. "We know you were not at the country house," Ainsley said after a long pause.

Lady Marshall's expression did not waver. "Where else would I be, Peter?"

His mother looked older somehow, not as youthful and vibrant as he remembered. Weathered. She looked like the grieving mothers who came to the hospital to claim their dead. Those women forced themselves to smile, pushing down a catastrophic pain in order to appear strong for the sake of everyone else. Ainsley saw that look in his mother, not in her mouth and cheeks that smiled on command, but in her eyes that did not sparkle as they should.

"Margaret saw you," he said at last, knowing she knew what he meant.

"Saw me do what, dear?" Lady Marshall sat on the edge of her settee again and, struggling against the tightness of her corset, she pulled up the hem of her skirts to unlace her shoes. "Oh, where did Violetta go?" Her face fell, no longer able to keep the demanding charade.

"She must be taking some items to the laundry," Ainsley answered earnestly.

"Of course." She laughed then, finding her strength for more false smiles. "Be a dear and ring the servant bell," she commanded. "Unlace these boots for me, please. I haven't the patience to wait."

Ainsley hesitated but relented quickly enough. He did not want to give her any more leeway to avoid his pointed questions. Slipping into the sitting room for a moment, he pulled the brass lever installed over her mantel, knowing it would ring the bell in the basement letting them know her ladyship needed assistance. Upon his return, he knelt down at his mother's feet and began pulling at her laces.

"You always were such a blessing to me," she said, reaching out a hand to cup the side of his cheek. Her face looked somber when their eyes met. "Look at you, all grown up and following your heart. Such courage." Ainsley could feel her thumb on the side of his face as he pulled the boots gingerly from her slight feet. "A courage I never had."

Ainsley could see her eyes turn red suddenly and he expected to see her cry at any moment, but she turned her head away and stood. He watched from his spot on the floor as she pulled her earrings off and then her rings, placing them on a cushion of blue velvet on her vanity.

He heard the door open and a few moments later Violetta appeared. "Ma'am," she said, bobbing a curtsey. She looked travel-weary and tired.

"I wish to take a bath," Lady Marshall said without apology.

"Mother, it's past nine o'clock," Ainsley replied in defence of the maid, who had no doubt been up since before dawn.

Lady Marshall smiled, somewhat wickedly. "What should that matter? Violetta is accustomed to drawing me many late-night baths. Isn't that so, Violetta?"

"Yes, ma'am." Violetta curtsied again and turned to leave.

"No." Ainsley walked to the maid to prevent her from going. "Mother, she is tired as are you. She must be eager to retire for the night." He looked to Violetta's face but the maid did not betray her true feelings. She waited for final instruction though Ainsley wished she would give him some sort of sign of gratitude.

"Retire? Then who shall draw my bath?" Lady Marshall nodded to the maid. "Water, please."

Patience wearing thin, Ainsley barred her path with the full extension of his arm. It seemed cruel to punish the staff because Lady Marshall was angered with her husband.

"Mother, be reasonable."

Lady Marshall stepped forward, her mouth pressed together in anger. "I am being reasonable. I have been travelling for hours and I am dusty and filthy. I would like a bath." She punctuated her last sentence with marked annoyance.

Ainsley looked down to the maid, who gazed at him imploringly to let her do as her mistress bid. Disappointed, Ainsley pulled his hand from the doorframe, allowing Violetta to exit.

"Someone has been in my room," Lady Marshall said

before the sitting room door fully closed behind the maid.

"Mother—"

Ainsley watched his mother sifting through papers and envelopes on her desk. She opened the single drawer of the desk, and looked over the contents. Lady Marshall grabbed a fistful of papers, crumpling them in her grasp. "Who had the gall to go through my things?"

"Mother, calm yourself," Ainsley began. "Margaret was looking—"

"Margaret!" Lady Marshall crossed the room quickly to her bureau and opened the drawers with a thunderous noise that accompanied her panic. "What right has she to go through my belongings?"

Ainsley laughed. "You were missing, for days. We thought you might have been dead."

Lady Marshall turned to him. "Don't be so stupid!" The level of her anger surprised him. Never had she behaved so erratically. It was the opium, he reasoned. She was worried they would find it, that they *had* found it and her secret would no longer be hidden.

She turned back to her drawer, and shifted her clothing, most likely trying to remember where she had stashed her bottles. "I was at The Briar," she said, while she frantically searched. "Alone," she emphasized, and then her voice fell, "as always." As if giving up her search, Lady Marshall slammed the drawer shut and turned, crossing the room to her toilette table.

A deep, concerted silence fell over them. Ainsley watched as his mother brushed the ends of her curls before flipping them over her shoulder and then pushing some waves of hair from her face. He caught her glancing up at him, her eyes lifting slightly in the mirror, but upon catching his gaze she immediately turned her eyes toward the table in front of her.

"So what have my beautiful children been doing whilst I was in the country?" She looked at him purposely then, eyebrows raised and giddy. She wanted him to drop his line of questioning and behave as if nothing was amiss. Ainsley's shoulders slumped at the realization that her denial had rooted and taken hold. There would be no way of coaxing a confession or even an admission of guilt.

"Perhaps in the morning, Mother," Ainsley answered, a feeling of weariness sweeping over him. "I suddenly feel very tired."

"Very well then," she said with a hint of relief. "At breakfast then." She winked at him teasingly. He planted a quick kiss on her forehead and gave her a pat on the shoulder before turning to leave. In the hall he encountered Violetta, who had returned with two pails of hot water. She bowed her head as she passed and Ainsley could not help but feel an overwhelming sense of pity for the woman.

Chapter 9

All things must die.

"She's in denial," Ainsley explained.

"Or delusional," Margaret offered, throwing the book she was reading on to the small table beside her bed. Ainsley had found her in bed with a book open but he could tell she had just been staring at the words and not actually reading them so he hadn't felt sorry for interrupting her. "What does she think we have been doing for the last few days?" she questioned.

Ainsley shrugged and shook his head. Her disbelief mirrored his. Their mother had acted selfishly and her self-centered view continued even now when they all demanded answers.

"Suppose they had a falling out," Margaret suggested. "Her lover, I mean. What if they argued and she decided to return, hoping we'd all be so glad we wouldn't question her?"

"I suppose it's possible," Ainsley conceded. "She was terribly concerned when she couldn't find her laudanum."

Margaret sniffed but did not reply. "I only wish I saw his face," she offered after a moment's pause.

Ainsley shifted uncomfortably. The thought of their mother's infidelity had been nagging at him, eating him from the inside out since he had heard confirmation from Margaret. It was a discomfort that he had been successful in suppressing for over a week and he feared his will was crumbling. He almost expected as much from their father, but coming to the realization that their mother was in the wrong was almost too much to bear.

"I remember so little," Margaret continued, either not noticing her brother's discomfort or choosing to ignore it. "It was dark, and naturally I left the room as soon as I could."

"And Jonas?"

Margaret started at the mention of him. "What do you

mean?" she asked quietly. "I haven't seen him since we returned to London."

"I am aware," Ainsley said. "I wasn't speaking of your affection for him."

"You spoke clearly on the subject once or twice before," Margaret answered with a sneer. "I don't see how—"

Ainsley raised an eyebrow, surprised at her defensiveness. He watched as her face became lighter, sudden realization spreading over her features and she smiled at her epiphany. "He saw!" she said, sitting up straighter in bed. "I asked him if he had seen and he said yes. Peter, he might recognize who it was." Margaret's face lifted with excitement.

"To what end?" Ainsley asked. "Mother has come home. Hopefully, you are right and they quarrelled, causing her to return. What good could come of tracking him down?"

Margaret's excitement was tempered quickly and Ainsley watched as her face fell somberly. "You are not curious?" she asked.

"Certainly not!" Ainsley nearly laughed at the suggestion. "I have no desire to meet the man. And if he is another man of society don't you think it best if we all just get back to normal?"

There was a strained silence between them when Margaret started to stammer out a retort before giving up and looking away all together. Perhaps she was looking for vindication for her anger, or even a second person to blame for the scandal. Ainsley's interest remained in mitigating damage to their family's reputation, only for Margaret's marriage prospects if nothing else. And perhaps in the same token, he hoped to protect Evelyn, who unwittingly would be part of their disgraced family if confirmation of the affair were ever made public.

"Leave it be," he said. "Allow Father to deal with it, if he chooses. For us, we should continue as per usual and corroborate the story in the paper. If only for Evelyn, so she does not know what kind of a family she is marrying into." Ainsley gave his sister a teasing smile and knocked her gently on the chin.

Margaret's smile was forced and Ainsley knew she would not heed his advice. So headstrong and judicious, she would not smile and lie for the sake of family, not when there was a mystery to solve. As he left the room, Ainsley thought he should not be surprised if he saw her the next morning at the hospital, looking for Jonas.

৵   ৵

Inspector Simms was standing in the foyer when Ainsley came down the next morning. The detective turned to him as him descended. Ainsley's waistcoat was draped over his crooked arm as he used one hand to fasten his cufflinks.

"So you have heard?" Ainsley asked, unable to help smiling as he made his way to Simms. His elation could not be hidden. Since the moment he had awoken that morning he had been smiling, assured that his mother was safe among them.

"I have yet to meet with Lord Marshall," Simms said, a look of confusion coming over his face.

"It's Mother," Ainsley explained. "She has returned. You are off the hook." Ainsley's grin somehow widened still.

"Indeed." Simms' reaction was not from elation. He was confounded, uncertain how to interpret the latest turn of events. Ainsley could tell he had questions, though Ainsley himself was not in a position to answer many of them. His own confusion was moderated by the high spirits brought on by his mother's return.

"Inspector!" Lord Marshall appeared in the foyer. He clapped his hands together, and then noted Ainsley's presence. "Has my son told you the great news?" Lord Marshall's excitement jolted Ainsley, as he knew the man to be far more cynical and had witnessed the less-than-pleased response his wife's sudden, unexplained return had elicited. Lord Marshall offered a hand to the detective, which Simms shook on reflex.

"Your wife has returned," Simms answered, doubtfully.

"That she has," Lord Marshall exclaimed triumphantly. "Unfortunately, we have bothered you these last few days without cause. She was in Edinburgh, you see," Lord Marshall explained. "Tending to her ill cousin." Lord Marshall let out a breath and grimaced. "She sent word but it did not reach me. I hope we have not inconvenienced you terribly."

"Not at all." Simms gave a glance to Ainsley, who stood numb, unable and unwilling to support or condone his father's spinning tale.

"If it is all the same," Lord Marshall continued, "we could keep this event to just us, can we not?"

"Naturally," Simms answered. "I am glad for the positive outcome."

"As are we." Lord Marshall clapped his hands together. "Well then, I bid you good day." He gave a cautionary glance to Ainsley before turning to Billis. "My man here will make sure you are compensated for your troubles." Billis bowed his acknowledgement of the order as his master walked by, disappearing into his study.

Simms turned to Ainsley. "A formidable man, your father," he said.

Billis appeared at their side, holding a bank note. Simms waved a hand of dismissal. "I am a man of the law," was his simple refusal.

When Billis had left, Ainsley retrieved his overcoat. "Can I walk with you?" he asked.

"It's a chilly morning, sir," Simms said.

Ainsley nodded knowingly "It always is."

On the street, they walked with hands shoved deep in their pockets and faces bent against the oncoming wind. "I apologize for my father, and his butler. He believes anyone can be bought." Ainsley saw a smile touching the edges of Simms' lips.

"Is it not every rich man's privilege to believe such things?" Simms answered.

"It's happened before?" Ainsley asked, sensing the detective spoke from experience.

"More than once."

Ainsley nodded, yet did not want to believe that certain members of society believed themselves to be above the law. He hoped the circumstances were similar to those of his family, a request for discretion, not a request to look the other way.

"I won't be investigating the matter any further," Simms said, after a pause passed between them. "You can tell your father that I have no desire to impede upon the matters of his marital affairs."

"No doubt he will be glad to hear it," Ainsley answered with a slight laugh. Ainsley, on the other hand, felt like nothing had found resolution. His mother's real whereabouts during the last few days remained a mystery, as did the reason why she had neglected to return home for so long.

"You still have questions?" Simms asked.

"Yes." Stopping, Ainsley reached into his inside pocket and found his mother's laudanum bottles and presented them to Simms, who had stepped slightly further before turning. "I fear there is more to this story than she says."

Simms took the bottles and held them to the dim December sun. "Laudanum."

"I fear she has been prescribed them unnecessarily," Ainsley explained.

Simms cocked his head, indicating they should begin walking once more. The bridge was in view and the winter wind was picking up where they stood.

"You have not prescribed them?" Simms asked, bracing against the onslaught.

Ainsley shook his head. "She may be addicted. I have read some articles on the matter. It would explain her odd behaviour."

"Odd in what way?"

Ainsley looked away for a moment, glancing to the throng of people ahead of them on the bridge. "I questioned her last night, rather thoroughly, but she is in full denial. Flat out refuses to admit anything is wrong. She claims she had been at The Briar this entire time."

Simms chuckled. "I sent a man there. He interviewed the staff, who all claimed she departed shortly after your sister did."

Ainsley flinched at the remembrance and he found himself stopping on the bridge to look at the murky Thames below. Margaret had sought him out while he was on assignment in the north. The news she brought was of seeing their mother and her lover in the parlour in a less-than-discreet coupling.

"What is it?" Simms asked, no doubt seeing Ainsley's face. He too leaned into the railing but stared at Ainsley.

Ainsley hesitated. With his mother home, safe and sound, he wondered what good it would do to drum up her sins, but then he remembered who he was speaking to and decided the detective might have some light to shed on the situation. "Margaret found my mother...with..." His conviction weakened and Ainsley found that he could not say the words aloud.

"She was having an affair."

Ainsley nodded.

Simms drew in air, pulling his shoulders back. "I wish you or your sister had told me before. Now that Lady Marshall has returned, there is little I can do to assist you."

"I am aware of this," Ainsley answered. "Would it have changed your investigation?"

"Absolutely." Simms bore a look of sheer disappointment. He began to walk again once the crowd on the bridge had thinned and Ainsley was quick to keep pace. "Had I known, I could have had more direction."

Ainsley knew this to be true but his loyalty to his sister trumped all. And despite her sins, Ainsley felt he owed as much to his mother as well, to protect her reputation. Scotland Yard had yet to distinguish itself as having tight scruples. However, he was not about to say as much to the detective beside him.

"Did your sister recognize the man?"

"No," Ainsley answered.

Simms gave him a look of doubt. "Let us hope Lady Marshall has come to her senses and has returned for the well-being of her family."

Ainsley gave a half-smile, unsure if the tale of woe she inflicted on them was truly at an end.

Chapter 10

Spring will come never more.

Margaret stood outside her mother's closed bedroom door for some time wondering whether she should knock and request admittance or if she should avoid her mother all together. She had not spoken with her the night before; in fact, Peter had requested she stay away, which was for the better considering how angered and hurt she was. Even now, Margaret wondered if she was in any mood to approach her mother regarding her absence or if she should again heed her brother's advice and pretend as if nothing had happened.

But something *had* happened, and it needled Margaret considerably to think that their mother could simply put on a performance, knowing everyone would keep up the charade for the sake of pretense.

Margaret knocked weakly and regretted it as soon as she had done so.

"Come in."

Margaret found her mother seated at her toilette table, patting the mounds of her hair and adjusting a curly tendril she allowed to fall near her ear. Lady Marshall smiled at the mirror when she saw her daughter walk in the room, but Margaret felt a pang of annoyance at the sight of it. Lady Marshall turned, clasping her hands in her lap and preened at Margaret, who realized as she entered how much she was not in the mood for her mother's antics.

"Good morning, Margaret, my dear," Lady Marshall said, leaning into the back of her toilette chair, one arm positioned over the top of the decorative wood. "You look rather resplendent. Must be that dashing young man you brought to The Briar last week." She smiled, pressing her lips together tightly as if she were the demure, bashful mother who dare not speak of men and their lustful attractiveness.

Margaret shook her head slightly, then stopped, suddenly remembering the kiss they shared on their last meeting. A panic rose within her, wondering if it was to be the only kiss they would share. Jonas had been like a dream to her, out of her life as quickly as he had entered it, leaving only the vague remembrance of his lips touching hers. Peter had been right, though, no relationship could ever come of it. Jonas' social standing was so beneath hers that it was more than a miracle that they had even met.

But then what greater reason could there be to believe their lives were meant to be intertwined?

Margaret found herself smiling slightly at the prospect and then she heard her mother's teasing laugh.

"I thought as much," Lady Marshall said, waving a pointed finger in a jovial way. "So tell me then, which family should I be inviting to tea? Oh, don't give me that look. There is no need to be shy. We mustn't delay if we expect—"

"Expect nothing," Margaret said at last. "Jonas is a friend of Peter's."

"From what I saw you two were quite... intimate." Lady Marshall practically giggled at the suggestion.

"Intimate? Nothing like you and your little extramarital liaison!" Margaret spoke before she could censor herself. She would clasp her hand over her mouth if such actions had not already been trained out of her as unladylike.

Margaret watched as her mother's face hardened at her words. Lady Marshall raised an eyebrow, a challenge to her daughter to continue, if she dared. She would not apologize, Margaret decided, even though an uncertainty clung to her as her mother attempted to stare her down. Now that the subject had been broached, however, there was no point in holding back.

Margaret took a breath and stood taller. "I did not come to talk about Jonas. I want to talk about the disgrace you have caused Father."

Margaret watched her mother smile on one side of her mouth and recognized the look of amusement. Her mother seemed to be rather enjoying the disquiet she was causing. It seemed to arouse her sense of accomplishment. It was a side of her mother that Margaret had never seen before. Despite her ill-advised challenges to London society, by and large Lady Marshall had conformed enough to simply be gossip fodder, and was able to avoid scandalous disaster. Now she seemed to be courting it.

Suddenly Lady Marshall put her hand to her temples. "You must forgive me, my dear, I seem to have a headache." Margaret watched her mother wince in pain, wondering if she was witness to an act, a tactic to change the subject or if her mother truly was suffering.

Lady Marshall stood up from her chair, and staggered to her bed.

"Mother?" Margaret went to her mother's side.

"My bag, my bag," Lady Marshall said in a husky voice. She waved her hand toward a small valise near the sitting area of her room. Lady Marshall climbed into bed while keeping one hand over her eyes, as if shutting out the early-morning light.

Margaret brought the valise and laid it on the foot of the bed. "Mother, what do you need?" she asked sifting through the contents. There was a panic in her voice that she could not quell. "Mother?" She looked up and saw Lady Marshall recoiling as though in pain into the mountain of pillows arranged on her bed. "Mother?"

"My pills. My tonic." Lady Marshall waved her free hand, but her movements gave no indication which she meant. Finally Margaret brought the bag to the head of the bed just as her mother recoiled again, as though in reaction to some unseen searing pain. Desperately, Margaret searched. Whatever anger she had had for her mother was now gone as she found it impossible not to believe, by the excruciating look on her face, that her mother was in sheer agony.

With fumbling hands Margaret retrieved a small vial, similar to the ones she and Peter had found in their mother's hatboxes, and then she stumbled upon the delicately engraved gold pillbox. Medicines in hand, Margaret climbed onto the vast bed and placed herself beside her mother, who was hiding her face in the pillows.

"How many do you need?" Margaret asked, aware of the weak way in which she spoke. Her feeble attempts at bravery were failing her and all she really wanted to do was ring the servant's bell and summon more capable help for her mother. Without any answer forthcoming, Margaret attempted to release the pillbox clasp with shaky fingers and when it finally gave the pills rolled out on top of the sheets. While Margaret tried to gather them, her mother pulled her face out from the pillows and reached a hand into the pile that Margaret had collected. Unsure how many pills her mother had taken, Margaret tried to stop her before they hit Lady Marshall's mouth.

"Mother, no. That's too much." Margaret grabbed for her mother's wrist but lost the brief struggle. Lady Marshall poured the handful into her mouth and turned from Margaret, but not before grabbing the vial that lay next to her on the quilt. She stumbled off the bed, walking toward her wash basin, and opened the vial.

"How much does the doctor recommend you take?" Margaret asked feebly. Her mother took one sip, then another before she finally put the bottle down. Margaret realized it was almost empty.

Lady Marshall kept her eyes closed for a few minutes, leaning over the basin, as if she expected to vomit, before finally returning to the bed.

Margaret had never seen her mother in such a way; perfectly coherent one moment and then incapacitated the next. It took a moment before Margaret realized she was shaking, disturbed by her mother's sudden illness and her own inability to assist. If their mother had a reoccurring condition, it could explain why she and Peter found the laudanum and it would also explain the frantic search for her medicine Peter had described from the night before

Margaret began stroking her mother's disheveled hair, pulling out the pins that had become loose among the pillows. And then Margaret heard the distinguishable sounds of sleep escaping with her mother's rhythmic breathing. The medical concoction must have worked and the pain sufficiently subsided enough to allow Lady Marshall some rest.

Slipping from the bed slowly, Margaret covered her mother with a blanket and quietly left.

On the stairs she met Violetta, with a full pitcher of water, no doubt warm from the fires of the kitchen. "Her ladyship is not well," Margaret said, pausing on the stairs as the lady's maid approached her.

Violetta nodded to Margaret and hastened her pace up the stairs. "She is resting," Margaret said, quickly seeing the look of alarm on Violetta's face.

"Thank you, Miss Margaret," Violetta answered, avoiding Margaret's definitive gaze. She tried to continue up the stairs but Margaret called her back. "Violetta, what are the pills Mother takes?" she asked, being careful to lower her voice in case any servants lurked below them in the foyer.

"They are what the doctor prescribed, Miss," Violetta explained. "Her ladyship requires them for headaches and..." Her voice trailed off as the maid lost her conviction.

"And what?" Margaret probed.

"Violetta!" The sound of Lady Marshall's painful bellow erupted throughout the house. Violetta's eyes grew wide and she turned. "Excuse me, Miss," she called down the stairs as she ran to her employer's aid.

Margaret stood on the stairs for a moment, her hand on the handrail, her feet stuck between one step and the next. Of all the siblings, Margaret had spent the most amount of time with their mother and yet Margaret had never seen her in such a state. She hadn't the faintest clue her mother fought such unspeakable and sudden pain. The laudanum was her mother's cure and suddenly Margaret felt ashamed for assuming something untoward was happening.

"Margaret."

Snapped from her reverie, Margaret looked down to the foyer where her father stood sternly.

"A word with you, please."

Margaret swallowed. It was not a request. Lord Marshall led her into his study, where Billis was setting a tray of tea and accompanying paraphernalia on Lord Marshall's mahogany desk. "Thank you, Billis." Lord Marshall pulled a slim, folded newspaper from under the crook of his arm and slapped it onto the bare wood next to the tray. "That is all," he said to his servant.

Billis turned to Margaret, who hovered at the door, and bowed slightly at the waist.

"Come in, Margaret," her father said gruffly. He indicated a chair on the opposite side of the desk to his and let out a great exhale of breath as she slipped into it. For a moment he stood, fists on hips and eyes fixated on the steam slipping from the spout of the teapot. Margaret readied herself for reprove, and began mentally sifting through all of the possible events he could be cross about.

"I apologize for not speaking to you about this until now," he said in a surprisingly soft tone. He gave a forced smile. "I have had other things to consider."

Margaret nodded, cringing on the inside and preparing for his reprimand. She watched as he twisted his mouth, most likely contemplating his words carefully.

"Given recent events I have decided to hire you a lady's maid of your own. Someone who can act as your companion and—"

Margaret's face fell, "But Father—"

"This is not a punishment," he said. "It's for your own safety. I have been too lenient. I cannot have you going about town without someone whom I trust at your side." His voice grew quieter as he spoke. "She will help you dress, direct the other staff in the keeping of your rooms and ensure that you are well looked after. And, when the time comes, she can follow you to your husband's house, where she can be some comfort during the transition."

"My husband's house?"

"Yes." He put out a hand in a placating gesture as he moved for his cushioned leather chair behind the desk. "I have no plans to marry you off anytime soon; however, let's face facts, I have had some enquiries and before long we will be faced with the very real possibility—"

"Father, is this about my trip to help Peter? About my friendship with Jonas Davies?"

Her father grew quiet. "Need I be concerned?" he asked after a moment.

Margaret hesitated. There was no understanding between them. Jonas had kissed her, nothing more, a simple act he had most likely perpetrated on other willing girls whose knees were made weak by his presence— as Margaret's had. She was unlikely to see him again, at least not in the same informal circumstances, and there could certainly be no possibility of them ever marrying. Jonas was a doctor, born to a much lower class, certainly not the type of young man her father had in mind for her. In any case, she had no doubt that Jonas had moved on. He had kissed her because she let him, not because any feelings existed on his part.

Margaret shook her head in answer to her father's question. "No, no need to be concerned."

"Good. I hired a woman named Julia and I sent her down to get to know the kitchen while I spoke with you."

"You hired someone already?" Margaret asked, suddenly aware of the smothering nature her own lady's maid would have on the freedom she currently enjoyed. She saw a smile spread over her father's lips. "I am nothing, Margaret my dear, if not efficient."

∂∂   ∂∂

Margaret was told to wait in her room and Julia would be sent up to meet her. Pacing the length of the room, Margaret could feel her throat tighten as if a noose had been thrown over her. She had no desire to meet the woman, who in effect would serve as her jailer. No doubt her father would expect whoever this lady was to report to him on her every move. The freedom to move about on her own accord felt threatened and she didn't like the idea of her entire life being monitored with such close scrutiny. She had always employed the other maids to help her dress or straighten her rooms if need be. Never had she needed a dedicated maid for such chores.

She envied her mother and Violetta's relationship. They shared a trust that no one in the family could penetrate. Margaret doubted such a bond could form between her and a woman working for her father. It was clear to Margaret that her father intended to tether her to a servant in an effort to keep her from running off as she had done with Jonas.

Suddenly, the house seemed stifling and she needed an escape, and quickly, before she would be tied to the woman she did not even know. Margaret hailed a hansom and cursed the driver under her breath for not moving at a faster pace. The streets were cluttered with traffic, carriages and pedestrians alike jamming the roadways like rats fleeing a fire.

Finally, she arrived at the hospital, but her mission to find Jonas was halted when she stumbled into Lady Brant at the doorway.

"Margaret!" she said exuberantly. Smiling broadly, Lady Brant reached out a hand, inviting Margaret to follow her inside. "What brings you here?" she asked. Margaret could feel Lady Brant leaning in closer, whispering as a conspiring gossip might. "Perhaps you and I have come to see the same young man. A Doctor Peter Ainsley perhaps?"

Margaret dare not correct her. It would be improper to admit to seeking out an unmarried man, unchaperoned as well. It did not matter why she sought him out, only that it would appear unseemly. Before their travels together Margaret had viewed Jonas as if a brother and so appearances had not mattered, but now she realized she should take more care than allow herself to be seen with a bachelor unsupervised. She knew all too well what fallout a damaged reputation could bring.

"You must miss him, dear," Lady Brant continued without missing a beat. "You two were almost inseparable in your youth."

"I am accustomed now," Margaret admitted. "Peter has been away from home for some time now, though I must admit, seeing him in the evenings is better than haphazard letters from Germany. There is so much more to look forward to when he is around."

Lady Brant smiled pityingly, no doubt amused by Margaret's quaint little life. Always the academic, the female trailblazer, Lady Brant often spoke with contempt of lazy socialite wives and grown unwed daughters, wondering what could possibly prevail them to get out of bed in the morning. Such domesticity was the furthest thing from Lady Brant's mind and Margaret knew it. She had heard her mother's friend speak often of the dreariness she felt her life would be had her husband survived longer than the first year of marriage. Margaret had not realized she said something trite and inconsequential until she saw that disparaging look on Lady Brant's face.

Not knowing what to say, Margaret remained quiet. Everything she could think to comment on sounded like the sort of thing Lady Brant would despise. Thankfully, she did not have to say anything because she saw Jonas exit a door down the hallway to their left and begin walking toward them in the lobby. He smiled broadly when he saw her but was careful not to behave too familiar.

"Margaret, I do believe this young man knows you," Lady Brant remarked as Jonas walked toward them.

Margaret could not alter the rapid beating of her heart and sudden shortness of her breath. His approach sent warmth up the core of her and, without warning, she became flustered and unsure. She had driven all this way to see him but Lady Brant's presence caused her to lose her nerve and she fell silent.

Jonas stopped and Lady Brant spoke first, saving Margaret from the embarrassment of stammering.

"Good day, young man. Lady Brant. I serve on the Board of Directors here." She spoke with authority and offered her hand for him to shake. "This is my niece in all ways but blood, Margaret Marshall."

Jonas' lips rose into a smile but his gaze avoided hers. "I am Doctor Jonas Davies, ma'am. But I am afraid Miss Marshall and I are already well acquainted."

A single eyebrow popped up on Lady Brant's forehead. "Are you now?" she said knowingly. Margaret knew what she was insinuating and, despite it being close to the truth, she was still annoyed at Lady Brant's forwardness in teasing her so openly.

"Peter," Margaret said, halting Lady Brant's forthcoming needling, "he is a friend of Peter's."

"Oh." Lady Brant's smile changed, as if disappointed that her fun had been spoiled. "You must be a surgeon then. How come I have never met you until now?"

"I just began as assistant to Dr. Lehmann."

Margaret smiled openly then. "Dr. Davies had been working at the university for some time before taking his position here," Margaret offered. "Peter is very proud of him." Even though Margaret looked to Jonas she could not look directly at him and always turned back to Lady Brant before their eyes could meet. It was the only way, she reasoned, that she would be able to keep herself from behaving foolishly. He had this jarring effect on her, a way that made her feel self-conscious and unsure.

"I am glad my good fortune pleases you," Jonas said, his tone denoting a hint of anger.

Suddenly, Margaret felt ashamed. "Jonas, I didn't mean—"

"There's Doctor Crawford. Would you excuse me, Miss Marshall? I must speak with him before he leaves for the day. A pleasure to meet you, Lady Brant." Jonas was gone and down the hall before Margaret could protest.

She watched him walk away, swallowing hard as she recalled the words she had said, and worse, the way she had behaved.

"Margaret, do you think it was appropriate to address the doctor by his first name?" Lady Brant asked, stepping further along the hallway. She turned slightly, inviting Margaret to keep pace with her.

"He's always been Jonas to me. He's like a brother."

"A brother does not cause a lady to blush as you did," Lady Brant answered slyly. "Come Margaret," she coaxed, "confess."

Margaret shook her head slightly, embarrassed by Lady Brant's willingness to speak of such things. "I have nothing to confess."

Lady Brant waved her hand in the air, dismissing Margaret's reluctance to confide in her. "Suit yourself," she said. "Let us go see what your brother is up to today. Something riveting, no doubt."

Chapter 11

O, vanity!
Death waits at the door.

Ainsley ignored his mounting work, preferring to remain perched on a stool next to his empty examination table. The sheet-covered bodies around him could wait, he told himself. Truth be told, his mind was awash with thoughts of his mother and the questions she allowed to go unanswered. He found it hard to concentrate and he knew he needed a deeper challenge if he was going to forget the tribulations of his family.

Laid out on the wooden surface of his examination table were the shards of mirror he had found at the boarding house, and he had spent the better part of an hour piecing the triangular slivers together like a complicated puzzle, a puzzle that he was not even sure he possessed all the pieces for. He had determined the shape to be a rectangle, though a large chunk of the mirror was missing. He only had a few pieces left to place and a large part of the mirror remained empty.

The break in the glass fanned out like a spider web beginning at a point that was off-centre from the middle of the rectangle and, as Ainsley placed the last few pieces, he realized there were no clues to tell him what the broken pieces had come from or whether one of them had been used as the murder weapon.

"Dammit!" Ainsley pounded his fist on the table, causing the pieces to jump. He grabbed one of the shards and, balancing it on its point, he turned it in place. Absentmindedly, he watched the mirror reflect back the light on the table as he turned it and became entranced by the shadow and light playing on the wooden surface. Without a speck of blood on the surface of the mirror, there was no way to know whether a piece of it was used to kill the woman.

As he turned the shard, careful not to cut his fingers on the sharp edges, he began to bore a hole into the wood of the table. He watched small particles of wood dust accumulate around the hole for a few turns before he realized what he was seeing. And then he had an idea.

He stood suddenly from his stool, letting the glass in his fingers drop to the table. Grabbing a pair of leather gloves, he took one of the largest pieces of the mirror and headed for the very back of the morgue. Along the wall, in the darkest reaches of the morgue, the bodies of the criminals were stored. No dissections would ever be done on these bodies. They died in their cells awaiting the end, often not eating or defecating as they should. Ainsley had seen it often enough, the way the minds of the condemned slipped away, their bodies following suit, but slowly, clinging to life long after the mind no longer proved effective. In those cases, Ainsley wondered if hanging wouldn't be a more humane end than the slow starvation the bodies endured physically and mentally.

The bodies of criminals were brought to St. Thomas Hospital as a formality and, when there was time, one of the morgue doctors would issue a death certificate. Sometimes it would be more than a week before the bodies could be released, but the one that Ainsley stood before was fresh, only a day old or so.

The shard of mirror in his gloved hand, Ainsley pulled back the sheet and positioned it above the slightly sunken stomach. With one swift motion, he drove the pointed tip into the obliging flesh then quickly pulled it out. The result was an inch wide gash. Ainsley placed the shard down and ran to retrieve a lantern and ruler from his cache of equipment. For the next half an hour Ainsley made notes on the depth and shape of each puncture with the intent to compare them to the wound on the brunette brought to him two days before.

That was how Margaret and Lady Brant found him, hunched over the corpse of the unnamed criminal, measuring each gash with precision.

"Peter, dear." Lady Brant stood a few feet away, Margaret beside her. "Is this hospital-sanctioned?"

Ainsley straightened his stance, and looked over the body

in front of him. There were at least twenty cuts in the flesh of the abdomen but Ainsley had been concentrating so hard, so keen on extracting as much information as he could, that he had not realized the damage he was doing. He pulled off his leather gloves and threw them down near his notes, and returned to cover the body with the sheet again.

"I am assisting an inspector," Ainsley answered, raking his hand through his hair, "On a murder case."

Lady Brant raised her eyebrows, her interest piqued.

Margaret walked around the table and reached over the body for Ainsley's notes. The paper had a few smears of blood, as if his hands had been marred by the body he was handling. As Margaret began to read them, Ainsley noticed what she had taken. "They are just notes." He snatched them from Margaret and turned from both women.

"I had not realized bodies were used in such a way," Margaret said, pulling back the sheet, her curiosity getting the better of her.

"Oh yes, Margaret," Lady Brant chimed in. "Doctors are granted a special privilege, are they not Peter?"

Ainsley nodded but he knew Lady Brant was doing him a favour. He was not sure how the other doctors would view his experiment. Most would have been keen to use whatever bodies they could find for medicinal purposes, including their own medical training, but with the changing views of society at large, he was not sure his tampering with a non-bequeathed body would have been acceptable. Lady Brant's explanation to Margaret showed Ainsley that she was on his side, and would cover for him if the need arose.

"So let's see this murdered soul, shall we?" Lady Brant breathed deeply, her curiosity overriding her sympathy.

Ainsley led them to the body of the brunette. "I was told she was identified as Lady Charlotte Marshall," he explained, as he began to pull back the sheet.

Margaret took in a quick inhale of breath. "Peter!" She raised her hand to her chest.

"When was this?" Lady Brant asked.

"Two days ago," Ainsley said. "Before we knew." He pulled back the sheet, revealing the woman's face and upper abdomen.

Lady Brant clicked her tongue and shook her head. "And that, Margaret dear, is why I do not trust law enforcement. This girl looks no more than twenty years old. Look at her. And your mother is far more beautiful."

Margaret nodded, but Ainsley could tell she was reluctant to speak. She appeared out of place and was clearly disturbed by the thought of the body belonging to her mother.

"You can imagine what a shock it was," Ainsley explained.

Margaret shook her head in disbelief. "Oh, Peter, how wretched."

Lady Brant leaned over the abdomen and looked at the gash that was the women's death sentence. "What did it? A knife?" she asked.

Ainsley shrugged. "That's what I was trying to determine," he said. "We found these in her letted room." He indicated toward the unorthodox puzzle of mirror pieces. "I thought one of them might be the murder weapon."

Lady Brant and Margaret were quick to look away from Lady Marshall's look-a-like and surveyed the mirror pieces. "Any more pieces?" Margaret asked. She enjoyed a good puzzle just as her brother did.

Ainsley shook his head. "I plan to match my data with the size and shape of her wound—"

"What's this?" Margaret asked, pointing to one of the pieces. Ainsley approached her.

"What?"

"That right there. It looks like an etching." Margaret held up the piece of glass for them to see.

Peter leaned in and Lady Brant brought the light closer. The three of them crowded around, peering at one triangular piece. "It looks like a circle," Lady Brant said. There was no piece beside it, one of the missing pieces held the rest of the design.

"It's a petal," Margaret said after careful study. "Like in a flower. I am sure of it." Ainsley grabbed for the piece and carried it to one of the floor-to-ceiling windows at the side of the room to be held up to sunlight for closer scrutiny.

"How can you tell?" he asked.

"It's a teardrop shape," Margaret explained. "If you were

a woman you would see it. The most commonly etched design is of flowers."

Ainsley returned to the table and replaced the shard. "You, sister, are a genius." He planted a forceful kiss on her forehead and walked away. He removed his apron and grabbed his coat.

"Peter, where are you going?" Lady Brant asked.

"To tell Inspector Simms," he answered with a broad smile on his face.

Chapter 12

See! Our friends are all forsaking
The wine and the merrymaking.

Ainsley returned to the house late that night and found Daniel in the parlour enjoying a cigar. The sight of him there at their family's home at such a late hour, and not in his newly built home, caused Ainsley to start. "Is everything all right, Daniel?" he asked.

"Why shouldn't it be?"

"Has Evelyn called it off then? Is that why you have come?" Ainsley found himself surprisingly giddy at the idea of Evelyn coming to her senses and not marrying his brother.

Daniel scoffed and drew from his cigar. "Certainly not," he laughed. "My house is a quagmire of dust and noise. I have decided to remain here until that dirty business is at an end." Daniel eyed Ainsley suspiciously. "I must say, brother, your excitement at my possible misfortune is rather disconcerting."

"Not excitement," Ainsley lied, "surprise."

Daniel nodded, though he appeared unconvinced.

"You said so yourself, Daniel, the marriage was not your idea." Ainsley poured himself a drink of scotch before taking a seat in the chair placed before the fire across from his brother.

"That is true," Daniel conceded. "If our parents are any kind of example, I doubt marriage is a good prospect for anyone. Why should I feel excitement for something that has the potential to cause me such pain?"

Ainsley had never heard his brother speak like this before. Daniel was always the businessman with a stoic, unmovable outlook on life as being nothing more than a string of business opportunities; he surprised Ainsley by speaking, for once, from his heart.

It pained Ainsley to hear his brother so defeated, though,

before vows were even exchanged. It did not seem right for Daniel to view marriage so harshly, to see his future so drearily. Ainsley felt it was his duty to say something to lift his brother's spirits and so he too disregarded his own, sometimes brash, exterior and spoke a truth he had always held inside.

"You should be excited, brother," Ainsley began, "because the same potential exists for greater fulfilment than you or I could ever imagine," he finished with a breathy air.

Daniel fell silent at this and the two brothers stared blankly into the fire for some time as it crackled before them.

Their reverie was soon interrupted by the door opening behind them. In stepped Billis, a tray in his grasp and a young woman trailing closely behind him.

"A meal for you, sir," Billis said, placing the tray on a table beside Ainsley. "Miss Margaret made special arrangements for your meal."

Ainsley saw his brother smile, almost mockingly. "Who's the young lady, Billis?" Ainsley asked, peering around the butler to the woman carrying the tea tray.

With the tea tray in front of her, her slight form was exposed, revealing a tightly fitted bodice that narrowed at the waist before becoming a wide flowing skirt. She was young, perhaps twenty, with a mass of long wavy hair the colour of cinnamon which had been pinned into a tight bun as befit her uniform. Her skin was pale, perhaps made to look even more so next to the deeply rich colour of her hair. With flawless skin and plump pink lips, she appeared to be just the type of girl Ainsley found himself drawn toward. But she was a servant and, for all that, she was protected by her position.

"This is Miss Julia Kemp, sir," Billis spoke with his hands clasped behind his back and he moved at the waist, shifting from the young Marshall men to the young woman as he spoke. "She is to be Miss Margaret's new lady's maid."

Ainsley and Daniel exchanged intrigued glances, raising eyebrows in surprise. When Ainsley looked back to the woman, she was looking at him. He smiled but it quickly faded once he saw the flirtatious look on his brother's face.

"Lovely," Daniel said, a hint of laughter on his lips, which caused her to become shy and drop her gaze to the floor.

Ainsley lowered his voice and directed his words to Daniel. "Margaret functions rather well with just one of the house maids to assist her. I wonder why Father chose now to hire a dedicated lady's maid?"

Daniel twisted his mouth into a half-smile and turned to his cigar. "Perhaps it has something to do with your little sojourn to the country," he suggested, looking at his brother.

Ainsley decided to ignore his brother's taunts and instead raised his head to address the butler. "Billis, surely serving tea is not part of her expected duties?"

"I asked for her assistance since all of the other maids are busy preparing food for tomorrow's event," Billis explained. He turned to the young lady as she placed the heavy tray on the table next to the fireplace but close to the brothers. "You may return to the kitchen once you are finished serving the tea," Billis told Julia before turning to leave.

"So Miss Julia," Daniel ventured devilishly, despite the disdainful look Ainsley was giving him.

Daniel was watching her intently as she gracefully lifted the china teapot and began pouring tea. It was a look that made Ainsley a little more than uncomfortable. He could only imagine how the girl must have felt. "Are you from the city?" his brother asked, an internal laugh threatening his attempts to remain serious.

"Do not embarrass the girl," Ainsley pleaded. "You know she is not permitted to speak to you unless necessary." Daniel raised his cigar to his lips but continued to look at the girl. Ainsley realized then that his brother did not care if he embarrassed the girl, not as long as there was sport in it.

"She could speak, if she would like," Daniel prodded while grinning.

Her face remained unchanged and she continued with her chore.

Ainsley saw her swallow hard, obviously trying to keep her composure. He saw the cup and saucer shake slightly in her hand as she crossed in front of him to present Daniel with his tea. When she turned back to her tray she kept her eyes to the ground and wiped her palms on the sides of her skirt. She glanced to Ainsley briefly as she passed. Clearly, his brother's attentions were unnerving her. He made a point to look her in the eyes when she approached him with a cup and saucer, and smiled warmly, hopefully giving her some measure of comfort.

She took a step back, straightened her skirt demurely and stared at the empty space between the brothers. "Will that be all, my lords?" she asked.

"Perhaps," Daniel smiled, "you'd like to help me draw a bath this evening, since everyone else seems to be occupied." His smile became crooked, as if he enjoyed her failing attempts to hide her shock.

"Oh, Daniel, that's enough," Ainsley said, unable to stand the awkward exchange another moment. After giving his brother a long, disapproving glare, he turned to Julia. "Thank you, Julia."

Her expression was stoic but it was her eyes that betrayed her despair. They glistened in the firelight, highlighting the lower lids as if she could cry at a moment's notice. She turned as soon as she was dismissed and Daniel's subsequent bemused laughter turned Ainsley cold despite the hearty fire.

Like a king on a throne demanding the jesters to dance, Daniel looked to others, the staff mostly, to provide him with entertainment, most often at their own expense. He must think himself witty, Ainsley thought, using his words to unsettle the female servants and watch them blush. Perhaps he fancied himself good-looking, or desirable, and took their shocked expressions and shifting gazes as confirmation that they found him irresistible.

In any case, there was no need to cause young staff members to cry. He was being a bully and Ainsley felt no better, as though being there made him a party to the rude behaviour. For the most part, he had just sat there and watched.

Ainsley sprung up from his chair suddenly and followed her. At the back of the house there was a long, narrow passageway that led to the stairs to the kitchen. It was here that he caught up with her.

"Julia," he said, reaching a hand to touch her shoulder. She swung around and he felt a sharp, stinging pain on the left side of his face. She had hit him, closed-fisted, and she looked as if she was ready to run but her hands went up to her gaping mouth.

"I am so sorry, Mr. Marshall," Julia said, her shock evident.

Ainsley nursed his cheek for a moment, the stinging continuing with the pressure of his hand. "I should not be sneaking up on you." He lowered his hands and noticed a slight ringing in his ears. It was a solid hit and, no doubt, her palm was on fire from the impact. When his eyes went to her hand he saw her shaking it, giving him reason to believe his guess was right. "Are you okay?" he asked. He held out his hand, offering to examine hers but she stopped short.

"I thought you were the other Mr. Marshall," she explained. She looked down the hall to the kitchen stairs.

"I only came to apologize," Ainsley said, struggling to keep her attention. "He won't be living here for much longer and..." His voice trailed off at the sudden appearance of Violetta at the top of the kitchen stairs. Her arms were weighed down by two buckets full of steaming water. She approached them and they pulled to the side of the hallway to allow her to pass.

"My mother is having another bath?" Peter asked Violetta as she passed.

"Yes, my lord," Violetta answered with only the slightest movement to meet his gaze as she passed.

Ainsley did not bother to hide his annoyance. His mother demanded an impossible standard of living. He was sure Violetta would collapse before long.

"Excuse me, my lord, I must return to the kitchen." He turned to see Julia drop a slight curtsey before turning. As he watched, he saw her hand rise to her cheek, as if wiping away a tear.

"No, wait." He didn't dare touch her again but she turned at the sound of his voice. It was undeniable. She could barely hold in her emotions, though she tried valiantly. She avoided his gaze, letting her eyes gloss over and then dropping them slightly to the floor.

"If my brother has upset you," Ainsley said, daring to take a step closer, "I can speak with him, tell him he is not to address you again."

The tears came then, steady and unmistakable. Ainsley pulled his handkerchief from his breast pocket and offered it to her. With a shaky, uncertain hand she accepted his silk handkerchief and used it to dry her cheeks and eyes. "Thank you, my lord," she said, her voice vibrating with either sadness or worry. "Will you tell His Lordship of my indiscretion?" she asked, sniffling slightly as she tried to hand back his dotted handkerchief.

Ainsley shook his head. "No, you keep it," he said. "There is no need to speak to my father, but you shouldn't be put off by my brother. If he rattles you again I have no doubt you could defend yourself." He raised his hand to his pulsing cheek and laughed slightly. "Who taught you to hit like that?"

She did not smile but rather returned to her statue-like exterior, using a unique ability to freeze her features and remain aloof. "Tonight was not the first night I have met men like your brother." She nodded and bending slightly at the knees in a curtsey turned to head down the stairs to the kitchen.

Ainsley decided his brother was a brute, inconsiderate and reckless. He was no longer the harmless flirt Ainsley grew up believing him to be; after that evening's exchange, he realized that his own flirtatious nature was nothing in comparison to Daniel's domineering ways.

Ainsley liked women, but only bothered them as much as they were willing to be bothered. He never teased or set out to embarrass them, as Daniel had done to Julia. He suddenly became very fearful for Evelyn, who would be celebrating her engagement to Ainsley's beast of a brother in less than a day. Ainsley thought he should warn Margaret, perhaps ask her to be more sympathetic to Julia and perhaps watchful. There was no telling how his sister felt about being assigned a lady's maid. When he went to her room to speak to her, he could not ask because she wasn't there.

Chapter 13

We are call'd–we must go.

Margaret stood under the curved brick archway that framed Jonas' front door and released the iron knocker, satisfied with the deep base sound which signalled her arrival. She glanced back to Jacob, her family's carriage driver, who stood next to the duo of horses. He looked at her with concern, no doubt questioning why she would request to come to such a place. Bonnington Square was not the sort of neighbourhood the Marshall clan was accustomed to visiting. Though pleasant enough with its two-storey row houses adorned with symmetrical arch windows and walled gardens, Margaret could have no doubt that her extravagant carriage had attracted a certain degree of attention from the middle-class families who lived there.

Margaret tried to look determined, if only for Jacob's sake, though she began to wonder herself whether she had made the right choice.

"Perhaps we should come again in the morning?" Jacob offered. Margaret did not reply.

"No one is at home, my lady," Jacob said, a trifle more panicked this time. He eyed the windows above them as if he were embarrassed to be seen in such a place. Most likely he was embarrassed for her, not realizing she had business with the occupant.

After another knock and a brief moment of waiting she almost resigned to leave, imagining Jonas back in his gambling den at the cards table. But then the door opened swiftly, catching her off guard. Startled she raised her gloved hand to her chest and inhaled.

"Jonas!"

Her surprise made her sound breathless, providing a cover for the real shock of seeing him with his shirt unbuttoned. He was hastily buttoning up as he stood before her. "My apologies," he said out of breath. Leaving the last two buttons undone, he raked his hands through his hair and smiled.

"I did not mean to interrupt," Margaret said, feeling heat rise into her face. It was anger more than embarrassment and it took all of her composure not to completely berate him. She wondered what he could have possibly been doing without his shirt on at such an early hour of the evening. Despite the fact that a winter night had settled, she had been careful not to call too early. She knew he was with a girl, a tart of some sort, the type of conquest that he and Peter always seemed jocular about whenever they were in each other's company.

"No interruption," Jonas answered, his breathing more controlled though still uneven. "Would you like to come—" he stepped aside but stopped himself. "Perhaps that is not gentlemanly." He bore a look of worry, afraid he had committed a deep *faux pas* and looked to Jacob as if to apologize.

Margaret hesitated to enter. She did not want to see the girl, whoever she might be, even if the trollop had miraculously dressed while they stood on Jonas' doorstep. After a moment's pause, she dared to ask what was nagging at her.

"Who is she?" Her voice was cold and distant.

Bewildered, Jonas looked at her, as if questioning the origin of her enquiry. "Pardon?"

She laughed and shook her head. "I'm not stupid," she said, momentarily forgetting the true purpose of her visit. "Whoever she is, I hope you have enough respect to make her breakfast in the morning."

Propelled by anger, she turned, much to the relief of Jacob, who seemed all too ready to help her into the carriage and leave.

"Margaret!" Jonas stepped out into the pavement, grabbing her arm to turn her around. "There's no girl, if that's what you're thinking."

Margaret swallowed, suddenly finding it hard to look at him, purposely avoiding the patch of bare chest she could see beyond the undone top buttons of his shirt.

"You cannot blame me for making that assumption."

For a brief moment, Jonas looked lost until Margaret's

eyes flickered to his chest and quickly moved away, staring over his shoulder. Doing up the last three buttons, he groaned, suddenly aware of his misstep. "If you must know, I performed a surgery today, a rather..."—he searched for the proper word—"messy one that didn't come to a happy end."

Margaret's face fell at the thought of it.

"I was changing my shirt because parts of the young man followed me home," he continued indignantly.

"I am sorry to hear that," she said. "It must be a hard time for you."

"It is."

He wasn't angry with her. Margaret knew as much but she felt completely helpless to comfort him, and even more silly for coming to bother him in the first place. The identity of her mother's lover seemed inconsequential now that she was home safe and sound, more or less, while Jonas treated dying men and women all day. A moment of quiet contemplation passed between them before Jonas' face softened.

"Why did you come, Margaret?" he asked.

She swallowed hard and looked back to Jacob, who waited expectantly. "Take a carriage ride with me?"

∿ ∽

A carriage ride with a bachelor, even with open curtains, was only slightly less unseemly than disappearing into his parlour without a chaperone. Jacob seemed determined to stay on the main, well-lit roads, though Margaret quickly drew the curtains to shield them and their conversation from inquisitive pedestrians.

Before they left Jonas had grabbed his jacket and a tie and within a few moments he was seated across from her, one leg bent and propped up on his knee, a hand purposely clasped on his ankle, while his free arm was stretched out across the back of the bench beside him. He looked so relaxed Margaret thought he would light up a cigarette at any moment. His nonchalance annoyed her greatly, especially since she felt like a tightly wound ball of wool.

Their relationship had been easy once, friends because

Peter wished them to be, but since that kiss and his subsequent desertion of her and Peter, Margaret could feel the strain. She had thought she loved him once, but finding him at home in such a state of undress reminded her that he was a ladies' man, a gambler, and a doctor. He could never be tamed. Even if they could be together, she would always wonder, never fully trusting him because of his past.

"Did you really think I was entertaining a woman?" he asked.

Margaret licked her lips, biting into the top lip slightly. "You have to agree it is not out of the realm of possibility."

Even though they sat with their knees practically touching, the distance between them was expansive. In the failing light she saw him shake his head in disbelief, glancing out the window momentarily before returning a hardened gaze toward her.

"It was all I could do to get out of the house without Julia knowing where I went." Margaret grew tense, remembering the afternoon she had had with Julia following her from room to room. Margaret had uttered less than four words to the maid and hoped the lady's maid would soon give notice so Margaret would no longer have such a shadow about her.

"Julia?"

"My new lady's maid. Father hired her. It's dreadful. She's quiet, reserved, and so very helpful. She does so much for me I think I will scream."

Jonas' lips curled slightly. "Dreadful."

"You misunderstand. She's my father's spy. She has access to my clothes, my trinkets, my entire life. I have to tell her where I am going so she can help me dress appropriately and all I can think is how unfair it is that my brothers can come and go as they please while I must be tethered to the house in some way. And she has such a nice demeanor it is hard to dislike her."

Jonas' laugh was one of amusement and arrogance. "Do not dislike her," he said with a slight shrug.

Margaret wished very much that she had not brought it up. She had not expected him to make fun of her.

"Become friends with her," he explained after some more laughter. "Switch her loyalty from your father to you."

"Could it be so easy?" she asked, already growing weary of his arrogance.

Jonas shrugged and the tension grew exponentally. Margaret thought it might have been a mistake to come see him. Their exchange was formal and controlled, and as much as she wanted to confess how much his kiss meant to her she held back. Seeing the way he was now and the manner in which he held her at a distance made her think that perhaps it was just a dream.

"Mother is home," she blurted out, deciding to get straight to the matter at hand.

Jonas smiled slightly. "I am glad to hear it."

"I should feel relieved but I don't," she explained.

"She is home, that is all that matters," Jonas said. "I had heard a rumour that Scotland Yard had brought in the body of Lady Marshall."

Margaret's face fell at the memory of Peter telling her just that at the hospital that afternoon. She nodded. "Peter told me about their mistake. Must have been dreadful for him."

"Be grateful it was an error and not your reality."

Margaret saw something in Jonas' eyes, though he tried hard enough to prevent her from seeing. There were tears, she thought, but when he looked back to her they were gone. What was it, she wondered, that struck him so harshly? He was angry with her for assuming he was entertaining a woman and now it seemed he was hurt by her inability to be appreciative.

"I am grateful," she retorted, perhaps a little too forcefully. "I am just not sure the worst is over." She expected him to have a quick retort, to offer some basic advice or easy solution but he remained silent, perhaps unable or unwilling to allay her fears. "Jonas, I need to know who he is," she said at last. "Did you see his face? Did you recognize him?"

It took him a moment to answer. He shifted slightly in his seat, which Margaret could not be sure was due to the movement of the carriage. "I don't think—"

"Jonas, please! I have to know."

"What will you do, chase him down and demand answers?" Jonas asked.

Margaret looked to her hands, twisted together slightly

on the folds of her dress. "No," she answered meekly. "I just need to know what kind of person he is. Is he the type to want to support her, to marry her? You can tell a lot by a person without even speaking to them."

"You mean judge them," Jonas said. He did not wait for Margaret to answer but she was so dumbfounded by his words she wouldn't have said much anyway. "I saw all I needed to," he said with a deep exhale of breath, "and then all I saw was the hurt on your face, that was all I could think about."

Margaret closed her eyes in disbelief. "I try to remember but it's all a fog. I can remember her," Margaret looked up pleadingly, "and you."

She did not know what she expected; perhaps she thought he would remember their kiss or take pity on her and soften his demeanor. Maybe she felt he would see how much she cared about him. Whatever she expected she was sorely disappointed.

He exhaled loudly and adjusted himself in his seat, pulling his coat in tighter around his body. It was as if he looked at her but could not see her. She knew then that he was truly lost to her.

"I don't remember," he said with a slight shake of his head. His tone was so definitive that Margaret did not press. "What does it matter, Margaret?" he asked. "She came home."

She found herself feeling angry, the red heat of frustration radiating from her core. Because it matters, she thought. It matters that she disappeared for days without anyone knowing where she went or how she fared, leaving their imaginations to assume the worst. It matters because the woman who returned did not resemble her mother in any way. It matters because something simply does not feel right. As much as Margaret wanted to feel the affair was over, in her heart she felt it was only the beginning of something much worse.

Chapter 14

Laid low, very low,
In the dark we must lie.

Ainsley had not ventured down to the kitchens of the Belgravia house since he was a young boy. Despite a near free rein at The Briar, all the Marshall children were promptly dispatched by Billis should they try to head down. The butler's office, which he shared with the head housekeeper, was set right at the bottom of the stairs. An open door was all Billis needed to ensure there was no unauthorized entry into his domain. That day, however, Billis was not in his office and Ainsley was able to walk past without being noticed.

The basement was a long hallway with the kitchens, scullery, and larder on one side and Billis' office and laundry area on the other. Ahead of him, Ainsley saw Julia walk from one of the rooms with a silver dress draped over her arm. She walked toward him with her head bowed and her hand running along the smooth satin fabric, a smile hinting at the corners of her mouth.

"Is Margaret wearing that tonight?" he asked.

The young maid stopped, suddenly aware she was not alone. "Yes, sir," she answered sharply. Her dreamy demeanor vanished and her gaze fell to the floor as he walked toward her. "I was just checking the hue against some ribbons I found..." Her voice trailed off, uncertain.

"Is Violetta about?" he asked, sensing her discomfort. He looked into the doorway of the kitchen but saw only the scullery maid at the sink.

Julia glanced up slightly and nodded. "She is down the hall, sir."

Ainsley smiled his thanks and continued down toward the far end of the hall. After a few steps, he looked over his shoulders to see Julia staring after him. It was not the fact that she was looking at him that unsettled him. He was used to that sort of attention. It was the look in her eyes, a look of sadness that came over her when she saw him. Ainsley felt as if he had seen it before.

Their eyes met for a brief moment, before she turned abruptly and dashed up the stairs, the long skirt of Margaret's silver dress rippling behind her as she went.

Violetta was seated near a long thin window that allowed in a small measure of light. A length of fabric in one hand and a threaded needle in the other, she strained against the dim light to sew tiny beads into the fabric. As he stepped closer, Ainsley recognized the fabric as a dress his mother was in the habit of wearing on special occasions. It became obvious the lady's maids were spending much of the day preparing for the engagement dinner later that evening.

Ainsley watched for a long while before Violetta finally looked up. "Mr. Marshall," she said, lowering the needlework that made her hunch over. She smiled at first and then it faded. "Is something amiss? The mistress?"

He shook his head. "No."

Violetta gave an audible sigh and raised a hand to her heart. "Even His Lordship does not venture down to the kitchens," she answered with a slight laugh.

"I have come with enquiries," he said, deciding he needed to take a firm tone with her if he expected her to give him the answers he needed. Her loyalty to his mother was commendable but it would not serve his purpose. "I need to know where Her Ladyship was."

He saw Violetta swallow nervously and then bite her lower lip. She shook her head and opened her mouth as if to say something but nothing came.

"You know my mother better than anyone," Ainsley coaxed. "And you were with her, Violetta."

Older than his mother, Violetta could have been a grandmother or great-aunt to Ainsley and his siblings. She could be both stern and loving within the same sentence. This instance was no different.

"Mr. Marshall knows better than to ask me for his mother's secrets," she answered firmly. "They are hers alone." She turned back to her needle and thread.

Ainsley hadn't expected his quest to be fruitful. His mother had a way of inciting loyalty as easily as she provoked smiles, but he knew he must try.

"I know about the laudanum," he said.

Violetta's work stopped, her hand frozen midair, her fingers pinching the needle. She remained quiet for a moment, her eyes trained on her mistress's dress and then she started again, saying nothing.

"She takes it regularly," Ainsley prodded. "I know this. Now that I have found her empty bottles I can see the signs clearly enough."

"I cannot say," Violetta answered. "Even if I wanted to tell what I know, you know I couldn't," she replied, looking up from her work briefly.

"She works you like a mule," Ainsley nearly yelled. He could feel heat rising into his cheeks and his hands curling into fists. "How can you be loyal to that?"

"Because convention—"

"Oh, damn convention!" Ainsley turned from her and paced the wide room. The smell of lye and ash invaded his senses as he walked to the corner. "Violetta, I am not defending my father"—a laugh accompanied his words— "but my mother—"

"Needs help. Yes, but I will not betray her confidence to open her to ridicule and abuse." Violetta spoke firmly, like any good matron would over her charges. Perhaps she felt his mother was in need of her care and, therefore, protection.

Her position seemed soli   d against Ainsley's barrage. He could not argue against such loyalty. It did not seem right that she paid such loyalty to his mother, forsaking everyone else.

"Your heart is placed right, Mr. Marshall, however misguided."

Ainsley nodded and turned to leave, stopping short at the threshold. With his head bent to the floor, his arms holding both sides of the door, he spoke in a near whisper. 'Was she with him?" he asked.

The maid was silent and he was forced to turn. He needed to see her face in response to his query. She had gone pale and her needlework nearly slipped from the precipice of her skirt.

His frustration was undeniable.

"She was, wasn't she?" he pressed. "She was with *him*."

"I do not have many more years on this earth, Mr. Marshall," she answered deliberately. "I simply could not live the rest of them in peace if I were to betray her ladyship's confidence." Violetta gathered her mistress's dress, stood and slipped past him. "I'm sorry," she said quietly as she went.

***

Later that evening Ainsley found Margaret seated at her toilette table staring blankly into the mirrored glass as Julia finished her hair. Margaret had the look of someone lost to another world, neither hearing nor truly seeing the activity around her. Ainsley hovered at the door as Julia placed a final pin into Margaret's hair, gingerly patting the secured curls with an open hand.

"How is it, my lady?" Julia asked, coaxing acknowledgement from Margaret, who refused to look up from the various bottles and jars on the table before her.

"Thank you, Julia," Margaret said by rote rather than genuine appreciation.

Julia gave a quick curtsey and turned toward the door where Ainsley stood, leaning against the door frame. Her eyes trained on the floor, Julia passed him.

Walking toward Margaret, Ainsley saw that her copious curls, pinned up from the neck with only a few tendrils cascading down, were dressed with silver ribbons twisted to look like rosebuds. The effect was quite stunning against her deep, chestnut hair.

Margaret finally looked up into the mirror, recognizing her brother standing behind her. "Beautiful, isn't it?" she asked, turning her head side to side to look at the elegant effect the tiny roses had on her hairstyle. "Goodness I hate her," she said with a scowl.

"Margaret," Ainsley said with a wide smile, "why would you say such a thing?" Ainsley found a seat on the edge of a chair at the foot of her bed. He took his place carefully, aware that his formal evening wear could easily be marred or wrinkled with any slight carelessness.

Margaret turned, throwing her arm over the back of the chair on which she sat. "Because she is so good. She can do everything and anything. I bet she goes to Whitechapel every Sunday afternoon to read to the orphans and brings them the crumbs from her week's worth of dinners!"

"Margaret, you are being unfair."

"Am I?" Margaret turned from him and grabbed for her silver, elbow-length gloves lying flat on her toilette. "Yes, well what do you expect from someone so inferior as I? I mean, really Peter, you'd think she was the princess of Norway the way you and Daniel fawn all over her."

"Daniel and I?"

"Yes!" Margaret began pulling on her gloves, careful to pull each finger into the formfitting satin. "I have seen more of Daniel in the last two days than I have the entire previous year."

It was worse than Ainsley had previously thought. He had never believed his brother capable of such philandering. His engagement party was hours away and he had been spending his time eyeing their family's newest maid.

Ainsley must have bore his concern on his face because Margaret's face fell and she grew serious. "Peter, tell me it's just a coincidence."

He wished he could, but he knew better. He had seen it in his brother's teasing tone and hungry eyes, and knew it was more than some slight flirting. He was to be a married man before long and already he was giving in to his wandering eye. He worried for Julia, but most of all, he worried for Evelyn, who truly had no idea who she was marrying.

Ainsley fell silent but Margaret must have been thinking along the same lines as he. "Poor Evelyn," she said.

"Perhaps I should warn her," Ainsley said, suddenly feeling a tightness at his collar.

"They will be in their own home before long and Julia won't be a distraction for him," Margaret reasoned, though she must have known her tone was less than convincing.

"Until another maid comes along that catches his eye?" Ainsley asked. He saw her press her lips together and her gaze dart to the floor. "Face it, Margaret, our brother is morally corrupt."

"Well, if Mother is his example, should we be surprised?"

"Father is not known for his moral choices either,"

Ainsley added, with a raised eyebrow.

❧ ❧

With Margaret on his arm, Ainsley headed down the stairs and saw Daniel waiting impatiently for the rest of the family to join him in the foyer. In full dress, he matched Ainsley almost exactly with black trousers and waistcoat, a pleated white shirt decorated with a pristine white necktie. He held his tall, silk hat in his one gloved hand while the other was thrust deep into his trouser pockets. A sigh of relief came over him when he saw Ainsley and Margaret walking gingerly down the imposing, curving staircase. "We have to only pray no one is about in the streets," he said, "Or Jacob will have a time of it getting us there on time." His tone hinted at annoyance. He appeared nervous, or so it seemed to Ainsley, who smiled at his brother's eagerness and then sneered at the memory of his ill-advised attentions to the newest housemaid.

At the base of the stairs, Margaret turned to the footman, Cutter, who waited with her evening cape. Billis stood at attention two paces off.

"Where is Father?" Ainsley asked his brother, but his question was almost immediately answered.

Lord Marshall exited his study door at the far end of the foyer, looking as if he had been ready for hours. He spread his arms out to the side and came straight for Margaret. Planting a kiss on each of her cheeks, he beamed.

"What a very becoming look for you, my dear," he said, surveying the ribbon roses in her hair.

Margaret patted her hair. "Julia did all the painstaking work this morning," she explained. Ainsley saw her look to Daniel, who appeared neither interested nor impressed by the maid's artistry. Apparently, he cared only to tease and taunt the girl relentlessly.

"She has done a mighty fine job, if I may say so," Lord Marshall said. He looked to Ainsley, pressed his lips in a tight smile. "Shall I keep my eye out for you tonight? I hear Evelyn has a slew of female cousins."

Ainsley gave a smirk. "No need, Father," he said, "I am quite capable of picking my own bride, should it ever come to that."

The fact had not been lost on Ainsley that Lord Marshall had pointed Daniel toward a young lady. Their union was not based on a mutual attraction, friendship, or any other fanciful notion of matrimony. Daniel and Evelyn were thrust together by the mutual benefit of both their fathers and if there were a more archaic means for soliciting lifelong disaster Ainsley was not aware of it.

Lady Marshall appeared at the top of the stairs just as Billis presented Lord Marshall with his hat and Margaret reached over to straighten Ainsley's necktie. Frozen in action, the family watched as Lady Marshall began her descent, clutching the handrail with a vise grip, smiling daintily though she wobbled slightly. Ainsley could only watch her take two perilous steps, each time fearing she would collapse down the stairs, before finally bounding up toward her two steps at a time.

"Thank you, Peter dear," she said in a quiet voice. She smiled at him as she gratefully took his arm and allowed him to anchor her as she stepped.

One glance to Margaret at the bottom of the stairs confirmed that she saw what Ainsley had. This woman, who had once been strong and formidable, had turned weak, seemingly overnight. She had always been the picture of grace and elegance but that facet of her seemed a distant memory. Even as Ainsley clutched her arm, grasping her hand to steady her, she faltered and would have fallen had Ainsley not been there to brace her. With just a few more steps to go, Ainsley saw his father turn from them, exasperated.

Once safely on the marble tile of the foyer, Lady Marshall gently placed her gloved hand on Ainsley's cheek and smiled. "You are too good for this family," she said, without any regard to the other family members who stood within earshot. Made uncomfortable by the slight against Margaret and Daniel, Ainsley said nothing. He stepped back, allowing his mother to turn into the fur-lined cape Billis held for her.

"Shall we go now, Mother?" Daniel asked, his words pushed out by a sudden exhale of breath.

Billis held the door, and the family filed out into the street, where their carriage awaited them. The ride was quiet and somber, despite Margaret's repeated attempts to lighten the mood and incite conversation. No one seemed in the mood for conversing and soon she relented, allowing the five of them to slip into an awkward silence.

Chapter 15

The merry glees are still;

The home where Evelyn lived with her parents was similar in finery and ornateness to Ainsley's family home, though it was farther from the heart of London. Not much could be seen on the outside due to the winter evening hour, but once inside the front door the building opened up into a three-story landing with a maze of arches and balconies circling above them. A large crystal chandelier hung somewhere between the first and second floors, suspended in place by a long, thick chain descending from the ceiling. When the Marshalls entered, only certain members of the staff were gathered, footmen holding trays of champagne and maids positioning exaggerated arrangements of flowers.

"Lord Marshall! Lady Marshall!" A petite womanly form approached them, arms outstretched before her. She grasped Lady Marshall's hands, squeezing them in greeting before planting a kiss on her cheek. An imposing man loitered behind her, reaching out a hand to Lord Marshall.

"A pleasure to see you again, Lord Marshall. I gather we will be seeing an awful lot of each other in the coming months," he said, smiling as they shook hands.

"Lord Weatherall, allow me to introduce my children." Lord Marshall turned. "You have met, Daniel of course. Here is my second eldest, Peter, and my beautiful daughter, Margaret."

Daniel was the next to offer a firm handshake and Ainsley followed suit. Margaret gave a slight curtsey when she was introduced and smiled demurely when both Lord and Lady Weatherall commented on the intricacy of her hair.

"I only wish I had another son," Lord Weatherall pronounced. "In a few years' time, our families could make a splendid showing in the House if another match between our houses could be made."

Lord Marshall smiled. "Pity, isn't it? No other girls either, then?" he asked, indicating Ainsley who found his father's attempt at matchmaking rather irritating. His father was not entirely joking, despite his jovial tone.

"No, afraid not. It's a matter of fate that I had a daughter at all," Lord Weatherall explained, giving a glance to Lady Weatherall. Ainsley saw his father's eyebrow rise, which caused Lady Weatherall to laugh.

"Evelyn is my daughter from my first marriage," she explained, "I was widowed whilst she was but a lamb. I married Ezekiel when she was twelve. Will's mother, the first Lady Weatherall, died when he was born."

"Have no fear, Jonas," Lord Weatherall said with a reassuring slap to the shoulder, "Our agreement on the dowry remains the same." His boisterous laugh filled the entire three floors of the foyer. "She is my daughter through and through."

"I do apologize, Lady Margaret, dear," Lady Weatherall said to Margaret, patting her gloved hands. "William has already promised himself but had I known, I'd have cast off that young lady and easily replaced her with you. You look so charming." She smiled and placed a cupped hand on Margaret's cheek.

Evelyn came down the stairs then and hurried to greet them. "Doesn't everyone look so dashing? I hope getting through traffic was not a chore," she said. She looked everyone over with only a fleeting glance to her fiance before letting her gaze continue to flit about.

"Come, Lord Marshall, Daniel, Peter, we shall have a drink in my study before our presence is required," Lord Weatherall said.

The three obliged, following him down a hallway to the right. Ainsley took up the rear, watching his father and Lord Weatherall chatting ahead of him and Daniel. Congratulating each other on the match made, no doubt. Daniel seemed to be taking it all in stride, neither interested nor overly worried about the coming weeks before the wedding. In the very least, Ainsley thought, he should consider the years that stretch out well beyond the wedding day.

Ainsley glanced back down the hall, expecting to give Margaret a reassuring smile but he was surprised when he saw Inspector Simms and who he believed was another detective standing at the threshold.

Ainsley retraced his steps down the hall. "Inspector Simms, can I help you?" He tried to look calm but all he wanted was to demand why the detective was bothering his family here on all nights. He could barely look at Inspector Simms for answers without betraying their working relationship.

"My apologies, Lord Marshall," Inspector Simms answered. "I was not aware of your relationship to the Weatheralls," he said, his tone apologetic.

"My brother is marrying their daughter. This is to be their engagement dinner."

The other detective spoke up then. "Inspector Wright," he said with an offered hand. "We have come to interview Lady Evelyn."

Behind them guests were arriving and even though the detectives did not wear the standard Scotland Yard uniform, their attire betrayed their profession. Ainsley gestured for the footman who was walking past. "Excuse me, can you point me to a room where I can meet with these gentlemen? Perhaps somewhere we will not be disturbed by guests arriving to the gathering."

The footman looked to the two men, knowing instantly who they were, and bowed slightly. "Yes, of course, follow me."

Once safely installed in the library Ainsley turned to the footman before he closed the door, "Please inform Lord Weatherall of our sudden guests and summon Lady Evelyn to come at once." The footman nodded with a "very well, sir," and closed the door.

Ainsley straightened his evening coat as he turned to the detectives. Wright had busied himself by surveying the room.

"We had no idea your brother was celebrating his engagement tonight," Simms explained. "My apologies."

"Justice does not wait because an aristocrat decides to have a party," Wright injected.

"What is this in regards to?" Ainsley asked. "My mother

has returned and I doubt the young Lady Weatherall has anything to add to your investigation of her disappearance. In fact, I don't believe she was aware of it."

"I am no longer investigating your family," Simms explained. "We have come in regards to a brunette female found stabbed in an east end rooming house—" Simms' deliberate voice was cut off by the clicking of Wright's tongue.

"We are not in a position to explain further," Inspector Wright explained. "I am sure you can understand."

Ainsley looked to Simms, who simply nodded slightly. They were referring to the woman he thought had been killed by a piece of a broken mirror. Simms thorough explanation was for Ainsley's benefit.

Evelyn entered the room, smiling, perhaps expecting a gathering of guests. Her smile faded quickly when she saw who it was. She looked to Ainsley, licking her lips anxiously. "You needed to speak with me, Mr. Marshall?"

"This is Inspector Simms, and Inspector Wright of Scotland Yard—"

"What is the meaning of this?" Lord Weatherall bellowed from the door, his jubilant demeanor disappearing immediately at the sight of the detectives.

"Lord Weatherall, Inspector Simms." Simms offered a hand, which Lord Weatherall just looked at, refusing to shake it. "This is my partner, Inspector Wright. We are investigating the murder of a young lady by the name of Clara Buxton."

Lord Weatherall scoffed, annoyed at the questioning. "You will find no one in this house who knows a woman by that name." Lord Weatherall turned to leave. "If you will excuse me, gentlemen, I have guests arriving. If you would be so kind as to use the servant's door on your way out." He was gone before anyone could protest.

When Ainsley looked to the detectives, he saw they were not overly displeased.

"I think Lady Evelyn knows exactly who Clara Buxton is," Wright ventured, a self-assured smile gracing his lips. "Don't you, Evelyn?"

Evelyn looked to Ainsley. There was a look of recognition in her eyes, and Ainsley felt she either knew the woman or felt a pity for her. "Do you wish me to leave, Lady Evelyn?" Ainsley asked but she shook her head quickly. "Please stay," she said in a near-whisper. "I would feel better if you stayed."

"I could bring Daniel for you."

Again, she shook her head. "I'd rather not trouble him, if you don't mind."

"Lady Evelyn, please take a seat," Simms offered.

Evelyn took a step closer to Ainsley, positioning herself just beside him but ventured no further. "I'd rather stand, if you please." Ainsley thought he saw her shaking, and it pained him to see her so upset on such a night. Surely, the detectives could have come in the morning when there wasn't the ever-present risk of public embarrassment. He wanted to reach out to her, or give her a look of reassurance, as he would do with Margaret, but he knew such familiarity would bring more questions from the detectives, so he remained quiet as they questioned her.

"Lady Evelyn, do you know the woman in question?" Inspector Simms asked calmly.

"I do, Inspector," she said, surprising Ainsley. "That is, I did, when we were young."

"She is your cousin, is she not?" Inspector Wright interjected.

Evelyn glanced to Ainsley, and he noticed she was twisting her fingers roughly in front of her. "I have not seen her in years. Was she truly murdered?"

Simms nodded. "I am afraid to say it, but yes."

"She knows it," Wright laughed, approaching her with a marked determination. "She was there."

"I most certainly was not!" Evelyn backed away and Ainsley stepped between them.

"Inspector Wright, that is quite enough!" Ainsley said boldly, holding out a hand to prevent him from coming further.

Simms walked toward them, as if he would pull Wright away but he didn't need to. Wright stopped in front of Ainsley and peered around him at Evelyn. "This will go easier if you tell us the truth."

"I don't know what answer you expect me to give. I was not there. I have not seen Clara in nearly ten years. I doubt

I would know what she looks like if I did." She swallowed and her eyes went to the floor. "Inspector Simms, may I ask how she died?"

The detective hesitated, not because he was afraid of revealing evidence but most likely because he felt her delicate state could not handle the shock. "She was stabbed, Lady Evelyn, in the stomach."

Evelyn raised a hand to her mouth and the tears came freely then. Ainsley turned to her, offering his silk handkerchief.

"I thought the lady had not seen her in ten years," Wright pressed. "Why such emotion for a woman you barely knew?"

Ainsley sneered at the detective. "I think your time is done. Evelyn, you do not need to answer any more questions. I will speak with the detective's superiors first thing in the morning." If Ainsley's threat affected Wright, he did not show it. Ainsley opened the door and guided Evelyn out with a hand gently laid on the small of her back. "Inspector Simms, remind your partner to whom he is speaking."

In the hallway, Evelyn nearly collapsed in his arms, forcing him to hold her up while he guided her toward another room, moving farther away from the guests who were steadily arriving for the engagement party. Not sure which rooms were behind the doors, he found the nearest one, opened it and guided Evelyn in. He was pleased to find it was Lord Weatherall's study, now empty, though the lights were still lit and the fire warm. Ainsley led her to one of the plush chairs and knelt before her.

"I should never have allowed them to speak with you, at least not without Daniel present."

Evelyn snapped her hand around Ainsley's wrist. "Don't tell him. I beg you, please." Her stare bore into him, wide and pleading. "I couldn't live if he knew."

"Knew that you had a cousin?"

"If he knew I had gone to that place, that boardinghouse. It was horrible, but when I left she was alive. I had no idea she was dead, let alone murdered."

"Then why did you tell the detectives you haven't seen her in ten years?"

Evelyn swallowed and her eyes drifted before coming back to search Ainsley's face. "I felt that is what Father would want me to say. He wouldn't want me to admit to knowing someone like that, not when he had forbidden all of us from even speaking of her." Evelyn hesitated, putting a hand to her forehead. "She came here a week ago asking for money. She said she had gotten herself into trouble and needed help. I knew she wouldn't be asking if it weren't life or death but Father didn't see it that way. He thought she was trying to capitalize on Mother's newfound fortune. He sent her away, not so nicely, and told her to never come around again."

"But you went to see her?"

Evelyn nodded. "Yes." She began to cry again, the redness marring her perfect skin. "I went, gave her what money I could. But when I left she was alive, I swear it." She looked up to him, her eyes wet and her cheeks blotched. "Please don't tell Father. He will think me wretched for disobeying him and Daniel would not marry me if he knew my past."

Ainsley involuntarily smiled at this. Would Evelyn marry Daniel if she knew his family's secrets?

"Your secret is not mine to tell," Ainsley answered in a reassuring tone.

The door opened behind them and they both turned to watch as Margaret slipped in. "Was that Inspectors Simms?" she asked. Her eyes found Evelyn in the chair, evidence of distress bore on her face and Margaret's eyes softened. After a slight pause, and a sideways glance to Ainsley, Margaret spoke. "What did they tell you about Mother?"

Ainsley stepped between them, preventing Margaret from moving closer and saying more, perhaps revealing their family's secret.

"Margaret, Evelyn has just found out her cousin was murdered," he explained.

Margaret stammered. "Oh...my. How dreadful."

Ainsley turned to Evelyn, who seemed too engrossed in her own tragedy to have noticed Margaret's slip about Lady Marshall.

"Why don't you take a minute?" he offered his hand and

assisted Evelyn to her feet. "Margaret can help you freshen up in your rooms, if you like."

Evelyn nodded feebly and slipped her arm into Margaret's. At the door she turned, peering at Ainsley over her shoulder.

"Thank you, Peter," she said with a demure smile.

The pair exited and Ainsley remained, a hand shoved in his pocket, the other scratching his chin and jawline.

Her initial tactic had been to lie to both detectives, he remembered, but she had confessed to him quickly enough once they removed themselves from the room. His position in society, not to mention his relationship to her future husband, would deem him the most undesirable confidant. She could not possibly know his involvement in the case; if she did, she would be just as wary of him as she rightfully was of Wright and Simms.

Ainsley drew closer to the side table; a decanter nearly empty of port remained, along with three crystal glasses. He poured the remaining contents from one into another and managed to serve himself nearly a full glass from the decanter. He drank eagerly while picturing Margaret and Evelyn preening themselves before a mirror. No doubt Margaret would apply a certain amount of powder to hide Evelyn's tear-stained cheeks.

How could Ainsley know if Evelyn's story was true? She could have very well been present during the girl's murder. The body was positioned on the bed in such a loving way; someone close to her, riddled with guilt no doubt, must have laid her out so thoughtfully. Could Evelyn possess the strength to move such dead weight? Of course. Ainsley grew angry with himself for such a thought. Recent experience had taught him that women were just as capable of murder as men.

His mind wandered, drawn back to Picklow and the young woman, Lillian, he had met there. He wondered how she fared, and then the guilt hit him. It was a feeling that he had evaded for some time since returning to London. Of all the times for these notions of guilt and responsibility to burst forth it had to be then, when he should very well be dancing, asking each young maid for a turn, as his duty required. Instead he was stiff with remorse, cloistered in the study, holding back what could be a flood of tears were he not careful.

One more gulp finished his port and he placed the glass on the table. He straightened his evening coat on his shoulders and checked the position of his tie, all the while steadying his breathing, pushing back any thought of Lillian, her sisters, and the horrors he witnessed while away from London. It was done, he told himself. They could not be saved.

Chapter 16

The voice of the bird
Shall no more be heard,

Margaret was already dancing by the time Ainsley emerged from the study. Evelyn had taken some time to allow her eyes to dry but had anyone looked closely they would have seen evidence that she had been crying. Thankfully, most of the guests were dancing, drinking champagne, or engrossed in jovial conversations, so no one noticed. Ainsley felt Evelyn squeeze his hand as she walked by him before drifting again into the crowd. He could see her greeting people and smiling without even a hint of the anxiety and fear that had engulfed her moments ago.

A footman appeared beside him with a silver tray adorned with flutes of champagne. Ainsley took one, though he cared little for that form of drink, and downed it rather suddenly.

"What did the inspectors want with her?"

Ainsley turned to see Daniel at his side, smelling of cigar smoke and brandy. He spoke softly enough so no one would hear, though Ainsley wondered if he also heard a hint of indifference.

"You knew they were interviewing her and you didn't come?" Ainsley hissed, though quietly. He glanced behind them, taking note of who may have been near.

Daniel shrugged dismissively. "Why should I? She's my fiancée, not my wife."

The pair bowed slightly as Lord and Lady Guilford walked in front of them. Lady Guilford, a cantankerous old goat, waved her lace fan before her face and only smirked as she paraded by.

"Sod-faced old crow," Daniel muttered. He tipped his fluted glass to his mouth. He turned to Ainsley, who had already finished his glass and was acquiring another. "Father has asked that we keep an eye on Mother."

Ainsley drew the glass to his mouth eagerly but found

the contents unsatisfying. He could not very well be everyone's secret keeper, not without something a mite bit stronger.

Seeing Ainsley's face, Daniel laughed. "Come," he said, tapping Ainsley on the chest, "follow me."

Ainsley followed his brother through the hall, dancing to their left and boisterous conversations on their right, until they were on the empty back veranda, the cold night making visible wisps of their breath. Ainsley watched as his brother pulled a bottle from behind one of the planters. "Evelyn's brother, Will, told me this is part of his secret stash." Pulling the cork, he offered Ainsley the first drink.

Whiskey.

"A likeable fellow," Ainsley said as his brother drank.

Daniel shrugged. "Likeable enough. Though I confess I don't plan on spending that much time with him, so it hardly matters."

Ainsley nodded, accepting the bottle again.

"Found my secret stash, huh?"

Ainsley turned to see a short man approaching them from the hall doors, a wide, amused grin decorating his face. He offered a hand to Ainsley, who shook it briskly. "Will Weatherall," the man said. Even his words seemed to smile.

"Peter Marshall." As they shook hands, Ainsley noticed Will kept his other hand in his pocket.

"My sister says you may be her new favourite brother," Will said warmly, accepting the bottle Daniel offered him.

"I doubt that," Ainsley answered, abashed.

"It is rather unfortunate those inspectors needed to come this evening," Will said, shifting his gaze from Daniel to Ainsley. "We are grateful for your fast action in getting them sequestered before too many guests arrived. My father tells me you are a man who commands and others follow. This is a good trait."

Ainsley did not know what to say. He looked to Daniel, who seemed unaffected by the praise being offered him.

"What did they want anyway?" Will asked.

"Yes, Peter, you never did answer my question," Daniel chimed in, his consonants blending together as he spoke. His eyes drifted, closing slightly before popping open again.

Peter looked around the veranda and then toward the door to the party, where they could hear laughter and glasses clinking, just to be sure there was no one else about.

"A cousin, Clara Buxton, was found dead, I'm afraid. Murdered. The inspectors had reason to believe Evelyn may have had contact with her recently."

Will laughed openly. "I highly doubt it. We have not seen the woman for... many years. I could scarcely say what she looked like anymore."

Ainsley shrugged. "Evelyn confirmed that point, though the shock of hearing of her cousin's death was a little too much to bear."

"She hardly knew the woman," Daniel said. "I cannot believe she feels much for her at all."

Suddenly, the alcohol was doing the trick. Ainsley could feel the tension slipping from his body, actually slipping from his fingertips and toes. The three of them drank the entire contents of the bottle as they stood on the veranda overlooking the family's back garden.

"Follow me, gentlemen," Will suddenly blurted out. "You strike me as the sort that will appreciate what I have to show you."

A few moments later, they were in Will's room on the second floor with the door closed. Ainsley and his brother watched as Will went straight to the table beside his bed and opened the drawer. He pulled out a small, wooden box and laid it on the bed. Opening the latch, he lifted the lid to reveal a gleaming silver pistol cushioned by a dark blue, silk cloth.

Both Ainsley and Daniel's eyes lit up at the sight of such a newly minted handgun. They drew closer as Will pulled it from the box and held it out for them in his open palms.

"Go ahead, take it," Will said, nodding toward Daniel, who was showing a keen interest.

Daniel grabbed the wooden handle and held it close as he ran his fingers over the engraved brass that adorned the sides. From his vantage point, Ainsley could see a marking of G & J Deane, and recognized the gunmaker to Prince Albert.

"I had it commissioned months ago," Will explained. "I

received a message yesterday that it was ready. Father would not allow me to wear it this evening," he said with a shrug, "but I intend to always have it on me."

"Peter, have you ever seen one so detailed?" Daniel asked, tilting it toward Ainsley.

"How does it shoot?" Ainsley asked, preferring to be impressed by its practical application.

Positioning himself ahead of the others, Daniel raised the pistol with an extended arm and levelled his line of sight with the opposite side of the room.

Will shrugged. "Haven't had a chance to test it. My stepmother hates guns and I need to wait until we are in open country. Though for the price I paid for it, I don't see how it could miss." He chuckled slightly and accepted the gun when Daniel handed it back to him. He placed it in its box and tucked it away in the drawer. "You should consider getting one Daniel, especially with my sister to protect."

Daniel nodded but Ainsley was weary. Exactly when did these aristocrats expect to need such weaponry?

❧   ❧

When Ainsley finally descended the stairs, he caught Margaret's eye on the other side of the room. She was speaking with Lady Brant, who appeared to be rambling without pausing for breath, and he made his way over to them.

"Peter!" Lady Brant grabbed him by the arms and leaned to the side, allowing him to plant a slight kiss on her cheek. "I was just speaking with Margaret about our scheme. Seems to have worked, no?"

For a moment, Ainsley hadn't the faintest clue what she meant until he saw the disparaging look on Margaret's face and he remembered the discussion they had at breakfast the day before.

"Everything has worked out then. Your mother has returned and everyone will think she was only out of town for a few days." Lady Brant looked overly pleased with herself. She patted Margaret's hand gently.

"I fear we have made things worse," Margaret confessed. "Who leaves and returns from Edinburgh in three days?"

"Four," Ainsley offered. His comment only incited raised eyebrows from Margaret.

"Don't you think people will wonder? Ask questions?"

Lady Brant smiled and waved off Margaret's concern. "No one pays that much attention."

Margaret sighed heavily and gave a look to Ainsley. They both knew how much attention was paid to such details. Lady Brant may not concern herself with the comings and goings of society folk, but there were individuals within society who were deeply concerned about the lives of others. There was no telling who would be keeping tally of Lady Marshall's returns and departures.

"Let us hope the family can avoid any further debacles," Ainsley offered with a forced smile. "We can repair with time."

"There's the spirit," Lady Brant said enthusiastically. "Nothing repairs scandal like a glorious wedding. I heard Lady Weatherall say your brother and Evelyn would like to marry within the fortnight."

Margaret looked startled at the idea. "So soon?"

Lady Brant laughed. "Is it not the bride's prerogative to choose the date?"

"But it seems so sudden." Margaret looked to Ainsley clearly in distress, but there could be nothing he could do. "Is it wise?"

"I say have it done with," Lady Brant leaned in to Margaret and Peter and lowered her voice, "before the girl gets cold feet, if you understand me." Lady Brant waved to a passing couple. "Excuse me, my dears," she said and slipped off in pursuit of them, leaving Ainsley and Margaret dumbfounded at the revelation.

Surveying the room, Ainsley could see Evelyn and Daniel standing together, smiling with guests he did not recognize.

"Why do you suppose she wishes to wed so quickly?" Margaret pressed, careful to keep her voice low.

Ainsley shrugged. "I haven't—"

"Unhand me!"

Lady Marshall was heard before she was seen being escorted down the main stairs, one of the Weatherall's male servants keeping a vise-like grip on her arm, more to keep her from falling down the stairs than it was to guide her.

Lady Marshall struggled relentlessly, trying to throw off the man's assistance. "I can do it!" she slurred.

Pulling against the servant Lady Marshall lost her balance and staggered.

It happened fast. Ainsley, who had been inching toward the bottom of the stairs to assist, had no time to react. Lady Marshall slipped and fell three stairs before stopping, having grabbed on to the handrail. A minor fall compared to the ten steps or more that would have brought her to the bottom. Her cry of pain rang out loudly throughout the party and everything went quiet as all of the guests turned to the staircase. Lady Marshall was injured somewhere beneath her bulbous hoop skirt.

Ainsley and Margaret were quick to come to her side, as was the servant who had tried earnestly to prevent that very thing from happening.

"Mother," Margaret cried, grasping Lady Marshall's hand. Margaret recoiled after her mother gave her a sneer, but she did not release her hand. Ainsley went to the opposite side. The normally dignified Lady Marshall hissed, pointing at her left leg. "My ankle," she said, writhing from the pain.

Ainsley went one stair below and found his way beneath the many layers of crinoline, hoops and fabric to her injured ankle. Sliding a slender shoe from her foot, he felt her ankle and lower leg, watching her reaction closely as he manipulated and pressed it.

"I am so sorry, my lady," the servant said, kneeling beside them.

"It's all right," Margaret said with a smile. "You were trying your best."

"What were you doing upstairs?" Ainsley asked Lady Marshall, as quietly as he could muster.

For a moment, it appeared as if his mother had not heard him. She looked down at her leg with a look of deep concern but when her eyes flickered up to him and then back down Ainsley knew she had heard him and was simply refusing to answer. Ainsley looked to the Weatherall's servant, who swallowed hard.

"I found her in Miss Weatherall's room," he said sheepishly. "She was opening the wardrobe and drawers, my lord."

Ainsley had little doubt as to whether the servant's words were true. Lady Marshall gave the poor man a look that ought to have turned him to stone.

"Mother!" Margaret's voice nearly cracked from the shock of it.

"I was just looking around," Lady Marshall said with a shrug, as if the proceedings bored her immensely. "I wanted to know the trollop your father engaged my favourite son to without my consent."

Ainsley failed to hide his surprise, though he tried. Did she say favourite son? Ainsley saw Margaret's apologetic gaze and shook it off. It was obvious their mother was drunk, and influenced heavily by her laudanum. It also became rather obvious that her fall had brought on a crowd who waited eagerly for word on her condition at the bottom of the stairs.

"Mother, please tell me you were not trespassing in the Weatheralls' private rooms?" Margaret asked.

"Only Evelyn's."

A muffled groan escaped both Margaret and Ainsley's lips. Ainsley slid his head into his hand and rubbed at his temples. She held no remorse whatsoever. Suddenly, all sympathy he had for her left him, influenced heavily by her slight against him. He could not understand how Daniel could be her favourite when it had been Ainsley who had kept her company at The Briar for all those years. Daniel was not the one who defended her when everyone else said such awful things regarding her character. In fact, where was Daniel now while she writhed in pain and public humiliation?

Perhaps Father was right, Ainsley thought. Mother was a blight on the family record, causing embarrassment and discord wherever she went. In his youth, he thought her fun-loving and jubilant, but perhaps he had been wrong. At that time, their levels of maturity mirrored each other, but now Ainsley was grown and finally seeing her antics as simply that, and he had far less desire to join in.

A murmur rose up in the crowd. Lord Marshall and Daniel emerged from those gathered, but remained at the bottom of the stairs as if establishing their distance.

"Nothing's broken," Ainsley said harshly, pulling his

mother to her feet abruptly. "Time to go home, Mother."

With the Weatherall's servant on one side and Ainsley on the other, they guided Lady Marshall down the stairs. Ainsley saw his father whisper into Daniel's ear and his brother left while Lord Marshall remained, looking ill-amused and somewhat hostile. He downed the remnants of a drink and thrust his empty glass toward a nearby valet. Ainsley struggled against the near dead weight of his mother, who clung to him, her least favourite son, as he tried to assist her down the stairs.

Just as Ainsley and Lady Marshall came to the bottom of the stairs Lord Marshall turned to the crowd. "My wife is all right," he said, giving the guests an easy grin. "We will take her home." As the crowd tapered off, Lord Weatherall appeared beside them and Ainsley's father turned and took his hand. "Thank you for your hospitality, Lord Weatherall,"

Ainsley passed them, their conversation falling into obscurity. His father was laughing at his wife's antics, showing little concern; no doubt, he had become an expert at such manoeuvres over the years.

At the door, Margaret placed Lady Marshall's cape on her shoulders before allowing the butler to help her with her own. Outside, soft wisps of snow drifted slowly in the blue night sky, covering the family's carriage, the backs of the team of horses, and the tops of the groom's hat.

"There's no need to leave," Lady Marshall protested as Ainsley led her down the few steps to the gravel drive. "We haven't made a toast."

"It is late," Ainsley lied. "You are overtired."

Lady Marshall pulled away from him and staggered back, unable to place her entire weight on her ankle. Ainsley grabbed for her but she fell backward and landed in the dusting of snow.

"Peter!" she screamed from the ground. "You dropped me!"

In an attempt to control his anger, Ainsley turned, running his hands through his hair. He walked to the front of the carriage, looking over the sleek, snow-covered backs of the horses as he paced.

"Peter!" Lady Marshall's screech was louder than before and held more of a shrill.

"Mother!" Margaret hissed. Ainsley saw his sister looking behind them to the darkened windows of the Weatheralls' manor, where the silhouettes of the guests could be seen against the lights inside. Clenching his jaw, Ainsley walked back to where his mother was crouched on the ground to offer a hand though he had little interest in playing into her shenanigans.

"Mother," he said, crouching down in front of her. Keeping his gaze square with hers he spoke in a low, commanding tone. "You are going to let me help you up and then you will get into this carriage. If you don't I will hoist you over my shoulder and throw you in, am I clear?"

Obviously stunned by her son's brutish threat, Lady Marshall nodded sheepishly and accepted his hand.

Ainsley positioned himself beside her in the carriage, strategically placing himself between his mother and the door. Margaret sat across from them and not long after Lord Marshall and Daniel filed in.

Ainsley watched as his father sneered at his wife, an unmistakable look of contempt for the woman who seemed hell-bent on ruining the small measure of respectability the Marshall name still held. At one time, Ainsley would have felt sorry for her, but he couldn't any longer. Any childish delusions he once held were long gone, replaced with his own feelings of scorn and anguish.

Everyone settled into an uncomfortable silence as the carriage jerked into motion. In the intermittent light of the gas lamps Ainsley could see his father's jaw clenched, his mouth pinched into a scowl. Lord Marshall's elbow was resting on the slim ledge of the window, his hand drawn to just in front of his mouth, quietly pensive.

When Daniel finally spoke, his voice echoed the anger evident in all of them. "Good God, Mother," he said, letting out a breath. "I have never been so embarrassed. I will be lucky if the Weatheralls don't call off the entire wedding."

"Perhaps we should," Lady Marshall said with a slight slur.

"I am sorry you don't approve," Daniel said with abject disgust.

"I was never consulted!"

"You were hardly available, Mother," Margaret said softly.

"Your opinion has no bearing," Daniel's voice bellowed in the small space. "I'll be damned if my wife ends up like you!"

Lady Marshall closed her eyes and turned away.

"We've heard enough," Lord Marshall said finally, turning toward his arguing wife and son. "We will talk about it in the morning."

Even in the dim light Ainsley could see his brother shaking his head, refusing their father's command for silence. "No," he said, with a marked determination. "She cannot expect us to play along, pretending nothing happened." His stare burned into their mother, narrow and concentrated, and would not relent even when she looked away. "Where were you, Mother?" Daniel asked coldly.

Her face fell, her gaze dropping to the tiny folds of her gloves. She bore the look of someone sober enough to know what Daniel asked and it seemed all her former vigour to keep the act had slipped away. Suddenly, she looked scared, lost in a maze of confusion and fear. She looked to Ainsley then, perhaps seeking a less-hardened face among those who had reason to despise her.

"I don't know," she said softly, giving a slight shake of her head. She laid a gloved hand on Ainsley's. "I don't remember."

Daniel was out of his seat and at their mother, hand clasped tightly at her throat, his face inches from her own. "You little bitch!" he spat. A vein on his hand protruded, pulsing even under the pressure of his vise-like grip.

Chapter 17

Nor the wind on the hill.
O, misery!

From his seat, Ainsley pushed him off, driving his fist into his brother's jaw and sending him back into his carriage seat. Even though he boxed, Ainsley was not used to the feeling of his knuckles hitting another man's skin and almost as soon as he had done it he could feel the heat rise in his hand; the swelling had begun, but in no way did Ainsley regret it.

"Touch her again and I will kill you!" Ainsley yelled with a pointed finger. He placed a protective arm in front of his mother. "And if I ever hear of you laying a hand on Evelyn, or any other woman on this earth, I will come after you."

From his seat, Daniel snorted and turned away, licking the blood from the corner of his mouth with his tongue. Ainsley turned to his mother and saw her hand at her throat. With his doctor's eye, he examined her neck and could already see a bruise forming where Daniel's hand had been.

"Can you breathe?" he asked.

His mother nodded and gave a slight gasp, more so out of shock than injury, Ainsley hoped. A few moments later, the carriage stopped and Ainsley opened the door and positioned the folding steps for Lady Marshall, not bothering to wait for the groom to descend from his perch. The first to enter their home, Ainsley guided his mother toward the stairs and as they climbed he could hear the other family members walking in the door.

"Still hiding under Mommy's skirts, I see!" Daniel's voice echoed through much of the house. At the top of the stairs Ainsley ventured to look down at the foyer, where Billis was accepting Lord Marshall's coat and hat. Daniel stared up at them without a hint of regret for his attack on their mother and Margaret looked uneasy.

Ainsley led his mother to her room, ordering Violetta to bring tea in as much of an even tone as he could muster. With the lady's maid out of the room Ainsley went to his mother, who had taken a seat in her settee before a small fire.

"Let me see," he said, drawing closer.

Lady Marshall swallowed and raised her chin as he crouched down. She was red and slightly purple though it was hard to tell in the firelight. After removing her gloves Lady Marshall reached to the back of her neck and fumbled with the clasp of her necklace, her hands shaking uncontrollably. Ainsley stood, offering to do it for her. With it finally removed he saw small scratches on her throat and his heart sank as his hands threatened to curl into fists.

"Damn it!" He turned, tossing a small pedestal mirror from his mother's mantel. The glass shattered on the floor before he realized what he had done.

"I'm sorry," he said instantly.

His mother smiled and gave a slight shrug. "I never liked it that much anyway."

Ainsley began to gather the pieces, throwing them in the empty bucket next to the fire meant for the ash. His brother was a brute and needed a good fight, from a real threat, to put him in his place. Ainsley traced his hand over his forehead, wiping sweat from his brow as he forced himself to become calm.

"He is angry," Lady Marshall said in a tone denoting a certain amount of resignation.

"I'll show him some real anger."

His mother simply shook her head. "Peter, please. He has a right to be angry."

Ainsley shook his head and knelt before her. "Mother, I don't care what you did or where you were. All I care about is that you are home and..." he stumbled, "well. You are well, aren't you?"

"Whatever do you mean?" She placed a cupped hand to his cheek. The inebriated, sullen, ungraceful woman he had helped navigate the stairs earlier was gone, replaced by the mother he could clearly recognize from his youth. Suddenly, he felt fourteen again, defending her against everyone who did not understand her unconventional ways or permit her expression of ideas. He was determined to guard her, though he felt completely helpless to save her at the same time.

"I know about the laudanum," he said. He began searching her face, determined to decipher each muscle movement as she looked at him.

"Peter," she sighed, turning her gaze from him. "I have far greater problems than that, my dear."

"I found a bottle," Ainsley said. "Margaret and I found it in this room. It was empty."

She avoided his eyes, though she looked uneasy and overburdened.

"Tell me," Ainsley begged. "Tell me and I can help you."

She smiled, but shook her head. "Oh, Peter, no one can help me now."

There was a knock on the door and Violetta slipped in, a tea tray in her grasp. Ainsley stood, pulling away from his mother and returning to the broken mirror that needed his attention.

"Can we talk about this in the morning?" Lady Marshall asked. "I'd like to take a bath." She nodded to Violetta, who dropped a quick curtsey and left. Ainsley wanted to protest, knowing the physical requirement it demanded of Violetta, but he stopped himself. The warm water might do his mother well for both her neck and her ankle. Besides, she needed some time alone and so did he.

Chapter 18

Hark! death is calling

Margaret was waiting for her brother in the family's private library, unable to shake the thought of her mother rooting through Evelyn's belongings. A swift shiver trailed up Margaret's spine and pulling her blanket tighter to her body did little to stave off the intrusive cold. She had already changed from her gown, preferring her nightdress and housecoat. Regrettably, she had pulled the pins from her hair but had been careful to save each silver rose with the intent to make an arrangement in the morning.

Such frivolous indulgences would have to wait. Much weightier matters demanded the majority of her thoughts, making her incapable of doing anything more than stare at the fire from her curled position in the cushioned chair. She did, however, turn the evening over and over in her mind. The way her mother needed Peter's assistance down the stairs before they left for the ball. The cool detachment with which her mother regarded her husband. And, worst of all, her loud and very public admittance to trespassing in a room that was out of bounds to her.

Margaret sighed involuntarily, hugged her blanket closer and pressed her lips together lest she yell out some profanity into the dark night air. She had no illusions as Peter had. He defended her blindly but Margaret was the one who was with Mother during the past many years while he was away apprenticing. While he was gone, she had been the one to guide Mother's drunken body back to her room at night. She had made excuses for her absence when people called. She often shrugged off her mother's strange behaviour with a laugh and some fun, but there could be no jokes of late.

She had caught her mother with her lover just a few weeks ago and the image would forever be burned into her memory. Try as she might, Margaret had to concede that the remembrance could not be banished. But now, after being gone nearly a week, Lady Marshall had done the unspeakable and spoken out against her future daughter-in-law. She was found to be publicly drunk and, worse still, trespassing in the Weatherall family's personal rooms. There could be no greater disgrace save for divorce.

Divorce.

Margaret could cry at the word. Could her parent's separation be any more damning to her future marriage prospects than her mother's unforgivable behaviour already was? She licked her lips, pulling at them with her teeth. Perhaps she could be free of a match in society. Such a development would open the door for Jonas, if he would still have her.

"You smile."

Margaret started and turned to see Ainsley standing over her, amused by her absentminded smirk.

"Do not let me disturb your enjoyment," he said teasingly. He made no motion to leave, fully expecting her to apologize and insist he stay.

"Tis nothing," she said with a slight shake of her head and a nervous laugh.

Ainsley rounded the end of the couch and took a seat near Margaret's feet, which were curled up almost beneath her, the blanket hiding her bare skin. She watched as he slipped into the cushions easily, resting his arm on the back of the couch and positioning himself so he could look at her as they talked.

"That was quite a show, was it not?" he asked, letting a long breath escape as he spoke.

"It may have been more humorous were it just a show," Margaret offered. "Are you not scared Peter, of the effect this will have on our futures?"

"In truth, no," he said, "I do not fear for myself. I have already chosen an unorthodox path. I admit, however, I am fearful for you."

"Do not bother to be fearful for me," she said, allowing a full smile. "I may well end up taking an unorthodox path as well."

"Then so be it. Let Daniel be good. He's the heir, in any case. You and I can do as we choose." He clasped a hand on her leg, squeezing it slightly while smiling teasingly.

"Do you mean it, Peter? I can do as I please?"

She saw his smile fade, reality being very different from the playful fantasies of free choice and unbridled futures. He did not have to say the words for she knew by the look on his face that he had been playing and hadn't meant a word of it.

They fell silent, the crackling of the dying fire the only sound in the entire house, or so it felt.

"I don't know what our future holds," Ainsley said at last. "Though I am sure Father will have much to say about it in the morning."

Ainsley lifted from his seat, and leaned over Margaret to plant a kiss on her forehead. He squeezed her shoulder as he passed the edge of the couch.

$$\approx \quad \ll$$

Margaret startled awake, her forehead bouncing off the wooden trim of the couch. Raising a hand to her pulsing temple she realized she had fallen asleep some time after her brother had left her. The fire had burned down to mere embers, glowing and receding in unison as a draft waxed and waned. Margaret rubbed her eyes, forcing them to focus but finding it difficult against the near blackness of the room.

One of the servants, Billis at least, should have woken her and escorted her to bed. They would have checked the fires in all the rooms before retiring. They would not leave her there, she thought, surveying the facts. It must have been well after midnight. She could tell by the slight presence of blue in the darkness beyond the window. A full moon was hovering over the cold, frost-encrusted city and Margaret realized she had been asleep on the couch for only a short time.

Uncoiling her legs from beneath her, she wrapped the blanket tighter around her body and slid from the couch. With all the grace of a four-year-old assigned to the task, Margaret banked the coals of the fire until they scarcely shone. Then she moved for the door as gingerly as possible so she did not injure a toe or series of toes while going forward in the dark.

Swinging open the library door, she heard movement on the storey above her; it sounded like sliding across the wooden floor with a slight drag. Her mother's rooms were just above the library but Margaret doubted she would still be awake. She imagined the alcohol, and perhaps even the laudanum, had taken their toll, putting Lady Marshall into a deep, comatose-like sleep. Pausing in the hall, Margaret listened, expecting to hear nothing, but after a moment her wait was rewarded and she heard footfalls on the boards above.

At the bottom of the foyer stairs Margaret heard a door being closed, slowly and carefully, as if the person closing it did not want to disturb the others already asleep. Margaret herself would not have heard it were it not for the latch catching with a distinct iron pang. Halfway up the stairs Margaret saw a shadowy figure passing in front of her on the landing. The figure was shrouded in darkness, and Margaret realized the person had just exited her mother's rooms.

"Mother?"

The sound of the steps did not quicken, they paused momentarily before resuming their steady pace down the long hall. Straining against the darkness Margaret scurried up the remaining stairs and looked down the corridor, seeing nothing but the slightest movement of the curtain next to the window.

Ainsley's room was down at that end of the hall but Margaret knew he had retreated to his bed long ago. Daniel might be sleeping in his old room, as yet unchanged since he purchased his new home, and that room was further down that hall as well. Lord Marshall also kept a room down there, preferring the morning light to wake him than any clock or servant. Only Margaret and her mother kept rooms on the opposite side of the landing, the other two rooms reserved for special guests or visiting family. Another floor of guest rooms existed above them, with only Billis having a sizable room to himself on that floor, since those guest rooms were so rarely used, and then the female servants' rooms in the attic, only accessed by a narrow, winding passageway hidden behind a false wall at the end of the hall. Once a fireplace and chimney, the rickety stairs became a joke to the Marshall family, who could always hear when someone was either walking up or down them despite the visual illusion of stealth.

A sliver of light could be seen beneath her mother's door. A lamp, Margaret guessed, or a small fire. And then she remembered the hour. It seemed impossible for her mother to be awake. Margaret crept for the door, leaning her ear toward it to listen for movement. There was nothing. No humming, shifting of sheets or creaking of floorboards Margaret turned the brass doorknob and slipped through the dim sitting room. Intending to turn off the lamp or bank the fire, Margaret crept into the bed chamber expecting to see her mother in bed, asleep.

She was surprised when she saw her mother's roll top tub near the window and her mother still in it. Margaret's face fell, unable to hide her annoyance. How could her mother justify having so long a bath, with Violetta no doubt running the stairs with fresh pails of hot water to keep out the winter chill?

Margaret abandoned her attempts to remain quiet. "Mother, it is well past—"

She stopped. There was something about the way her mother's head slumped to the side, so close to the water.

"Mother?"

Suddenly Margaret found it hard to breath; a lump grew in her throat, cutting off air and leaving her frozen. Her legs grew weak as she stepped further into the room, unable to take her eyes from the oddly positioned form in the bathtub.

Margaret gurgled slightly, choking on the tightness when she saw her mother, her face half submerged, her eyes fixated forward. Her eyes just above the waterline, Lady Charlotte Marshall stared blankly and Margaret knew nothing remained behind those eyes. The thin fabric of her mother's shift floated, moving without a clear direction as the current of the water swirled, disturbed moments earlier.

A panicked scream escaped her lips and Margaret backed away colliding with the fireplace mantel behind her. In a panic, she began pawing at the wall looking for her exit. A mirror slipped from its nails and crashed to the floor, which sent another scream into the night. Tears came then, streaming steadily as the cries escaped her lips. She needed to leave. She was desperate to get away and yet she stared unblinkingly at the body in the bath.

Her mother had drowned.

Chapter 19

While I speak to ye,
The jaw is falling,

Ainsley had fallen asleep on top of his bedclothes, neither attempting to get under the covers or remove the myriad of medical texts that surrounded him. After he left Margaret he had gone to his room, and pulled all of the literature he had on addiction from his shelves. It was not long however before sleep overcame him and he drifted off.

It was Margaret's scream that startled him awake. He tore from his room and ran down the hall toward the sound of her voice, first the screams and then the sobs. He found her backing out of their mother's rooms and into the hallway, hand over her mouth. She only turned away when Ainsley touched her and it was then that she buried her face into his chest. He hugged her close, looking over her head to see into the room.

He inched forward but Margaret pulled him back.

"Don't," she said in a near whisper. "Don't."

Disobeying her, he pried himself away and slipped into the room. Doubt plagued him with each step but he forged on, steeling himself for whatever awaited him in his mother's room.

"Oh, my God!"

Once at the threshold he ran for their mother, dead and nearly blue. The house was fully aroused, with Daniel and Lord Marshall arriving at the door as Ainsley pulled his mother from the chilled water. Her body kept slipping from his hands as he tried to locate her pulse.

"Daniel, help me!" he yelled, unable to pull her body from the water.

Daniel ran in but hesitated, unsure how to assist him.

"Grab her arm!"

Daniel nodded and together they were able to pull her from the deep water. The shifting of her body and the movement of Daniel and Peter sent waves of water over the edge of the tub and onto the rug and wooden floor.

"Someone call for a doctor!"

Ainsley looked up, startled at the sound of Julia's voice, and saw her at the door, her standard maid's attire ghost white against the darkness of the sitting room. Lord Marshall nodded to Billis and the butler took off into the darkness with Julia close at his heels.

Lord Marshall clung to Margaret's shoulders as she leaned into him. Her cries had subsided while she looked on with only one emotion in her eyes. Hope.

With his mother propped up over the side of the tub, Ainsley pressed on her back. "Clear her airways," he ordered.

Clumsily, Daniel pulled the soaked strands of hair from her face and bent over to look into her mouth.

"Is there air coming out?" Ainsley asked, trying desperately to remain calm.

When Daniel shook his head Ainsley pushed harder, using the edge of the tub and the force of his pressure in the hopes that the water would come out.

"Peter, stop that!" Lord Marshall cried from the farthest corner of the room. His voice lacked the harsh dominance he so often displayed.

"Father, please!" Ainsley growled against the physicality of his work. "I know what I am doing."

Lord Marshall pulled in air, no doubt trying to calm his own panic at the sight of his wife at death's door.

"Now?" Ainsley asked Daniel, who again looked for signs of life.

Again Daniel shook his head.

"Damn it!" Ainsley did not stop. He pressed and pressed remembering precisely how he had seen the act depicted in a medical journal. The pressure should force the water out but as each moment passed Ainsley's strength weakened. His mother was limp and cold to the touch, dead and most likely had been for some time. He grew weak with each series of thrusts but he continued, hopeful for a better outcome each time.

"Peter." He felt a hand on his back and looked up to see his father crouching over him. "You have been doing this for thirty minutes."

Had it been so long?

"Let her go," his father said quietly.

Ainsley shook his head. "No," he said, choking slightly. "no, I can't."

Lord Marshall looked to his dead wife, swallowed hard before looking back to his son. "You have to."

Ainsley fell back into the pool of cold water that surrounded them on the floor, exhaustion engulfing him. He ran his hand over his face and then put both hands up and began crying. There was no chance of saving her, and there never had been. If it weren't the alcohol it would have been the drugs or some disease given to her by her lover— Ainsley's face went pale at the thought of it. He pulled his hands away from his face and he looked to the body of his mother. Even in the dim light he could see red marks forming on her neck, those he recognized from Daniel's outburst, but there were also marks on her shoulders.

"What is it, Peter?" Margaret asked.

"Call Scotland Yard," he said, a sneer forming on his lips.

"Whatever for?" Daniel asked.

"Do it!"

❧ ❧

Ainsley began to shiver; the cold water that had seeped into his clothing began to take its toll and he was forced to leave the room. "No one touches her," he ordered, pointing a finger at his brother and father before leaving. Margaret pulled herself from her father's arms and followed him down the hall.

"Peter, what could the inspectors possibly do for her now?" Margaret asked as she practically chased him to his room.

Ainsley turned at his door, intending to bar her entry. He was in no mood to answer her unrelenting questions. Not only had he just found his mother dead but he was unable to save her. He pounded a fist into the door jam and turned. "Margaret!" He stopped, suddenly ashamed at his misplaced anger. She stood just a few paces away, a blanket tightly wrapped around her shoulders and she too seemed to shiver against the cold night air. Suddenly, he remembered she had just lost her mother as well.

He glanced down the hall and watched servants lighting the gas lamps in preparation for the soon-arriving constables. Their father must still be in the room with Daniel because he saw neither of them.

Ainsley cocked his head back, inviting Margaret in, and closed the door behind them. Margaret headed for the hearth, gingerly placing a log into the dying embers to entice larger flames.

Ainsley began to undress, first releasing his collar and pulling his shirttails from his trousers. "Don't turn around," he commanded to Margaret, who kept her gaze on the fire.

Within minutes, he was dressed in dry clothes and buttoning a new shirt, leaving the top two buttons undone.

"Something is not right, Margaret," he said at last.

Margaret turned and watched as Ainsley struggled to fasten his cufflinks. She walked toward him, reaching as if to help his shaking hands but he turned away. Dejected, she took a seat on the edge of his bed and watched him looking out his window.

"You are overwrought," she said at last. "She must have fallen asleep and drowned."

Ainsley shook his head. "No," he said with vehemence. "Did you see the marks on her shoulders?"

"Peter, what are you talking about?"

"There are marks on her shoulders," he said. "Someone held her under."

Margaret started to laugh but stopped herself suddenly.

Ainsley sneered again, glaring at her with little patience. "Laugh all you want," he said. "I know what I saw. Have you forgotten what I do for a living?"

"You made those marks yourself trying to pull her from the water. You and Daniel," Margaret explained. She walked toward him cautiously. "Perhaps what you do for a living has changed your world into a very dark place."

The chatter down the hall grew louder and Ainsley knew the detectives must have arrived. He went for the door, stopping before he reached it and looked to Margaret. "The world is a dark place Margaret, and no amount of money can cocoon you from it."

Ainsley was pleased to see Inspector Simms but not so pleased to see Inspector Wright when he reentered his mother's room. His mother's body remained in the white tub, repositioned as they had found her. Her white night shift acted as a shroud, billowing beneath the water's hidden currents created by Ainsley's attempts to save her. All the lamps in the room had been lit and Ainsley could see the marks on his mother's shoulders more clearly than he had before.

"Why was I taken from bed so suddenly?" Inspector Wright demanded as he stood over Lady Marshall's body. Hands in his pockets he surveyed her in a way that made Ainsley uncomfortable.

"Huh?" Wright looked directly at Ainsley. "Your idea, was it?"

Ainsley shifted his gaze to his father, who pursed his lips and shrugged. He turned away. "If you need me, gentlemen, you will find me in my study," he said in a steady voice. Daniel followed their father out of the room, leaving Ainsley there to deal with the detectives. Perhaps it was only fair, since he had been the one to demand they be summoned.

"Looks like she drowned," Wright said, wiping the corner of his mouth with his thumb.

"I believe she had help," Ainsley said, trying hard not to look to the body.

"To drown?" Wright chuckled. "What did you say she was involved in, Simms? Opium, was it? Laudanum?" Wright shrugged. "Under the influence. Fell asleep. That's it."

Ainsley was across the room in two steps, grabbing Wright's collar and steering him back toward the wall. The detective's back hit the doorjamb with a marked thud. Ainsley got in one square punch before he was prevented from delivering another when Simms pushed himself between them, grabbing Ainsley's shoulders to hold him at bay.

Wright doubled over, clutching his face. Ainsley saw the detective's hands ball into fists and struggled against Simms' tightening grasp. In the scuffle two other constables came into the room and waited to see if they needed to help restrain Wright. The wounded officer, in pride and person, looked to the two constables and Simms before letting his

TRACY L. WARD

fists fall.

"Contain yourself, Mr. Marshall, or I shall have to find a way to contain you," Wright said, laughing slightly. He pulled his hand away from his mouth and rubbed the smear of blood from his lip into his fingertips.

"It's not worth it," Simms whispered to Ainsley.

Ainsley shrugged Simms' grasp from his shoulders and adjusted his collar without taking his gaze from Inspector Wright.

Simms gestured to the two uniformed constables. "Remove the body," he said, gesturing to Ainsley's mother. "Respectfully." They nodded and turned to retrieve a stretcher. "Wright, wait for me outside."

Wright's mouth curled into a smile, the blood now drying at the corner. He pulled his handkerchief from his pocket and dipped the corner into the tub before placing it to his wound. Ainsley stepped forward as if to hit him again but Simms pulled him back.

With Wright gone, Simms turned to Ainsley. "You, my friend, have a temper."

"You have no heart," Ainsley answered. He slipped onto the edge of his mother's bed, using the post to prop himself up. He watched as the two constables returned and together with Simms they pulled Lady Marshall's body from the water and placed it on a wooden stretcher. They covered her with a sheet. With one man on each end, they carried her down to the waiting carriage.

"What did you see when you first entered the room?" Simms asked.

"She was submersed in the water. Her face completely under."

"And?"

"I tried to revive her—"

"How?"

"A technique I learned in school. You apply quick pressure to the back to force air in and out of the lungs."

"Like with a newborn baby who doesn't breathe?"

"Yes," Ainsley answered. "It didn't work." The outcome was obvious and Ainsley felt awkward for having pointed it out. He found himself tapping his leg nervously with an open palm and forced himself to stop.

152

"When you first arrived, had anyone else been in this room?"

"Just Margaret. She found her." Suddenly Ainsley felt ashamed of his earlier treatment of her. They had both lost a parent and Ainsley had treated her like a nuisance. He closed his eyes in an attempt to block out the memory.

"You will send her to my hospital," Ainsley said. In no way was he asking.

"If you like." Simms eyed Ainsley, as if questioning his reasons for such a request.

"Yes."

"You cannot be thinking of examining her yourself," Simms said, lowering his notepad.

"Who better?" Ainsley asked. He ran his hand through his hair, and shrugged when Simms' penetrating gaze did not relent. "I could not trust her to another."

"Was she behaving peculiarly last evening? Did she do anything out of the ordinary?"

Ainsley scrambled to find the words that could describe the events. Realizing there was no better way, Ainsley let out a deep exhale. "She was discovered trespassing in Evelyn's rooms," he said with resignation. He began to relay the tale beginning with his mother's uncertainty with stairs and ending with her slight against the Weatherall Family. "We left shortly after that."

"Did she steal anything?"

Ainsley found his jaw clenching as soon as the words were said. "What sort of question is that?"

"A natural one given her proclivity for certain substances," Simms said without missing a beat. He had obviously dealt with many irate individuals and was used to asking questions most would never dare to ask.

"We are not your typical east end family, Inspector Simms. We do not pick pockets, provide favours for payment, or filch from our friends. Whatever recreational activities my mother participated in I am sure she had enough funds to support it." Ainsley began to pace the room, steering clear of the bath but hearing the water under his shoes as he walked over the rug. He shook his head in disbelief, not at Simms' line of questioning so much as the fact that he was required to answer them at all.

"I am not asking out of mere curiosity," Simms said after a long pause. "You must believe that."

Ainsley nodded begrudgingly. "You want to know if my father had reason to cut short her allowance?" he asked, already knowing the answer.

"I should hate to ask myself," Simms explained. "A gentleman like your father might find such a question impertinent."

Ainsley nodded, allowing his gaze to wander. He knew what Simms said was true. If they were going to find out the truth to any of this, it was Ainsley who needed to do the sleuthing.

Chapter 20

The red cheek paling,
The strong limbs failing;

Ainsley chewed on his thumbnail with his other arm crossed over his chest. Leaning against the counter of autopsy tools, he looked over the body of his mother, which was covered in a sheet of pure white. His hands shook slightly and his mind fluttered from one subject to the next, never really gaining a grasp on any one thought. He had been dreading this day from the moment he heard she was missing and this time he knew it was not a case of mistaken identity. She was there beneath a thin layer of linen, laid out like all the criminals and cadavers he had examined before.

Ainsley let out a long breath, steeling himself against the task before him. With one motion, he pulled back the sheet, intending to get right to work, but he stopped. He found himself looking at her face, tracing her jawline, counting each freckle before stroking the hair away from her face. Another breath and he forced himself to look away, to concentrate instead on the body and what it could reveal to him. He used the white cloth to hide her face and decided to look at her as just another cadaver. Nothing more.

Scalpel in hand he hovered over her torso, poised and ready, but his hand shook. The more he tried to steady it the more it jumped. Breathing forcibly, Ainsley pressed his lips together and lowered the blade to her pale skin but stopped short of cutting into it. After a moment, he turned, throwing the knife to the counter behind him. Pounding his fists on the table, Ainsley cried out in frustration. "Goddamn it!"

He trusted no other with the task and yet he was unable to perform the act himself. Desperation drove him to cover her up and charge out of the morgue and into the main part of the hospital. He found Jonas bent over a patient in one of the charity wards.

Ainsley cleared his throat.

Jonas looked up, his pleased expression turning sour when he registered Ainsley's pained look. "Is it Margaret?"

Ainsley shook his head.

                                            ଛ   ଵ

Later that evening, with the other doctors long gone, Jonas met with Ainsley down in the underbelly of the hospital, chilled like an icehouse in the dead of winter. Ainsley stood back while Jonas looked over the body on the examination table.

"Peter, say it isn't so," Jonas said without taking his eyes from the body.

"Say you'll do it. Do it and I shall never ask another favour as long as I live." Ainsley bit his lip and shook his head slightly before closing his eyes. Denial eluded him. For as long as he lived, he'd never forget that image.

Jonas swallowed and spoke hesitantly. "I'll do it," he said, "But I beg you not to tell Margaret."

"Oh what difference does it make?" Ainsley asked, suddenly agitated and impatient. "Our mother is dead and I need to know if someone killed her or if it's the result of her own... dependency."

"What am I to look for?"

"Laudanum. Opiates. Alcohol. Just do it now before I lose my nerve." Ainsley raised his hand to his mouth and began working on his thumbnail again. "I need to know if she was with child."

Jonas looked to Ainsley. "What difference would it make now?"

"Is that not a possible motive for murder, an illegitimate child? A stain on an otherwise pristine pedigree?" Ainsley found himself sneering at the mere thought. His father was more than capable of murder and he had certainly been given sufficient reason by then to want to wash his hands of his infidel wife completely.

"You'll forgive me if I have little patience," Ainsley said.

Jonas nodded without hesitation and their gazes locked for a long moment. It was then that Ainsley felt his old demons of self-loathing rising up and ripping at his chest. In the six years that Jonas had been his friend, Ainsley had been unrelentingly harsh, judgmental, and demanding, and here Jonas was, willing to break hospital protocol to help him yet again. It was clear they remained friends because Jonas was able to overlook Ainsley's arrogance.

Their rivalry had started with good intentions. Neither one seemed to mind their competitive streaks—comparing exam marks, wooing women, gambling, and boxing. In fact, their friendship seemed to spur Ainsley on when his enthusiasm for his studies waned. For that alone Ainsley owed Jonas a tremendous debt. In recent months, though, their rivalry had taken a turn and their encounters had become strained. Ainsley realized his folly as he watched his friend set to work positioning lights around the body

"Is something wrong, Peter?" Jonas asked, looking up briefly.

"I was just trying to think of a way to say thank you," Ainsley said, allowing a small smile. "I don't think I say that enough."

Jonas was already hunched over, scalpel in hand. "You're right," Jonas said, "you don't."

***

Like many other things, Ainsley regretted the flask he had downed by the time the third punch connected with his face. Had he been sober he would never have allowed a boxing opponent so much leeway. Hit after hit struck him with unrelenting force and Ainsley swayed, unable to get a grip on his senses, unable to defend the barrage that was always one second ahead of his reflexes. The chorus of the yelling crowd, dockworkers and railway men mostly, became shrouded in a high-pitched ringing that only grew louder as seconds passed.

The next thing Ainsley knew, he was sprawled out on a cot in the hospital. Jonas was leaning over him, a bit too closely, and Ainsley tried to wave him away but Jonas caught his wrist.

"Do not touch it!" he commanded, holding fast as he stitched the long cut above Ainsley's eye.

And then the pain hit him. The ringing was gone, the crowd as well and all Ainsley could feel was the poke of the curved needle penetrating his tender skin and then the thread being tugged through.

"Just one more," Jonas said in deep concentration.

Eyes closed, Ainsley scrunched up his fists and clenched his jaw until Jonas finally tied it off.

"How many?" Ainsley asked, resisting the urge to put his fingers up to feel it.

"Four." Jonas handed him a small hand mirror before turning to clean up his table. "You're going to be quite the sight at your mother's funeral."

Ainsley looked at his reflection and cringed. The skin around one eye had turned black and the other was now marred by an unsightly cut just under his eyebrow. Despite Jonas' steady suturing Ainsley knew it would never heal flat. He slapped the mirror on to the cot beside him in disgust.

"It took myself and three men to bring you here. I had hoped you would stay out for the entirety. But the third stitch was troublesome." Jonas turned to Ainsley on his stool and let out a sorrowful sigh as he clasped his hands in front of him. "Why would you agree to such a match?" he asked, "One would think you have a death wish. You know the Queensbury's allow you to use gloves now?"

"They confine the hands," Ainsley explained. "Besides, it's not like you haven't participated in a fight or two of your own."

Jonas placed a small square cloth on Ainsley's stitches. "People mature, they find new pastimes," he said, taking on a fatherly tone. "You should consider it."

Ainsley disagreed and shook his head slightly. "There is no pain greater than growing up."

The pair grew quiet before Ainsley spoke up, "Speaking of which, what did you find about Mother?" His tone was resigned. He already knew much more about her character than he had ever thought possible and it pained him to know there was still more to learn.

"She was not with child," Jonas offered. He reached for his bag, pulling out pages of notes and diagrams he had scribbled earlier.

"Thank God."

"There was evidence of alcohol in her system," Jonas said

as he flipped the pages, searching for verification. He finally stopped and began to read. "I couldn't detect anything else," he said slowly, as if hesitating to go further.

"Tell me," Ainsley told his friend.

Jonas nodded and continued. "She drowned, but there was a struggle, like you said. I found bruising on her shoulders and a small fracture of the collarbone. And a nail on her right hand was broken, as if it had been under considerable pressure."

"She fought back," Ainsley breathed.

"Which part of the room was she facing?"

"Away from the door..." Ainsley's voice trailed off as the foggy realization hit him. "She wouldn't have seen who it was but it wouldn't be unusual if she thought Violetta had come back."

Jonas nodded with a sorrowful look on his face.

The world became silent and even the distant wails of suffering patients were enveloped by the altered reality. With his rapidly increasing heartbeat, Ainsley found himself struggling for breath. The pain in his face and head that had been so pronounced seconds earlier ended abruptly before returning with a pulsing to match his heart.

Father.

Ainsley raised a hand to his face, shielding the forthcoming tears from his friend and then turned his gaze. He wanted to ask more questions, hungered for the answers but only a choking noise escaped his throat, forcing him to take a moment. He felt Jonas' reassuring hand on his shoulder and closed his eyes against the pain.

Chapter 21

Ice with the warm blood mixing;

Ainsley lingered at the threshold to his mother's room, which had already been altered from its disheveled state. Everything was back in place and cleaned. The bath had been removed but the splashing water had left a waterlogged look to the grains in the wood. Ainsley approached, his hands in his pockets, and surveyed the site in front of the hearth where the tub had been. A flash of the morning before assaulted him.

Screaming from Margaret.

His own desperate attempts to revive his mother.

He gave a quick shake of his head to banish the memory.

The one thing he wanted to remember was the one that eluded him. When he first came to his mother's side had there been water on the ground? Those minor details, the ones which he would have remembered on any other occasion, were lost in the panic. He had never been witness to such a scene concerning his family and he found his normal propensity to remember minute details completely blank. He had been wet to the skin by the time he had finished, that much he remembered, but had he stepped into a pool of water already present?

Ainsley growled at himself and ran his fingers through his hair.

"You did everything you could," Margaret said from the door.

Ainsley started and turned, unaware that he had been watched.

"Was the floor wet?" he blurted at the sight of her.

Margaret's eyes went wide with panic and she shook her head but it appeared less than a committed response. "I don't know," she said quietly.

Ainsley let out another deep throaty growl.

"My apologies, Peter!" she yelled. "I am not used to such

scenes as you are." He heard the panic rising in her voice and she began to back away as if disgusted at his anger toward her.

"Margaret, no," he said quickly, putting out a hand. "I am not angry. Not with you. With myself for not remembering."

She lingered, but her expression was leery. When she finally spoke, her tone was soft and less sure. "I have been thinking of what you told me," she stopped suddenly, swallowing hard and licking her lips. "I saw someone leave her room that night."

"What? Who?" Ainsley stepped closer, unable to hide his desperation.

"I don't know. It was dark. I was too tired to think much of it." A tear slipped from her eye and cascaded down her cheek. "I fell asleep in the library and..." She began to sob more openly, "if only I had woken up a few moments earlier."

"You must remember who it was," Ainsley pressed.

Surprised, Margaret's eye grew wide. "I don't know! Goodness, Peter." She raised her hand to her face, pushing tears from her red-rimmed eyes. "I am frightened, Peter." She wrapped her arms tightly around herself and backed away when he approached. He wanted to hug her, hold her, and reassure her, but she wouldn't let him.

Her eyes lifted then, as if catching a glimpse of something she had not seen before. "What happened to your face?" she asked.

Instantly he raised his fingers to his stitches and regretted it once they touched his wound. Wincing slightly, he shrugged it off.

"Were you drunk again this time?" she asked disapprovingly.

"How else could I knowingly stand in front of a man who is vying to hit me as many times as he can?" his soft tone gave way to his annoyance at her meddling but Margaret seemed to be in no mood for their standard teasing. "Margaret, please."

She turned from him and retreated to her room, slamming the door as Ainsley tried to follow her.

For a moment, he hesitated in the hallway wondering if

he should step forth and barge in, like he would have done under normal circumstances. Things were different but not so entirely different that Margaret would not indulge him.

When he did open the door, he found Margaret seated on the edge of her bed, one arm wrapped around the wood post that held her bed curtains in place. A dress form was set up at the far end of the room, near the window, with one of Margaret's mourning dresses set upon it.

Margaret looked as if she were talking to someone and when Ainsley looked back at the dress form he saw Julia crouched down and concentrating on the hem of the skirt. As if caught trespassing, Ainsley stopped and set his shoulders straighter.

"Peter, I am in no mood to argue," he heard Margaret say from the bed, though his attention was placed elsewhere.

"I have not come to argue," Ainsley answered, turning his gaze to his sister. "I only thought you had been vexed with me."

"Why shouldn't I be? That which you men call sport is barbaric and reprehensible."

Ainsley could see her knuckles turn white as she gripped the post. He knew she did not agree with his liking for boxing but her protests had never been so forceful.

"You would not want to hear what I think of your drinking," Margaret nearly hissed.

Julia stood slowly, a needle carefully held in her slender fingers. "Perhaps Miss Margaret wishes to speak in private," she said demurely, her eyes to the floor.

Margaret let out a sigh and waved a dismissive hand at her lady's maid. "No, please stay. Forgive me." Margaret gave a forced smile. "I am overwrought."

Ainsley watched as his sister raised a hand to her face, rubbing her cheek with an open palm before resting her chin on it. Her hand lingered there, her eyes fixated on something in front of her and then he saw a tear slip from her eye and spill onto the fabric of her dress.

"Margaret," Ainsley breathed as he stepped forward, taking a seat beside her on the bed. By the time he placed a consoling arm around her, she was openly weeping, her body trembling with her sobs. She did not push him away but rather melted into him like she often did when they were small. It was then that Ainsley realized their once strong bond had fallen to the wayside under the expectations of adulthood. He had been neglectful of her in his quest for scientific excellence. It was a situation he remembered once reassuring her would never happen. With Ainsley's arms wrapped around her, she buried her face in his chest and gripped his lapel, using it to muffle her sorrowful cries.

Over the top of Margaret's weeping form, Ainsley saw Julia watching them, her task paused and her eyes glistening with sympathy. Their gazes locked for the briefest of seconds but it was when Julia turned away, using her sleeve to dry her eyes, that Ainsley felt his heart nearly stop and he was remorseful for allowing the moment to pass.

"What are we to do?" he heard his sister say from the folds of his jacket. She sniffled and Ainsley pulled out his handkerchief and held it out for her.

He wanted to reassure her, tell her everything was going to be all right but words failed him. If the Weatheralls decided to call off the wedding or society shunned the Marshall name completely, he cared little. He had his sights set on one thing, and one thing only: finding out who killed their mother.

Margaret's sobs grew stronger when he gave no immediate answer.

"Hush now," he found himself saying, though he could not say why it mattered.

"If what you say is true," she said, pulling her face from his shoulder to look at him, "and someone killed her—" Her words broke off as she cried forcibly.

Ainsley's eyes darted to the other side of the room where Julia was dutifully pretending not to hear.

"I will find out," he answered softly.

He saw Julia swallow hard at his words and she looked up to him nervously. Suddenly, she stood and made for the door. Ainsley was quick to step up, grabbing her arm before she made it to the door.

"Wait a minute!" he yelled, pulling her back with a forceful grip.

"You are hurting me," she cried, trying to gingerly pull his hand from her arm. She wriggled under his strength but he only pulled her closer.

"Peter, stop!"

Ainsley felt his sister at his side, pulling him back but he could not relent. "You know something," he growled, caring not how she cried.

"No," she answered, shaking her head furiously. "I was the one to draw her bath but I swear I don't know anything more."

Ainsley's grip loosened and Margaret, as well, appeared shocked at her maid's words.

"Where was Violetta?" Margaret asked, stepping between Ainsley and Julia.

"She had collapsed, my lady." Again, Julia tried to twist her arm free. "Please, you are hurting me."

"Peter, let her go!" Margaret demanded.

"What do you mean she collapsed?" Ainsley pressed, pulling Julia even closer.

The maid appeared panic-stricken. Her eyes grew wide and she looked as if she would weep under the scrutiny. "She was overtired, I suspect. I saw to her ladyship's bath. She was fine when I left her. I was in the kitchen but a minute when I heard Miss Margaret's screams."

A flash of the night before came to his mind and he remembered Julia and Billis standing at the door looking in over the scene while Ainsley and Daniel tried to revive their mother.

Suddenly feeling ashamed of his treatment of her Ainsley quickly let go. His anger had given way to remorse and then shame.

Julia turned to Margaret, openly crying. "I'm sorry, Lady Margaret," she said between sobs. "I should have told you. It was my fault. I should have been watching her. I knew she was not herself that night. I should have kept a closer eye. Forgive me."

Margaret shook her head. "There is nothing to forgive, Julia," she said, pulling the maid close.

Ainsley raised a hand to his mouth and then traced his jawbone to his chin. "Forgive me," he said, unconvincingly.

Julia swallowed nervously when she looked to him. Though she nodded, Ainsley doubted whether she truly did forgive him.

"Is Violetta recovered?" Margaret asked.

"Yes, my lady, though like all of us she is handling her ladyship's passing quite hard," Julia explained.

"Nay, I'd say worse," Ainsley offered, knowing how close she and his mother had been.

Julia nodded in agreement. "May I return later to finish your dress, my lady?" she asked between sniffles.

No sooner had Margaret nodded than Julia dropped a quick curtsey and left the room.

"Peter Benjamin Marshall!" Margaret snarled, using his name as if it were laden with curse words. "How could you do such a thing? Imagine the week that poor woman has had."

Ainsley was forced to admit her first week of employment with the Marshalls must have been hellish. It was a miracle she had not given notice and run for Canada.

"You have taken a liking to her then?" Ainsley said, admittedly changing the subject from his own misdeeds.

"Yes," Margaret answered without a thought. "She's been listening to me ramble for hours about Mother, and hasn't said a peep in return that wasn't amiable and uplifting. You are becoming a brute."

His sister's words stung, though he knew emotions were running high in the household. "Are you not suspicious? She starts working for us and then Mother is murdered?"

"Peter!"

"Do I not have a right to question?"

"Yes, but Julia?"

"I mean Father." Ainsley paced the room, hands on hips and looking to the window.

Margaret was quiet for some time, either stunned or pondering her brother's words. "Father?"

Without trying to hide his disgust, Ainsley nodded.

"But Julia couldn't do such a thing," Margaret continued incredulously. "I doubt she'd have the strength."

Thinking of the sting on his cheek Julia dealt him a few days ago, Ainsley had no doubt regarding her strength. "We do not know this woman from Eve," Ainsley said, "and remember Mother, remember how uncoordinated she was that night? I doubt it would take much strength if she was inebriated."

Margaret swallowed, her eyes scanning room. "You believe Father hired Julia to kill Mother?"

Ainsley nodded.

She closed her eyes. "What evidence do you have, besides circumstance?"

"Give it time, Margaret. All I need is time."

Chapter 22

The eyeballs fixing.

The following three days were a haze of flower deliveries, condolence cards, and funeral preparations. Ainsley tried to throw himself into his work but his usual methodical pace descended into a crawl. Eventually, he gave up trying to act normal and sent word that he was ill. As much as he mourned for his mother, he was also tortured irrevocably by the thought of his father's hands doing the deed, the only one with sufficient cause to want her dismissed from their lives.

Ainsley sat at the window seat in his room, knees bent and hand to his mouth. He watched over the street below. So unaffected were the passersby, he noticed, going about their daily chores, running errands, attending carriages, sweeping stoops, as if his entire world had not come crashing to an end. He closed his eyes against the image, willing his life to return to normal yet knowing it was useless.

His only way forward was simple. He needed to find the person responsible, even if it meant taking down his own family in the name of justice. As drunk and intolerable as his mother was, she deserved more than that ending.

The horse-drawn hearse arrived, pulling up slowly to the kerb before stopping at the front step. In another hour, his mother's body would be interred and his eyes would never behold her again. Ainsley watched from his window as Daniel came out to the street, Billis at his side. They greeted the undertaker as he stepped out of a carriage that had followed closely behind the hearse. Adorned with black and silver livery the two teams of horses stomped in place, bobbing their heads as if showing off the great black plumes that adorned them. Such pomp and circumstance was traditional, and almost essential for their neighbourhood. Ainsley had no doubt his father had gone to great expense to prove to society how deeply he mourned. A sound escaped Ainsley's mouth, both a laugh and growl, as he thought about it.

And then he saw his brother almost smile as he and Billis stood on the kerb discussing the coming procession and Ainsley's outlook changed. He wondered why it had never occurred to him before. Of course. His brother had the most to lose should his mother be shunned from society. Father had always cared little for it and yet he fit in as easily as anyone could, but Mother struggled. Daniel took after her in many ways but he possessed none of her nonchalance. His Achilles' heel was that he cared too much. The more he thought about it, the more Ainsley's stomach churned.

A knock on his bedroom door snapped Ainsley from his disturbing trance. He looked up and saw Margaret at the threshold. She did not look as if she had been crying that day but her eyes gave warning that it could happen at any moment.

"Will you walk down with me?" she asked. She reminded Ainsley of her younger self, demure and soft-spoken, unsure and lacking confidence.

Ainsley nodded, slipped from his seat and joined her in the hall.

ॐ   ॐ

The ceremony in Lambeth Church was short and somber. The turnout was respectable though Ainsley wondered if most of the attendees were there as spectators rather than mourners; fewer were gathered at the gravesite following the service. Lady Charlotte Marshall's remains were to be interred at North Western Cemetery, an imposing square stone erected to mark her final resting place.

All the family's servants from Belgravia formed a line behind Ainsley, Margaret, Daniel, and Lord Marshall. The Weatheralls, the Cumberlands, the Brants, the Bells, the Ashfords, and the Pennyfeathers, among other prominent families, lined the opposite side. Lady Brant stood alongside Margaret, holding her hand as women do to show solidarity. The men, however, betrayed nothing, standing at stoic attention, staring blankly as if unaffected and unconcerned. Inspector Simms stayed back but his presence was known. Ainsley knew why he was there. They both employed the same technique when flushing out the identity of a killer, it seemed.

At last, the vicar ended his reading, the family was invited to sprinkle fistfuls of dirt on the lowered coffin, and those gathered began to disperse. Lord Marshall and Daniel left quickly but Ainsley and Margaret lingered with Lady Brant at the cemetery, meandering through the paths and ignoring the coach that waited for them at the gates.

"That is Scotland Yard if I ever saw one," Lady Brant said, glancing behind them as they strolled.

Ainsley followed her lead and looked.

Simms lingered near a tree, watching the threesome as they made their way down the gravel path.

"This is so embarrassing. Do either of you care to share with me the reason why we seem to have a chaperone?" Lady Brant asked.

Ainsley pressed his lips together, stopping himself from speaking, knowing it would only upset her if he did. Margaret sighed, raising her gaze from her feet.

"Both of you hold secrets," Lady Brant said with a slightly stern face. "Do not make me bribe you with sweets like I would when you were knee-high to a grasshopper."

"Peter believes Mother was murdered," Margaret said without warning.

Lady Brant must have already guessed as much. She nodded with a stern face and slipped her arm into the crook of his. She pulled him along, leaning into his arm as they walked. "You have your suspects, I imagine," she said invitingly.

Ainsley nodded though he was unwilling to reveal his hand. Lady Brant seemed to sense this and became annoyed. "You may have your secrets," she said dismissively. "But I would wager your suspicions mirror mine."

Margaret gave Ainsley a panicked looked but he was quick to turn away, not wanting to fuel Lady Brant's blatant resentment for her best friend's widow.

"I have never appreciated your father," Lady Brant said

without solicitation. Their steps stopped short of her waiting carriage. "He and I have never gotten along and I doubt that is about to change. She deserved better in life and in death." She raised a gloved hand to the side of Ainsley's face. "I know you will do right by her." Patting his cheek gently she gave him a sympathetic smile.

Her footman holding the door for her, Lady Brant stepped up into her carriage but did not duck in. Instead, she turned to Margaret. "The dissection I told you about happens in two days' time, Margaret. You have not forgotten?"

Margaret hesitated.

"My dear, the man has donated his cadaver to the hospital. Wouldn't we be rather amiss to use an illegal specimen for such a public display?"

Still, Margaret displayed less enthusiasm than she would have months prior.

Lady Brant looked to Ainsley and then back again. "Very well then. What a morbid pair you two have turned out to be," she said with a sigh. Slipping inside her carriage, the footman shut her door securely. "I expect you to change your tune, Margaret," Lady Brant said peering out the window and eyeing Margaret as the carriage began to roll along.

❧   ☙

The cemetery was empty. The black carriages that had lined the meandering paths throughout were exiting the far-off iron gates by the time Ainsley escorted Margaret back to their family's conveyance. Lord Marshall and Daniel looked ill-amused at being forced to wait for their return.

"And what did *she* want?" Lord Marshall asked, unwilling to look his two youngest children in the eye.

"She is grieving, Father, as we all are," Margaret answered, her normal patient tone absent. She accepted Ainsley's steady hand and stepped up into the carriage before the others.

Ainsley glanced to a cluster of trees a few paces from his mother's grave, where Simms stood observing the family.

"Why don't you head along?" Ainsley said to his father.

"I'd like to walk."

Daniel rolled his eyes and turned away, disappearing into the carriage. Lord Marshall's gaze followed his son's and saw the detective loitering behind them.

"Be mindful of the company you keep," he warned sternly.

Ainsley found his mouth curling into a slight smile. "You as well." His words were meant as a warning, though he doubted his father would take notice. So self-assured was the man, Ainsley knew it would be impossible to unseat his composure.

The family's carriage began to roll away and Ainsley took a few steps to Simms, who waited by a large sycamore tree that was void of leaves and stood skeletal against the grey winter sky.

"Who was that woman your sister and you were walking with?" Simms asked, gesturing to the path where Margaret and Ainsley had walked with Lady Brant.

"She is a longtime friend of my mother's," Ainsley explained matter-of-factly. He pressed his cold hands into his pockets and hunched his shoulders against the biting wind. "Lady Gemma Brant, widow of the Marquess of Exeter."

Simms raised his eyebrows.

"My father despises her."

Ainsley saw a slight smile touch Simms' mouth. "I will not pretend to concern myself with the rivalries within the peerage," he said in a very policeman-like manner. "I need you to do something for me," he said, glancing around as if to assure they were alone. "Evelyn has a brother, has she not?"

"Yes, Will is his Christian name."

Simms nodded. "Speak with her about him."

"Along what lines?"

"I understand he held an appreciation for Clara Buxton," Simms explained. "Those I have interviewed describe him as sullen, would you say the same?"

Ainsley shrugged. "Not my sort of company, though he seemed amiable enough. Do you think he has a connection to Clara's murder?"

"Witnesses only describe a woman leaving Clara's room

on the day she was murdered, but I cannot discount other leads. I need you to speak with Evelyn, and find out if Will and Clara were intimate."

"And how should I ask?" Ainsley asked, laughing slightly. "How does one broach such a private subject?"

Simms smiled. "Such is the nature of police work."

Chapter 23

Nine times goes the passing bell:

The operating theatre was connected to the hospital on the south side, a perfect position for curious Londoners to come witness the macabre dissection of a willing cadaver. Such scenes had become popular among elite society and it developed into a great way for the hospital to raise funds and favoured opinion among possible benefactors. The operations themselves had developed over time, slowly becoming evenings filled with theatrical playacting, turning surgeons into thespians as they displayed each action and subsequent organ as if it were a showpiece.

At first, Margaret found the evenings riveting, and she could easily understand why her brother had been drawn to the profession and all its scientific precedence. As of late, however, the operations had become more and more gruesome, which generated a more boisterous response from the gathered socialites but it put Margaret on edge and sometimes left her wondering why she had come. Ainsley would never show his face as either surgeon or visitor; he could not risk either side of the theatre recognizing him.

Lady Gemma Brant practically pulled Margaret around in the theatre, directing her from one group of friends to another. A certain segment of the London elite ventured to these affairs and for Lady Brant it was all the more interesting for its chances at social achievements as well as simple professional curiosity.

"Miss Margaret, how do you find these sorts of engagements?" a friend of Lady Brant asked.

Margaret was snapped from her thoughts and forced into conversation. "I am not sure," she replied, unwilling to concede absolute fascination for the proceedings. She had little doubt her very presence was *risque* enough for her teetering reputation. Her response aroused boisterous laughter from the mixed group of five standing around her.

"Isn't she precious?" Lady Brant asked in a somewhat disparaging way. Lady Brant pulled her close and gave her a gentle stroke along her back, meant to coax out the Margaret of old who was not so dreadfully dull, before pulling her arm away to shake the hand of an approaching physician.

"Dr. Lehmann!" she called. "So lovely to see you this evening. Are you performing the procedure?"

He gave a quick nod. His eyes darted to Margaret and away again quickly.

"Oh," Lady Brant started, "you remember, Lady Margaret Marshall, the daughter of Lady Charlotte Marshall, don't you?" Margaret offered her hand and he bowed his head slightly as he shook it. He was a tall man with dark hair and dark eyes. He had a somewhat imposing posture and yet lacked refinement. He avoided her gaze, looking away and fidgeting as if afraid he would miss another important visitor. It was only a moment before Margaret was completely put off.

"You have heard of her recent departure from this world?" Lady Brant asked, coaxing him into a conversation that he very clearly did not wish to engage in.

Forced to look back at them he nodded and then spoke in a diluted German accent. "Yes, my heartfelt condolences, Lady Marshall. Your mother..." he looked away, easily distracted it seemed, "was a great patron of this hospital."

Lady Brant smiled, nodding her agreement. Margaret pressed a quick smile but could muster no more. He was gone quickly after that, muttering some regrets.

"I find him rather disagreeable," Margaret said quietly to Lady Brant soon after he left. She did not try to hide her annoyance. Lady Brant laughed but people began to claim seats and they were forced to do the same.

The operating theatre resembled a Greek stage, with a platform placed in the centre and seats arranged in the round, ascending with each row to allow as many as possible to see the performance. Despite the black metal railings to distinguish the stage from the audience, Margaret and Lady Brant had a rather good vantage point with seats in the front row and slightly to the side. Margaret watched closely as the recessed area filled with doctors, and bit her tongue once Jonas stepped out among them. She felt Lady Brant lean into her, keeping her eyes trained on the front of the theatre.

"Is that not Peter's friend?" she asked.

Margaret swallowed hard, looked to her fidgeting fingers, and decided to change the subject. "Dr. Lehmann, have I made his acquaintance before?" she asked.

Lady Brant shrugged. Neither one took their gaze from the sheet-covered stretcher that was escorted into the theatre by two porters in crisp white uniforms.

"Perhaps you have seen him at the last public dissection?"

Margaret searched her memory, unable to place where she had seen him before. "No," she said at last. The general murmur of the crowd, a packed house with standing room only, died away and the room became eerily quiet.

Dr. Lehmann spoke first. "Welcome." After giving general remarks, addressing the donor's time in life and the purpose of the gathering, Jonas was instructed to remove the sheet from the body. Noise rose from the crowd, and people began to crane their necks for a better view.

"Please," Dr. Lehmann said, raising his hands to subdue the eager crowd. "We will proceed slowly so everyone may see what we are doing." He introduced the four doctors behind him of whom Margaret only recognized Jonas and Crawford. Jonas saw her and smiled and Margaret was grateful he did not do anything else, as anything more would be improper.

Though it was Jonas' steady hand that made each cut, Margaret soon lost all interest in the cadaver and began to focus on Dr. Lehmann. Her gaze followed him as she recalled each word he had said and tried to decipher their meaning. He knew her mother, knew her enough to remember her and her contribution to the hospital, if any such contribution existed. Margaret could scarcely recall.

Dr. Lehmann must have felt her gaze and he looked over, his narration to the audience faltering when he did so. Margaret kept her stare trained on him and he continued to stammer.

"Margaret, please, you are unnerving the man," Lady

Brant whispered.

"I know him," Margaret hissed. "He knows my mother."

Lady Brant exhaled deeply. "Margaret, please," she said through gritted teeth.

His jawline, his dark curls, and even the deeper tones of his voice seemed ever so familiar and yet she could not yet place him. Each second that passed felt like a curtain being pulled away from the cloudiness of memory until finally all that remained was him with her mother.

"That's him."

She knew she had seen him, though it had not been him her attention was on. "That's her lover." Margaret felt her composure slipping away as the panic set in. The relief at finally finding him faded into anger and frustration. Margaret felt Lady Brant's hand on hers and she was forced to look away from Dr. Lehmann, who was stuttering with greater pronouncement.

"Margaret, please be quiet, you are embarrassing both of us." Lady Brant looked around, concerned with the people who were beginning to take notice of the scene.

Keep quiet. Don't make a disturbance. Act like a lady. It all rushed over Margaret, making the anger boil and spill over. Without care or concern, Margaret stood, shaking Lady Brant's hands from her own. "I will not be quiet!" she yelled.

All eyes in the theatre quickly turned to her, a soft but audible gasp escaping some of the women.

Margaret felt her cheeks go crimson at the sudden attention but she did not relent. She leaned into Lady Brant, her anger fuelled by her own embarrassment.

"He killed my mother."

She spoke quietly but not quietly enough and the people in the immediate vicinity heard. Lady Brant reached for Margaret's hand, as if to pull her back to her senses, but Margaret ruefully pulled herself away. A murmur started as Margaret climbed the stairs that would take her from the room and she heard the whispers of the gossips starting. "What did she say? Did she say the doctor killed her mother?"

By the time Margaret reached the door her face was flush with tears. Unable to head for the street, she turned, opening a door to the hospital and charging down the hall without a care to where she went. Eventually she found a dark stairwell, secluded and safe from the noxious smells and sounds of the hospital itself. There on a step she cried, hiding her face with her hands and deeply regretting not listening to her instincts by remaining home that night.

After a while, Margaret heard someone open the door from which she had entered and she looked up to see Jonas walking toward her. He had cleaned up, trading his soiled smock for his regular tailored suit. In fact, it was the most impressive suit she had ever seen him in; it appeared as if his new position at the hospital suited him rather well.

"I do believe you upstaged me, Lady Margaret," he said as he approached her, a teasing smile on his lips.

Margaret stood, wiping the remnants of her earlier tears and tried, unsuccessfully, to resume the dignified heiress she was supposed to be. "I—"

He did not let her finish; instead, he used his thumb to brush the peak of her cheekbone, allowing his hand to rest on the side of her face as he looked at her. "You are a force to be reckoned with, Miss Margaret."

Margaret laughed. She shouldn't have been surprised. He was not like the gentlemen she knew who would have denied ever associating with her had she behaved like that in their presence. As a woman of society, she was expected to look beautiful, act elegantly, and remain quiet. Perhaps it was her mother's influence but she had always had trouble with such things. Jonas, however, hardly noticed her many beaches of proper conduct. In fact, she greatly suspected he liked her all the more for them.

He smiled and it did not take long for her to see their earlier spat was history. He had never stopped caring for her, like she had feared. She moved to lean in to him, hoping he'd kiss her and then resolved to kiss him if he didn't, but she stopped short when Lady Brant walked through the door.

Her face was stern and unforgiving. "Dr. Lehmann is this hospital's most celebrated surgeon."

"He's also married," Jonas offered.

Margaret started at the words. It had never occurred to her that two marriages had been destroyed by her mother's impropriety, but now with the facts so clear she wondered how she had not thought of it sooner. Close at her side, Jonas' hand found hers behind the deep ruffles of her skirt. Fingers locked, his thumb rubbed the back of her hand, a gesture that sent both shivers and thrills through the core of her.

Lady Brant clenched her jaw even tighter and, as if deciding Jonas was not to be acknowledged, she looked to Margaret. "I'm surprised he was able to keep himself composed. After your little outburst his face went as red as a beet."

"I'm surprised he dared to show his face," Margaret said, anger interlaced with her words.

Lady Brant laughed and crossed her arms over her bodice. "Margaret, stop this. Dr. Lehmann is an amazing man and you are acting like a spoiled child."

Margaret shook her head. "How can you defend him? For all we know he killed her."

Lady Brant's tone softened and she walked toward Margaret. "Margaret dear, please, end this nonsense." Lady Brant reached her hand toward Margaret but she dodged her touch. "Margaret!"

Jonas moved to step in front of Margaret, a protective gesture that was not lost on her as she reached up a hand to hold him back. "I saw him in the parlour at The Briar with my mother," Margaret said sternly and deliberately. She desperately wanted Jonas' hand again but dared not reach for it. "He was her lover and judging by his behaviour I suspect he knows where she was when she disappeared and has the most reasons to want her dead."

The threesome became quiet and the air around them grew thick with a haze of suspicion and doubt. Margaret could not fathom any reason for her mother's dearest friend to wish to deny the possibility her lover was involved.

Margaret's throat seized, growing dry as each second passed. Her eyes became locked on Lady Brant as she contemplated if she were somehow involved. The possibility that Lady Brant was the murderer seemed unlikely, but what else could explain her defence of such a man? There was something sinister in her demeanor, something unfamiliar and suspect. In truth, Margaret liked Dr.

Lehmann as the culprit more than she liked to think her father had something to do with it. If the latter were true Margaret believed she would never recover.

A loud sigh of resignation from Lady Brant pulled Margaret from her dark thoughts. "Very well," she said. "I think this warrants a family meeting. Dr. Davies here will fetch your brother and we will all meet at my house. Is that agreeable to you, Margaret?"

After a moment of thought, Margaret relented and gave a slight nod.

"Let's get to it then." Lady Brant laughed heartily, and began to guide Margaret through the doors to the front of the hospital. "Really, Margaret, you have become such a disagreeable child."

Chapter 24

Ye merry souls, farewell.

Ainsley smiled as Jonas walked the perimeter of Lady Brant's parlour, taking in the artfully displayed anatomy as if he were a kid in a candy store. Ainsley himself had seen her collection many times and though she often had new pieces that he could appreciate, it was clear that Jonas had never seen such a display.

"Lady Brant, I think you may have an eager apprentice," Ainsley said, nodding to Jonas, who was surveying a square glass box with a dissected foetus inside.

Lady Brant's face lit up at the idea. "Truly?" She looked to Jonas with a sudden admiration. "It's not as difficult as it seems," she said, hopefully. "All you need is some resin, wax and a few other ingredients but the steady hand is hardest to come by. Have you a steady hand or are you one of those quick, slash and dash type surgeons?"

Jonas looked up and glanced to Margaret as if concerned the topic of discussion would alarm her.

She sat daintily in one of Lady Brant's chairs, her elbow propped up on the arm, her hand held to her face as she looked out the window. It was clear her thoughts were not in the room.

"He's one of the best," Ainsley offered, with a benevolent smile, trying to lighten the dark mood that Margaret's demeanor cast in the room.

Jonas shrugged dismissively.

"I do believe your sister finds us irritating," Lady Brant said, slipping into the chair opposite Margaret, her close movement forcing Margaret to break from her deep train of thoughts. "She made quite a spectacle of herself at the operating theatre this evening," Lady Brant said with a sigh.

Ainsley smiled. He wondered if Lady Brant expected him to chide his sister or, in the very least, side with her disapproval. He did neither, and decided it was best not to feed in to Lady Brant's overreaction.

"Lady Brant, we are not strangers to spectacles," he said, winking at Margaret. "After all, you remember what my mother was like."

"Yes, and that's precisely why I am warning you against it. We are trying to repair a great deal of damage." Lady Brant sat so close to edge of her seat Ainsley wondered why she did not fall off completely.

"We?" Ainsley asked with a raised eyebrow.

"Yes, me, you, all of us. With your mother gone—"

"She no longer has a say," Margaret said raising her gaze from the floor. She spoke as if it were an epiphany, a realization that she had slightly more control over her life than before. Margaret turned to Lady Brant. "And you never did." She may have been in deep mourning but Ainsley saw Margaret's strength swell in those simple words and he could not help but be pleased by it.

Lady Brant sat with her shoulders straight, her gaze shifting from Margaret to Ainsley and back again. She opened her mouth to speak but closed it again, having changed her mind.

"Now, Jonas fetched me here, tell me why," Ainsley demanded.

"Dr. Lehmann," Jonas breathed.

"What about him?"

"It's him," Margaret said.

Ainsley nodded, though he did it absentmindedly. Dr. Lehmann was his highest superior, the one who had ultimately recommended him for hire.

"Peter, a week ago you were begging me to remember!"

"I know! I wanted to track her down and make sure she was safe. I had no idea it would be Dr. Lehmann, of all people!" He raked his hands through his hair and turned from the gathering. His heart rate quickened and he suppressed a frustrated growl.

"I do not see how it matters now," Lady Brant interjected. "It's all water under the bridge. What's done is done."

Ainsley rounded on Lady Brant with a slow deliberate step. "You knew," he said quietly.

She avoided his gaze, pressing her lips together as she

scanned the room. When her eyes came to Jonas she spoke. "Perhaps you should leave us now."

Jonas appeared more than willing to oblige and took a step toward the door but Margaret stood. "No, Jonas is thoroughly trustworthy," she said in protest.

"Margaret, it will be all right," Jonas answered.

"There is no need for you to leave." Margaret stepped toward him, "only that Lady Brant is worried for our family's reputation, which by all accounts has suffered enough scandal there is no need to be so secretive."

When Jonas and Margaret looked to Ainsley for reassurance he shrugged, caring not if his friend left or stayed and knowing if Jonas stayed he'd not tittle-tattle to the papers the next day.

After a drawn out sigh, Lady Brant relented. "She begged me never to tell you," Lady Brant said, raising her eyes to meet Ainsley's. "How was I supposed to know any of this would happen? Your mother was miserable in that marriage. I warned her not to marry him. I told her she would never find peace. It was Dr. Lehmann she loved."

Ainsley laughed bitterly. "She was married to a miserable man with three grown children. She sought solace in something new, something foreign."

Lady Brant shook her head gently. "No, Peter. He and your mother had plans to marry long before you and your siblings were even born. Lord Ainsley, your grandfather, refused to give his blessing to such a match, even after Charlotte became with child."

"What do you mean?" Margaret asked in a far-off voice. Her gaze was vacant, lost in thought, before she turned to Ainsley suddenly. "We have another sibling?"

Ainsley turned from them and walked toward the farthest end of the room, running a hand over his face and trying unsuccessfully to control his breathing.

"She must have put it up for adoption or... worse," he heard Margaret say from behind him. She must have been looking at him but he dared not turn around. "There are ways right, Peter, ways to prevent a pregnancy from developing?"

Ainsley turned, crossing his arms over his chest. "I don't think that is what Lady Brant means," he said.

"What else could it be? There's only the three of us... oh dear God," her voice suddenly grew quiet. "Daniel."

Ainsley watched as Margaret closed her eyes momentarily, flexing her hands at her side. "It cannot be true."

"We must never tell him," Lady Brant said.

"But Father knows," Margaret said looking to Lady Brant. "Doesn't he?"

"He knew," Lady Brant conceded. "He also knew it would be his only way to marry the woman he loved who didn't love him back. Lord Ainsley, your grandfather, approved the match and they married within a fortnight, hoping her pregnancy would appear legitimate. Your father agreed to keep it a secret and she agreed to never see Dr. Lehmann again."

Everything changed with those sentences. Suddenly, Ainsley's hatred for his father, though very real, seemed unjust. He wasn't sure if he felt ashamed of himself or angry that such scandal had been plaguing their family since before Ainsley was even born. Lady Charlotte Marshall had never fit into society because society never forgave her and eventually she must have given up trying. Her marriage was not happy because she had never wanted to be with him. And Daniel remained as a daily reminder to the life that could have been.

"She broke her promise," Ainsley said at last.

Lady Brant nodded, her gaze avoiding his. "Yes, her fidelity lasted until a few years ago. I believe the demands of society became too much for her and she needed an escape. Your family's estate in Tunbridge Wells proved most useful in that regard."

The pieces of the puzzle fit so snugly it nearly gave Ainsley the chills.

Chapter 25

The old earth
Had a birth,
As all men know,
Long ago.

The bell at Daniel's house, nearer completion, sounded strong and commanding, like Daniel himself. Ainsley had never imagined himself to be in a position of knowledge such as that which Lady Brant had told them the night before. Standing on his brother's doorstep with sweaty palms and rapid heartbeat, Ainsley wished he had never been told. Their relationship had been so easy, so concrete; this new revelation threatened to change it all.

Some things could never really change, of course. Daniel had been his older brother all of his life. Often a sobering presence, Daniel demanded attention as soon as he entered a room. His departure from the Briar to live in London with their father while he attended school allowed the country estate to come back to life. The family and staff did not fear Daniel, not the way Lord Marshall made them fearful. It was only because Daniel was less forgiving of both himself and others. Any transgression was to be treated seriously and any deviation from the norm was intolerable.

These characteristics which Daniel possessed had released Ainsley from any guilt. He could study medicine, travel extensively, and only converse with their father when absolutely necessary, with the knowledge that his brother was required to be the responsible one. Being the second son, Ainsley felt no guilt for not following his father's wishes, or heeding his father's cautions. All these years Ainsley cared nothing for his father's pride, knowing his father had an eldest son in whom to take solace. It had never occurred to the young doctor that he was his father's real legacy. Lord Marshall's blood coursed through his veins and not those of his brother.

The door opened after a long wait and Ainsley forced a benevolent smile when he saw Evelyn's maid, Esmie, open the door.

"I see Lord Marshall has not acquired a proper butler or footman," he said in jest. The maid shook her head. "His lordship is away this evening," she answered without hesitation, paying no attention to his attempts at informality.

"Did he give an indication where he would be? Lord Marshall's family home perhaps?"

Again, she shook her head. "He did not say, sir, only the Lady and I are within."

"I see," Ainsley answered. Before he turned away, he thought of the task Simms had charged him with and realized it was serendipitous that his brother was not home. "May I speak with Miss Evelyn then?" he asked before Esmie could close the imposing wooden door.

Protocol required that she allow him admittance but he could tell she was not often trusted with such duties. She hesitated.

"She is to be my sister-in-law," Ainsley said with a smile. "I assure you there is no need to fear."

Briefly looking to the street behind him, the maid pulled the door to open wider, revealing a strikingly dark foyer, and closed it as soon as there was clearance. As he walked in, Ainsley saw each room that exited the foyer was dark as well. The maid disappeared, walking the flight of stairs to alert her mistress of his presence, and Ainsley was left there to wait in the near dark.

He wondered how long it would be before the house would be ready and the pair could be settled and, of course, married. That is to say if Evelyn still wished to marry his brother after she found out Lady Charlotte Marshall's death was not an accident and that Daniel was one of Ainsley's suspects.

Within a few moments, the maid returned. "Her ladyship is on the second floor."

Ainsley nodded and followed the maid as she led him up the stairs. They walked an equally dark corridor and approached a dim room to their left. The maid entered first and Ainsley slipped in behind her.

The room looked to be her bedroom, a large ornate poster bed dominating the relatively small space compared to his own room. Without a mattress, the ropes could be seen already strung and tightened, a tower of quilts and sheets lay freshly laundered and folded on a chair beside it. There was an abundance of wood crates strewn about, some empty but most unopened and yet Evelyn already had her mantel and furnishings cluttered with vases, peacock feathers, paintings, and portraits.

"Lord Marshall, how nice for you to stop by," Evelyn answered graciously. "I am afraid your brother is not home."

"Yes, your lady here has so informed me."

"How do you and Margaret fare?" she asked. "Daniel is greatly pained by Lady Marshall's passing."

"Is he?" Ainsley asked, not intending it to sound so indignant.

Evelyn gave a slight chuckle. "I have made an observation."

Ainsley raised an eyebrow.

Evelyn turned to her maid. "I'd like a tea, Esmie."

"My lady?"

"Thank you," Evelyn said solidly. With the maid gone, Evelyn spoke. "It has become clear that you bear some ill feelings toward your brother. I saw as much during the funeral."

Ainsley set out to protest but found his energy for such things missing. "My brother and I are not chums, if that is what you imply. He and I disagree on many things."

"Such as?"

Reluctant to speak, Ainsley paused and reached for a trinket poking out of a nearby crate. Fingering it, he tried to formulate a dismissive remark but found his resentment too strong. "Because he is a womanizer and a brute and does not deserve to be wed to anyone, least of all you. His attentions are always directed toward the maids, very inappropriately, and while he is my brother, I must warn you. Do you realize the nature of the man you are pledging to marry?"

He expected Evelyn to be reproachful but instead she remained thoughtful, as if carefully considering his words.

186

"I thank you for your concern." She smiled slightly and began to pace the room, walking toward the window next to her large, imposing bed. "Your concern is charming but unnecessary. I am aware of the reputation of the man I am to wed."

"He will bring you nothing but heartache, I assure you," Ainsley said.

"You underestimate me, Lord Marshall," she said with a smile, "I am not a young girl, smitten by your brother's charm or promises of undying love. I am a woman rapidly approaching spinsterhood."

"So you would marry him for what? ...children?"

"In part, but you must consider my family's past to understand my true meaning." She looked out the window briefly, watching over what Ainsley guessed to be the yard, perhaps the carriage lane that would lead to a small carriage house beyond, given the location of the room they were in. When she turned back her expression was sad. "When my father died I was very young. I had no recollection of him and my mother had nothing to remember him by, not money nor property. We were destitute, as difficult a situation as you can imagine, particularly for my mother, who had been raised in a lavish home. She married for love and he died within two years. The second time she married for money."

"Lord Weatherall?"

"Correct. My mother has taught me that love and sweet nothings pay neither baker nor undertaker. My children will be earls and countesses and my purpose will be fulfilled."

Ainsley tried to suppress a crooked smile. He had learned his brother was not the rightful heir, and by rights he could demand the title be passed on to him. Evelyn and Daniel were planning a life under the impression that he was to be Earl of Montcliff when in reality he was nothing more than a doctor's son. Ainsley reined in these thoughts, deciding that was another task for another day.

"Are you confessing to marrying my brother for our family's money?"

Evelyn shrugged and began to walk slowly back to him. "You could tell me your brother wished to marry me for something other than the generous dowry Lord Weatherall is providing, but I would know you to be wrong. My money is just as alluring as your brother's money and, naturally, his eventual inheritance of your father's title, though I confess I am glad it will not be for some time. The time will give me more practice."

Ainsley shoved his hands deep into his pockets and exhaled. "You care nothing for the possible lovers my brother will take?"

"No," she answered plainly. "He is welcome to take as many as he likes, as long as my children are his rightful heirs." She paused and regarded him a moment. "You thought me more sentimental?"

"I had, yes."

"I am aware of the workings of this world. I know the minds of men, the evils they perpetrate. As a woman, I cannot change the system of this country but I can learn to play it to my best advantage."

Ainsley pressed his lips together, more than a little put off by her confession. She had grown up poor, it was clear she had no desire to return to that state. Lord Weatherall's money gave her the opportunity to rise in rank and secure a future for her children. It seemed sensible enough to him, though he wondered if she was discounting the most important ingredients to long-lasting happiness, friendship and mutual respect. He had seen the effects of the business-driven marriage and it had ended in his mother's early death. No one deserved such a fate. Was he concerned Daniel and Evelyn's marriage would end the same way?

"You may tell your brother my reasons for marrying him," she said, breaking his reverie. "I am sure he will see it as sensible, just as I see nothing amiss with his expectations of my dowry."

Ainsley began to nod. "And so is the way of the world," he said quietly.

He turned, glancing over the half-empty crates and unwrapped belongings when something on a nearby table caught his eye. It was a mirrored vanity tray, with cut glass bottles of perfume and scented oils laid out on top. It had silver-plated handles intricately designed with swirling ivy and bulbous flourishes. But it was the etchings on the surface of the mirror that caught his eye. On it were clusters of five petal flowers framing the corners in a decorative fashion.

He felt the warmth drain from his head and through his body as if it were seeping into the floor and spilling out all around him. It was the very copy of the etched mirror he had found in Clara's letted room. Ainsley looked to Evelyn, her usual composure lost when she saw what had caught his eye.

"A gift from my brother," she said quickly.

"Why are you shaking?"

She shook her head, unwilling to reply.

Ainsley began quietly "Evelyn, you know a mirror like this was found in Clara's room."

"How do you know that?" Her face looked pained.

Ainsley sighed, wanting to keep his own secrets. "Evelyn—"

"I told you all I know," she answered emphatically.

Ainsley shook his head. "I do not doubt your insistence," he said. "I believe you do not know of her death. Did Will give her one as well?"

She shook her head and avoided his purposeful gaze. She pulled a cloth bundle from a crate and unraveled it to reveal a medium-size vase.

Ainsley continued. "Your brother, he viewed her rather fondly, did he not?"

"Will would not hurt a soul," she said quickly.

Ainsley smiled and tried again. "What were you both doing at Clara Buxton's room?"

She remained silent, looking at Ainsley sideways. Her hands shook slightly and the vase she held in them looked as if it would completely shatter should she lose her grip. Ainsley walked to her and gingerly slipped the vase from her grasp and placed it safely on the mantel, all the while keeping his gaze trained on her faltering expression of innocence.

"Evelyn, should I be concerned for my brother and the true nature of the woman he intends to marry?" Ainsley raised an eyebrow.

It was the only card he had to play. She had already expressed her desperation to marry for their family's money and rank. She had even confessed to being able to overlook

Daniel's wandering eye for the privilege of being the next Lady Marshall. Could she have conspired with Will to murder Clara to prevent the troubled girl from speaking of their family's past? Had Clara threatened such an action Evelyn could very well have neutralized the threat by killing her.

"I do not comprehend your interest in this personal family matter. I think it best if you leave, Peter," she said forcefully, though a slight flicker in her gaze gave Ainsley reason to believe her confidence wavered.

He did not immediately leave. He stood in disbelief, his options turning over in his head as they looked each other over. With a sudden-found vigour she repeated her command, "I am telling you to leave, do so now or I will summon a constable."

Ainsley gave a smirk at this. It was a higher-ranking police officer who had sent him, but of course she could not be told this. "Very well," he said, resigning to his failed mission. "But understand this, the detectives who came to your engagement ball will be knocking on your door again. They will not be charmed as my brother and I first were and they will not be bought with your family's money. If you had a hand in that girl's death you will be apprehended and tried and maybe even hanged."

Evelyn quivered slightly at his words, shivering against the realism he presented and the abrasive manner by which he said them. Suspected of murder he could no longer treat her with kid gloves or ask special treatment. Too many clues had been uncovered for that. She needed to trust him enough to tell him what really happened lest she be imprisoned or worse.

The terrified look on her face made him soften. "I only tell you so you can prepare. If something happened I can help you," he said.

"How?" Tears threatened her composure but as quickly as they came, they left and she reverted to her original stance. "It happened as I said," she answered stoically. "I was not there."

გ❧   ☙

By the time Ainsley arrived at home, he was chilled to his core. The temperature had taken a sharp dip when the sun went down and the frigid wind proved capable of piercing his overcoat and gloves. After giving a hasty greeting to Billis, foregoing their usual banter, he went straight for the parlour, where he found Margaret, Father, and Daniel set before a healthy fire.

"Look what the weather blew in," Daniel muttered when he saw Ainsley walk into the room. He gave a slight sneer, turning from Ainsley, disinterested. Margaret was seated away from the men, having chosen a place near the lamp, a book lying open in her lap. She gave Ainsley little more than a pressed smile, causing Ainsley to wonder at the moods of Daniel and their father.

"I'm afraid your sister neglected to instruct the staff to lay a plate aside for you," Lord Marshall said, a slight slur proving they had been drinking for a while.

"Peter, I—"

Ainsley cut Margaret off. "It's all right," he said, unbuttoning his jacket. "I admit I haven't any interest in food at the moment."

He warmed his hands briefly in front of the fire, rubbing them together and moving them to coax back some feeling. Purposely, he moved, ignoring the gaze of his father and brother. Removing his jacket he laid it on the arm of a chair placed against the wall and decided to join Margaret, slipping into the empty space next to her on the couch.

He saw her give him a glance and open her mouth as if to say something but then her eyes darted to their father and her confidence retreated. Her gaze returned to her book.

"I was looking for you, brother," Ainsley said, "Had I known you were here I would have saved myself the trip. I found Evelyn at the new house alone."

Daniel gave a slight chuckle and took a drink of what Ainsley guessed was brandy. "She's quite eager, isn't she?" he replied. "She asked me if she could have her father's men bring over some crates." He placed his glass on the table. "Why did you seek me?" he asked. "Let me guess, you have found Mother's killer?" Daniel laughed heartily at his own joke, which produced a smile only from Lord Marshall and a look of shock from Margaret. Ainsley saw her give him an apologetic look before lowering her gaze again. She had told them, at least about the findings of the examination, if nothing else.

"You do not believe my suspicions then?" Ainsley asked.

"She drowned of her own doing," Daniel said quickly. He waved his hand dismissively.

Ainsley leaned toward them, sitting on the edge of his seat using his knees as a brace for his elbows. "There was suspect bruising on her shoulders and two nails were broken on her right hand—"

"Suggesting what?" Lord Marshall asked, not bothering to turn to his son.

"Suggesting a struggle," Ainsley answered indignantly.

Daniel let out a huff. "Move on."

Ainsley shook his head. "I won't."

"You will, and that will be the end of it!" The voice of their father reverberated throughout the room, and no doubt the house. He did not turn to even look at Ainsley, who sat in quiet disbelief, unsure how to handle such a confrontation.

"I have made a decision," Lord Marshall said. He finally turned and pointed a finger at Ainsley. "Your work at the hospital has come to an end. I need not appease your mother any longer."

"And what of your son?" Ainsley did not dare say only son, though he wished he were ruthless enough to do so. Wouldn't that wipe the growing smirk from his brother's face?

Lord Marshall shook his head. "I am master here," he said.

"Is that why you killed her?" Ainsley asked, squaring his shoulders, preparing to be rebuked. "So you could be master and commander once and for all?"

Lord Marshall rose and turned, his form silhouetted by the light of the fire behind him. Dark shadows crawled over his face, the light of the lamp next to Margaret making him appear more like a devil than a human. "I will not be spoken to in such a way!"

Ainsley stood, squaring against his equally tall father. "And I won't be ordered about like a prepubescent boy!"

"Perhaps if you ceased to behave as such—"

"Please stop!" Margaret yelled, coming between them. She held a hand to Ainsley's chest, touching him as if knowing her presence would make him behave. "Mother is gone," she said, as if only to Ainsley. "Nothing good will come of this argument."

For a moment, Ainsley forgot all others in the room and focused on Margaret, wondering what she expected him to do. There was evidence enough to prove their mother was forced under the surface of the water, but the findings ran cold when he tried to pinpoint the murderer.

When Ainsley looked from Margaret he found his father had retreated to the fireplace, setting his tumbler beside an ornate gold leaf frame on the mantel. "I did not kill your mother," Lord Marshall said, his voice quiet and his gaze concentrated.

Ainsley remembered the portrait well, a small painting of his mother in her wedding dress that had sat on that mantel since before he could remember. He distinctly recalled he and Margaret, no more than five, pulling a chair beneath it just so they could climb up and behold it. Of all the portraits of their mother it remained the only one that held a true likeness. It had been a shame it was so small but the artist commissioned to do it died a year after.

"I loved her."

Ainsley and Margaret stood stunned, unsure how to react to the sound of their hardened father crying.

"I loved her but she did not love me like I thought she could one day." He pulled the small frame from the mantel and turned it toward the fire as if using the light to look upon it. His free hand wiped a tear from his cheek.

A groan escaped Daniel's lips. "Enough, Father," he said, standing suddenly. "She was a fool and an adulteress. Good riddance to—"

Ainsley charged, pushing his brother from his feet and together they fell over the small table between the chairs, the wood splintering under their weight. On the ground they struggled but Ainsley had the upper hand. He had no drinks that night to impede his hits and he got three solid blows in before he felt the strong arms of Billis pulling him away. Ainsley struggled against Billis' grasp, unable to accept that his vengeful moment had ended.

Daniel sat up, lifting a hand to his nose just as a trickle of blood seeped onto his upper lip.

"You are despicable!" Ainsley yelled, pulling on Billis' tight grasp around his midsection. "Mother was good to you. She was good to all of us!" Ainsley yelled.

Billis turned Ainsley around, positioning himself between Ainsley and his brother. His imposing body served as a wall but Ainsley still tried to breach it.

"You don't deserve to call me brother, you selfish prat!"

He could feel Billis pushing him from the room and into his father's study, despite Ainsley's attempts to confront his brother. "Move, damn it!" he yelled at the butler.

"That is a command I cannot heed," Billis answered.

Ainsley heard the door to the study close and secretly wished his brother would come for him. His anger had not been satisfied and his temper raged on.

"He is a fool!" Ainsley said to Billis, as he straightened his shirt. It was then he realized two buttons were missing. He loosened his tie and threw it aside.

"You are a fool," Billis answered evenly. "Your mother hardly deserves such a fuss."

"Pray, choose your words carefully. I am in no mood." Ainsley gave the butler a pointed finger.

"I have served your father for many years and my loyalty remains with him. I have seen the pain she has inflicted on him." Billis glanced to the closed door and looked back. "I see it still."

"She was murdered, Billis," Ainsley said, struggling to keep his own tears at bay.

The butler nodded, his gaze somber. "I know, my lord."

The door opened and Margaret slipped in, a look of worry on her face. "Good God, Peter, what were you thinking?" She did not need an answer. Margaret was at his side and looking him over, most likely searching for swelling or cuts as she did when he would return from boxing fights. She raised her hand as if to touch his ear but he brushed her away. "I am fine, Margaret."

While they spoke, Billis turned to the door. Always the same, never changing, Ainsley and Margaret saw that he had aged a great deal in the last few days. He walked to the door as if defeated, his pace slow and his gait haggard.

Always brisk and spry, this change startled Ainsley.

"Did I hurt you, Billis?" he asked, suddenly aware that he could have injured the ageing butler in an effort to harm his brother.

At the door, Billis placed a hand on the knob and turned to them. "No, my lord." Ainsley watched as Billis left the room, closing the door behind him.

"I think he fibs," Margaret said. She was not sweet or doting; she looked angry and annoyed, her patience drawn thin by her brothers' row.

Ainsley said nothing. He went to their father's table of liquor and poured himself a generous glass of whiskey, downing it quickly and pouring another.

Margaret let out a long sigh. "You truly think this is the time?" she asked.

Ainsley shrugged and put the glass to his lips. "I don't see how it matters?" he asked. "You heard Father. I'm done."

"Peter."

Ainsley shook his head, unwilling to accept her sympathy, and turned to the window just as the icy mist turned into snow. He did not need any more reasons to drink.

He knew his father was ruthless enough to renege on their agreement. Working under his mother's name had given everyone what they wanted, but now Lord Marshall seemed panic-stricken. Ainsley himself realized the position they were all in and felt the panic rising in him as well. Technically, Ainsley was the eldest, the sole heir to the Marshall fortune and his brother had no legal claim to any of the money or the title he had grown up knowing would be his one day. Should their family secret be revealed, by anyone involved, they'd all be called to task. Ainsley would no longer be able to practice medicine once his presence was requested in the House of Lords. Although certainly not penniless, Daniel's world would be shaken and in truth Lord Marshall was under no obligation to provide their brother with anything.

Lord Marshall would be made a fool, and Margaret would be labeled wanton. Two glasses later and Ainsley wondered what anyone would have to gain from revealing their family's darkest secret. Lord Marshall said it himself: without his wife to appease, there was no need to condone Ainsley's work at the hospital. When he thought himself the second son, the spare, Ainsley had never understood his father's pressure. With this new information it made sense. Ainsley was Lord Marshall's only true heir and it must have pained him greatly that the boy who would take his title was not his, and the boy who was his had no interest in his title.

"What are you thinking?" Margaret asked.

"I'm thinking he did it."

"Who? Daniel?"

Ainsley shook his head, remembering she was not privy to his thoughts unless he expressed them. "Dr. Lehmann. What if their relationship turned sour, bitter? He must have been supplying her with drugs for years, Margaret."

She shook her head in disbelief. "What would he have to gain from her death?"

"Revenge? For wanting to return to her family." Ainsley set his glass down sharply on the desk.

"She was his willing partner." She closed her eyes as if trying to suppress a memory. "She showed no remorse."

"She wouldn't, would she? Especially if her eldest was a result of her affair."

"What are you saying, Peter?"

"I am saying that judging from Dr. Lehmann's behaviour the other night he knows something and your presence made him uncomfortable."

"We have no proof," Margaret pleaded.

"We will before long."

Chapter 26

And the old earth must die.

Of all the hospital, the east wing was the quietest, with the apothecary and its laboratories buffering the wails of the pain-ridden and dying for the head staff that had offices there. A long, well-lit corridor displayed portraits of notable surgeons and physicians, chief benefactors and contributors. Like a hall of note for the rich and richer, the pictures were commissioned by the very men they were meant to honour, an odd arrangement, Ainsley realized as he walked the length of the hall. He wondered if he too, in the evening of his life, would feel the need to commemorate himself with a portrait and a brass plaque.

At the end of the hall and just before Dr. Lehmann's door Ainsley saw the surgeon's own portrait, his name neatly embossed and a quote underneath.

In nothing do men more nearly approach the gods
than in giving health to men.
-Cicero

Ainsley snorted when he read the words, knowing the damage this man had done to his mother and the Marshall family as a whole. It was that vengeful spirit that spurred Ainsley on to what he was about to do.

Glancing up and down the hall, Ainsley stood at Dr. Lehmann's door. He knew the doctor was not in, having checked with Jonas. Ainsley knew the doctor had a full morning of surgeries and would not venture back into his office until the afternoon. Had Jonas known what Ainsley was about he would not have been so obliging, but that was why Ainsley had formed a ruse under which to enquire.

Pulling his hand from his pocket, Ainsley held a long, slender blade and slipped it into the iron keyhole. It did not matter to him if he damaged the lock. He planned to be long gone before anyone noticed. With a quick thrust of the blade, the lock broke and Ainsley was able to turn the knob and step inside.

Dr. Lehmann's office was a decent size, with floor-to-ceiling bookshelves along one entire wall. There was an unusually neat desk with a tall, brown leather chair on the opposite side, and two less impressive chairs on the side closest the door. There was little light but Ainsley scarcely noticed. He went straight for the desk, pulling open each of the five drawers and rummaging through them. There was nothing but medical notes, patient files and office supplies.

Leaving the desk, Ainsley moved to the bookshelf and quickly surveyed the leather-bound collection, which did not have the look of the oft-used volumes Ainsley had at home. They were all evenly placed, lining the very edge of the shelf. And everything looked in order. It seemed odd for a surgeon's room to look so neatly placed. There were no portraits or artwork as Ainsley had seen in other offices.

And then Ainsley reached behind the line of books to the back of the shelf. Nothing. Systematically he looked behind each row of books on each shelf, feeling nothing until his hand graced a bundle. At first touch, it felt like a tight bundle of papers, cards perhaps, until Ainsley pulled them out and saw that they were envelopes and letters. The addresses had been written with slanted writing and then he noticed the return address.

The Briar. Tunbridge Wells.

His persistence had paid off and for a brief moment he forgot that he was searching out proof of his mother's infidelity and Dr. Lehmann's motive to kill her.

Untying the bundle, he laid the envelopes and letters on the desk and began flipping through them, searching for dates, recent ones if they could be had. All he needed was one letter to prove they had fought, to solidify his hunch that Dr. Lehmann, not his father, had killed his mother.

Scanning the dates, he saw the letters were old. The paper was faded to near yellow and some showed signs of water damage. Looking at the envelopes again he noticed the forwarding address was to Germany. Discouraged, yet hopeful, Ainsley opened one and confirmed it was his mother who wrote to the surgeon and his curiosity overtook his better judgment. He began to read.

...Peter has never forgotten your lessons. Wish I could say the same for our son, who appears so unlike us in all respects... It pleases me that Peter should take after you. He told me the other day he'd like to attend a medical school...

The rest of the letter was unremarkable save for some love notes and such. A few letters later Ainsley found another one that mentioned him.

Your university is held in the best regard, most likely due to your management... I would like to send Peter before long. I beg you to help him gain entrance. He is keen to learn all he can but I doubt he has the stamina for such work...

Ainsley felt his grip tighten involuntarily. He resented how she spoke of him, as if he needed such assistance. Truth be told, he had wanted to study in Edinburgh but she had pushed him to apply to the University of Freiburg in Germany. He never knew her stake in the school he would choose to attend. Suddenly he felt idiotic for following her suggestion so blindly. At the time, she spoke of the school being the best in the world, and he did not doubt the claim but it had seemed odd to push him outside of Great Britain.

Then he read the next letter.

...Abraham is beside himself. I must admit I am pleased that he is so vexed...I know Peter would not have been accepted were it not for your recommendation and for that I am grateful...

He could not read any more. He slumped in Dr. Lehmann's chair, letter still in hand.

His mother had thought him so incapable she sent him to a school where her former lover could vouch for him. The concept was so devious and underhanded, and completely insulting. Had Ainsley known, he doubted he would have held such a high regard for her.

The doorknob turned and Ainsley sat dumbfounded and unable to prevent himself from being discovered. Dr. Lehmann walked in, and stopped suddenly at the sight of Ainsley seated in his desk chair.

"Dr. Ainsley, you have ventured far from your dungeon," he said.

Ainsley sneered at the slight.

It had been three days since Margaret had seen him at the dissection and any panic he may have felt that night must have dissipated by the time Ainsley ventured to his office.

The senior surgeon's eyes fell on the stack of love letters, some opened, another in Ainsley's hand.

"Anything in particular that you seek?" he asked, laying the papers he held in his hands on his desk. Removing his blood-spotted lab coat, Dr. Lehmann hung it from a hook behind his door and turned to Ainsley.

"May I?" he asked, gesturing to his chair.

Begrudgingly, Ainsley stood, but gathered the letters in his hand, unwilling to give over the possible key to his case against the doctor.

Dr. Lehmann sat in his leather chair, pulling it in close to his high desk and indicated a chair on the opposite side, closest to Ainsley.

Ainsley remained standing.

"I have come about my mother—"

Dr. Lehmann shook his head. "I know nothing."

"She was your lover. My sister saw you," Ainsley said, his jaw tight and his fists tighter. He had not been sure how he would react upon seeing the man who helped destroy his family. Ainsley had expected he'd be more controlled and struggled to push the need he had to throttle the smirking immigrant.

"Did you come here to hurt me?" the doctor asked, taking up his pen. He displayed no fear and seemed to be fully recovered from any shock he may have had at finding Ainsley in his office. "You have developed quite a reputation. I'd warn you to pay that some heed." He pointed his pen at Ainsley and spoke as if he were a close friend giving a warning.

"I need no advice from you," Ainsley answered with disdain.

Dr. Lehmann shrugged slightly. "I realize you are upset but breaking into my office will not bring Charlotte back, nor will it do your fledgling career much good."

"Fledgling?" Peter grimaced.

"Yes, of course. I doubt this hospital will employ you long after it is discovered that you broke in and began rooting through my personal belongings. You are not that valuable to us."

Ainsley grew hot and his heart raced as the head surgeon spoke. Of course the elder surgeon was right. Ainsley had scarcely taken a moment to consider such an outcome. His rage burned so deep that considering the man's connection to the hospital and his work eluded his conscience.

"And what of your career?" Ainsley pulled his mother's bottles from his pocket and placed them on the desk with a purpose-driven thud. Dr. Lehmann looked at them for a minute before he spoke, his previous disinterest vanishing. "Sit, please."

After a moment of hesitation, Ainsley took a seat, but did not soften his hardened stare.

"I did not give her those," he began.

"Will the hospital logs support your claim?" Ainsley asked.

Dr. Lehmann nodded. "Yes, I believe so." He dropped his pen on the paper in front of him and laced his fingers together. "I had been working with her to try and break the habit but your mother was quite dependent. We tried substituting other substances with little success."

"If your work was so benign then why hide the fact?"

Dr. Lehmann licked his lips. "I am a surgeon, not a physician. My involvement with your mother would raise suspicion. I couldn't risk her reputation."

Ainsley laughed. "More likely, you could not risk yours."

"I have no need for reputations," Dr. Lehmann answered. "My work speaks for itself. Not even your sister's outburst has marred people's opinion of me." He smiled slightly. "You and your sister know I had nothing to do with your mother's death."

"She was gone for nearly a week," Ainsley said. "I know she was with you."

Dr. Lehmann nodded. "Yes, however not of my invitation."

Ainsley raised an eyebrow.

"She came to my house after some argument or such with her husband. Thank goodness my wife was not at home. Charlotte was in such a state I could not simply send her away. I was afraid for her. She shook uncontrollably and was running a very high fever. Vomiting. Clearly her body was craving her drugs. Last summer I had seen a young lady die from her convulsions. I could not very well send Charlotte away, now could I?"

"You kept her at your home?"

"No!" Dr. Lehmann began to wring his hands as he recalled the memory. "I took her to a church hospice run by the Sisters of the Holy Trinity. I visited her every day and when she was well enough I arranged for her ride home."

"When my mother returned home she could not tell us what happened or where she was. I thought she was lying."

"She wasn't. Under my guidance, the sisters administered careful doses of a tonic I have been developing for her, and others like her, to suppress her movements. I had hoped her body would use the rest to learn to live without the opium. I know now it did not work. She must have returned to her habit."

"Dr. Davies found no traces of laudanum or opiates in her system."

A smile began on Dr. Lehmann's face. After a moment of bliss, his face turned sober. "She must have been intoxicated. Why else—?"

"She was forced under the water," Ainsley answered reluctantly.

"Oh, dear God!" Dr. Lehmann raised his hand to his mouth.

"I had thought you had done it. Perhaps you had quarreled," Ainsley suggested, suddenly unsure.

Dr. Lehmann nodded. "We had the night your sister came to the Briar. She felt I had seduced her again, using the treatments as an excuse to see her. I admitted it was the truth." The surgeon smiled and his gaze wandered. "We had planned to be together, her and I, but her father would not hear us out. I was a doctor, and she was a well-bred society lady. To say nothing of the fact that I was also a foreigner." His voice softened. "I never stopped thinking about her. I did check in to see if her husband was treating her well."

Ainsley shifted uncomfortably in his chair, unsure of how to feel about this man speaking of the intrusion into his parent's marriage.

"I remember you," Ainsley said suddenly, his eyes widening as the memory came to him. "You came to The Briar when I was a boy. We caught frogs."

Dr. Lehmann nodded. "And do your remember the fate of those frogs?"

Ainsley did, indeed. Sacrificed in the name of science. He remembered himself and Dr. Lehmann under the yew tree, crouched over the specimens. Ainsley made each cut slowly; even at the age of nine he was meticulous. His first dissection very much like the ones he performed still.

"I had forgotten."

"But I didn't. When your mother told me you wanted to go to medical college I made arrangements at my alma mater. I was able to forge your papers and erase your lineage without sacrificing your credentials. My recommendation saved you when you failed that exam. Do you remember?"

Ainsley did indeed. He had been too slow. Had his cadaver been a real person she would have died, bleeding out through the leg he had been assigned to amputate. That botched procedure and the resulting grade remained etched in his mind permanently.

"You are a brilliant mind, but not a very good surgeon."

This Ainsley already knew, but the pain of hearing the words spoken out loud was like a knife gutting his stomach. Any effort he had made to make himself faster, all the assistance Jonas had given him, had been for naught as he was cursed with a methodical mind and an inquisitive heart. He hadn't the stomach for hacking away at flesh and bone while the patient writhed and gasped in guttural pain. Ainsley had been accused of being too soft, and he blamed that too on his sheltered upbringing.

"It was all I could do to get you a position here," Dr. Lehmann continued, "and your mother was displeased. I imagine she wanted you as far away from your father as possible, but the relationship she and I had was already strained under the secrecy and fear of discovery. I am afraid you must advance on your own now. I can no longer help you."

Ainsley snorted. "Your duty to my mother is done now that she is gone."

Dr. Lehmann's gaze remained unchanged. "No. I doubt your father appreciates my help. I wish you were the eldest."

"You knew about Daniel? You knew he was yours?"

A slight smile began to form and then vanished. "I wish I could say I was proud," he said with a distant look in his eyes. "He is more Lord Marshall's son than mine." His expression perked up and his gaze met Ainsley's again. "An interesting case study into nature versus nurture, I suppose."

Ainsley hardly knew what to say. He had learned so much about his family and why they were the way they were since his mother's death. There was so much to seep into his understanding, so much that he knew was there but that he could not fathom while his mind reeled from so much change. Everything he knew had been altered and the pieces still moved in his mind to form a full picture.

"So," Dr. Lehmann broke the silence, "if you have come to ask if I killed your mother then the answer is no." The senior surgeon took up his pen again and turned his attention to the papers in front of him. "And if you wouldn't mind," Dr. Lehmann looked up and pointed at the bundle of letters in Ainsley's hand with his pen, "be sure to leave those."

Ainsley did not remember leaving Dr. Lehmann's office and could not recall how he had made it back to his morgue but once there he opened one of the drawers beneath his cache of tools and found the full bottle of scotch he had left there weeks earlier. Seated on a stool, and using his unoccupied examination slab as a table, Ainsley drank half and was sufficiently drunk by the time Frisker approached him.

"Mornin'," Ainsley slurred. "Care for a drink?" he asked, moving the bottle toward the morgue porter.

"No sir," Frisker said, "There is a lady here demanding admittance. Shall I—"

The door to the morgue could be heard slamming back into place, followed by the voice of Margaret. "There's really no need for an introduction." By the time Ainsley looked up she was only a few steps from him. Ainsley expected a gasp, a reprimand, something to mark his disgraceful condition but she offered none of these.

The porter hesitated but eventually relented. "I will be out at the desk, sir."

Ainsley nodded and waved a loose hand in the direction of the door. "Just go," he said. He looked up and saw Margaret standing over him. "You as well," he said, with little conviction. He reached for the bottle but her hand was quicker and she snatched it away. Without warning, she raised the lip of the bottle to her mouth and took a long, drawn out drink. "What is this? Scottish?"

Ainsley gave a smirk. "German."

The silence that followed was impenetrable. Ainsley was now privy to information his family had worked hard to keep secret. There was nothing left to say. Ainsley's career was a joke. His mother was gone and her killer remained unknown.

"Daniel has set a date," Margaret said suddenly. Placing the whiskey bottle back on the table, she pulled a small square of paper from her pocket and handed it to him. "I received that by messenger this morning."

It was a wedding invitation, elegantly scrolled in black ink on a pure white paper embossed with filigree around its edges.

"It's in three days?" Ainsley's shock was only tempered somewhat by the alcohol that swam in his veins.

"I couldn't believe it myself." Margaret said. "Seems... rushed, if you ask my opinion."

Ainsley pushed the paper away and grabbed the bottle. "What of it?" he asked roughly. "His decision."

"And you don't think it was Evelyn who pushed for this date?" Margaret asked, waving the invitation in the air in front of her. "Is there anything she could gain from rushing things?"

Ainsley shook his head but when the room began to spin he stopped suddenly and raised his hands to his face. "He said she was eager," he mumbled in reply.

"My question is why?"

"Why not? If they are both willing parties to their mutual gain, what does it matter?"

"It matters because Daniel has no idea about Clara Buxton," Margaret answered sternly. "Peter, you cannot just sit there and pretend none of this matters to you."

"What do you want me to do?" Peter bellowed. "It's their bed, not mine!" He reached for the bottle again but Margaret snatched it out of his hands before it found his lips. With great force she threw it to the ground, shattering the glass and sending the whiskey all over the floor.

"One day you are going to have to stop feeling sorry for yourself!"

She was halfway out of the room before Ainsley had gathered his wits enough to attempt to apologize.

"Margaret," he called.

She continued walking.

"Margaret! I'm sorry."

The door closed loudly behind her and the room went quiet. The sheets on the corpses moved slightly, swaying in the turbulence of Margaret's sudden departure.

She was right. Margaret was always right.

Ainsley gathered himself together, splashed cold water on his face from the trough sink in the corner and headed for the door.

"Tell Dr. Crawford I went home ill," he said as he passed Frisker's desk in the hallway. Almost at the stairwell, Ainsley turned to him and added, "And I'm sorry about the mess." Ainsley did not stay to explain and he pretended not to see the look of confusion on the porter's face.

Ainsley tore up the stairs of the hospital and out the front doors just in time to see Margaret stepping into their family's carriage. "Wait. Wait!" he called up to Jacob before the groom had a chance to urge the horses into motion. Ainsley jumped into the carriage, closing the door quickly. Margaret just shook her head as he entered and turned to look out the opposite window.

"You are right," he said, slightly out of breath. "Forgive me if I don't understand what you expect me to do about it."

Ainsley's words only seemed to anger Margaret more. Her jaw clenched, she turned her head slowly to look at him. "If I were a man I'd be able to go where I want, find the answers I seek, and no one would think the worse of me," she said coolly.

"All right then, if you were a man what would you do to

solve Clara Buxton's murder?" Ainsley asked.

"Clara and Evelyn were cousins. Didn't Evelyn say she grew up in Aldsgate?"

"Yes."

"Then your trail leads you there."

Chapter 27

So let the warm winds range,

The name and address that the workhouse matron had given Ainsley cost him ten shillings and his word to never reveal her involvement should the origin of his source be questioned. The neighbourhood he found himself in was filthy and overcrowded, a far cry from the one he would have imagined a refined lady like Evelyn growing up in. As he walked the streets, sidestepping heaps of horse dung and human excrement, Ainsley could see how an advantageous marriage would appeal to her.

At the indicated address he was directed up three flights of rotting stairs to a dark door with the letter 'C' painted crudely on its weather-worn surface. His knock made the door rattle on its loose hinges before being opened abruptly.

"I said I don't have it today—" the woman's voice cut off, and a look of fear came over her.

"Lizzy White?" Ainsley asked.

Propelled by fear she moved to step back into the house, reaching a hand to close the door, but Ainsley stopped her with a hand firmly placed on the door.

"I am not here to harm you," he said quickly.

"Yeah, what do ye want then?" she asked, her voice rising in panic.

Ainsley stepped inside and closed the door behind him. Once he did, he wished he hadn't. The musty smell of the room was only somewhat masked by the smell of wood burning in a small, potbellied stove in the centre of the room. There was only one window, broken and patched with a muddy board no doubt scavenged from the streets. There was a small, narrow metal bed pushed close to the stove, a worn blanket over the flimsy mattress. A single, off-white man's shirt hung from a thin line fastened in front of the stove.

"I have come to ask some questions," he started after

realizing he was staring.

"Men dressed like you only come to ask for favours," she answered with disgust. "At least that's what the lady downstairs tells me."

Ainsley was quick to shake his head. "I just want to know about Clara Buxton."

"What about 'er? I 'eard she was dead. That true?"

Ainsley nodded. "Yes."

"Then I see no need to speak of 'er," Lizzy replied.

"She was murdered," Ainsley said quickly, with the hopes it would spur on some concern, or in the very least pity for the girl with whom she had been friends.

Lizzy dropped her eyes, "I 'eard that too."

"Did she ever speak about Evelyn Weatherall?" Ainsley asked.

A slight laugh escaped Lizzy's mouth before she looked up and met his gaze. "She was Clara's favourite."

"Favourite what?"

Lizzy shook her head. "You think you men are the only ones inclined to have favourites."

"You mean, Clara fancied Evelyn? I was told they were cousins."

Her unladylike laugh filled the room. "God, no. Favourite," she said, with a raised eyebrow. "They were the best kind, if you ask me. Men bring you nothing but pain." Lizzy glanced around the room as if memories brought on her words. When she looked back she tilted her head upward to him and pulled her shawl tighter around her shoulders. "If you know what I mean."

Ainsley could well imagine, but in truth his attention was fixated on the information she had given him. Had this friend of Clara's openly admitted that Clara and Evelyn were closer than friends? That would explain Evelyn's disinterest in love and even fidelity. She cared more for security and perhaps children than she did about a loyal husband. It suddenly all made sense and Ainsley found himself smiling at the thought. His brother's marriage was a business deal and Evelyn saw it the same way.

"When did you last see Clara?" he asked.

"A week or so ago," she said with a shrug. "She 'ad been living in Manchester, working at a mill but I saw 'er a coupl'a streets over in the Borough. She said she'd been sacked on'a 'count of her smoking. Lighting a match in a place like that is deadly and she should 'ave known better."

"Did she say anything else? Where she was going? Who she had been seeing?"

"She was all dolled up and said sump'in about see'en an old friend, perhaps Evelyn, but I dunno, she never said." Lizzy shrugged slightly and turned to a large pot on the stove. With a long-handled ladle she stirred a watery liquid with scarcely anything inside. "We don't pry too much 'round 'ere," she continued, "Not unless something is owed us."

"And you haven't seen her since?"

Lizzy shook her head and her face fell. "Next thing I 'eard she'd been killed, 'er body found at the boarding'ouse."

"Anyone mad at her? Perhaps someone still holding a grudge from the last time she lived in London?"

"The only person I'ze ever known to hate 'er is Evelyn's new Pa. He married Evelyn's Ma and Clara weren't welcome no more. She lived with 'em before that and said she expected to go with 'em when they moved to that fancy house, but next thing I know she's cryin' on my stoop, saying he threatened to kill 'er if she ever came around again."

Ainsley straightened his stance, remembering Lord Weatherall's reaction to Inspectors Simms and Wright's visit.

Lizzy shrugged. "I guess he weren't keen on his new daughter's friend. Why you wanna know anyway? You a Bobby or some'pin?"

Ainsley smiled, and realized he should depart before he outstayed his welcome. "Thank you for your time," he said tipping his hat.

On the street, Ainsley made his way through the maze of alleys and passages to get back to the carriage and driver he had left at a less-conspicuous location. Despite an extreme focus on his footing, careful to avoid any gutter filth, Ainsley was lost in thought pondering the tidbits he had just learned. Was it possible Lord Weatherall knew his daughter had gone to see Clara? Had he followed her there and proved good on his previous threat? It seemed unlikely;

a man of his stature and prominence would be noticed and no one at the boardinghouse had admitted to seeing him there.

Ainsley had expected to unearth a relationship between Will and Clara. Never had he imagined Evelyn having a tryst of her own. Evelyn's reaction to the news of Clara's death was painful to witness, and now that Ainsley knew her better, it seemed out of character for her normal docile demeanor. He knew her to be quite even-tempered and less inclined to dramatics. At the time, he thought it was a natural reaction to news of a cousin's passing, but it was more than that. She was mourning someone she loved.

Chapter 28

And the blue wave beat the shore;

Once home, the sound of Lord Weatherall's boisterous laugh met Ainsley in the foyer. He guessed that Evelyn's father and Lord Marshall were in the parlour smoking cigars and sharing a drink, congratulating themselves on a match well made and nearly consummated. Two more days and their families would be tied forever.

Ainsley found himself reluctant to join them. Despite his need for a drink, he had no need for talk of business or politics or their latest speculation, rightly chosen or otherwise.

"Is everything well, sir?"

Ainsley turned. Billis had caught him staring at the door to the parlour. The butler looked at him without judgement but with genuine concern.

"I doubt things will be well for some time," Ainsley answered quietly.

Their conversation was ended abruptly when the door to the study opened sharply.

"Peter," Lord Marshall said with surprise.

Lord Weatherall looked at him over Lord Marshall's shoulder, as if amused by his damp, dishevelled state. Beyond the two men, Ainsley could see Will and Daniel seated, once in conversation but now looking over to Ainsley.

"Father," Ainsley answered with resignation. There would be no escaping now.

"I was just about to show Lord Weatherall the new cellars. He does not believe I have an 1812 Scotch. Care to join us?" Lord Marshall asked.

"No—"

"His lordship was just asking for a plate of food to be brought to him," Billis broke in. "Shall I serve it in the dining hall?" the butler asked, turning to Peter.

Ainsley smiled. "Yes, Billis. The dining hall, thank you."

Billis bowed slightly and took a step back before turning to leave. Ainsley stepped out of the way as his father and Lord Weatherall stepped out from the study.

"You are home rather late," Lord Weatherall said, indicating the darkness outside a nearby window.

"My son has an affinity for the card tables," Lord Marshall answered quickly for Ainsley. "I suppose it is better than some pursuits."

Ainsley knew his father was speaking of the time he spent at the hospital. It was amusing that his father would rather have a son who gambled than a son who assisted humanity. He wondered how long he could defy his father's wishes before he would disown him entirely. That eventual outcome was what Ainsley had been slowly preparing himself for—the day when he would be forced to choose between medicine and his inheritance. But now he realized that Lord Marshall wouldn't disown him, he couldn't. Ainsley was his only true heir and Lord Marshall could no more disown Ainsley than he could declare Daniel was not his son. The disgrace on both accounts would be his undoing.

Lord Marshall and Lord Weatherall began to walk down the long hall toward the stairs that would take them to the new wine cellars installed the previous year. Before leaving, Lord Weatherall turned suddenly.

"Peter, my daughter tells me you were going to look at the case of Clara Buxton?"

"Yes, sir," Ainsley answered, squaring his shoulders as he faced the man.

"Any news on that front? Any developments my family should be aware of?" The manner in which he asked his questions was casual, if not flippant, but Ainsley knew the stake his family had in the investigation's outcome. Lord Weatherall wanted everyone to believe he held little concern for finding the girl's killer, but Ainsley knew better. Someone in his family had murdered that girl.

"News, sir?" Ainsley asked innocently.

"Have they reached a conclusion? Found the scoundrel who did it then?"

"No, sir," Ainsley answered. "Nothing yet, though they tell

me very little."

Lord Weatherall nodded, looking down his long nose at Ainsley, his mouth partly open. "Is that so? Well, thank you all the same. Your words were a comfort to Evelyn."

"Of course, sir."

Lord Weatherall nodded and turned from Ainsley, joining Lord Marshall at the end of the hall. Ainsley was in no mood to entertain Will or converse with his brother. He left them drinking in the study and enjoyed a quiet dinner in the dining hall where he could think over the case.

The exchange he had had with Lord Weatherall left a bitter taste in Ainsley's mouth and a sour scowl on his face. It surprised him that Weatherall would consider bringing the matter up in front of his father as well. For a family in such a hurry to marry off a daughter Ainsley wondered why he wouldn't be more guarded about such information and less inclined to remind new family ties of their involvement with a murder.

Weatherall couldn't have known he was a suspect in Ainsley's mind. Had his words been meant as a warning? Perhaps Ainsley had dodged a bullet by answering and eluding his questions. Then again, his words were not malicious in the slightest way. Perhaps he meant to publicly soften his stance on the issue of Clara to alleviate suspicion.

Then again, Will was another likely suspect. Or had been until Ainsley met with Clara's friend earlier that day. Given their intimate history, Clara's murder could be the culmination of a lovers' spat, a final solution to a problem that could bring an end to Evelyn's marital ambition. She was more than capable, Ainsley concluded, and experience had taught him never to dismiss one who weeps openly.

❧　❦

"Margaret, you must help!" Ainsley burst into Margaret's room, without a knock or even a care as to what would be found inside.

Margaret, Evelyn, and Julia turned, a look of surprise on all their faces. Evelyn was standing on a stool or some such thing, while Margaret crouched in front of her. With a few pins in her mouth, Julia was sitting on her heels, pinning Evelyn's hem.

"Mother's wedding dress," Ainsley breathed as he took in the scene.

"Margaret said I may wear it," Evelyn answered with a smile, her joy slipping from her features as Ainsley walked into the room. "I suppose I should have asked everyone."

"Nonsense," Margaret blurted out. She stood up from her stooped position beside Julia and gave a disapproving look to Ainsley. "It's been sitting in Mother's wardrobe for nearly thirty years. All it needs are a few alterations and we are set. Don't you like it, Peter?"

Ainsley stammered. He could barely look at the woman in the same way, knowing what he knew of her past and the marriage ahead. "Yes, yes of course. I just... well, I was just struck by the resemblance. Forgive my intrusion."

"See," Margaret turned to Evelyn, "nothing to fret about."

Evelyn nodded though her expression remained somber. "I suppose it is a bit hasty of Daniel and I to set the date so soon. All the dressmakers in London nearly laughed in our faces when Margaret and I enquired. So close to the holidays too."

Margaret and Evelyn exchanged slight smiles.

"I was so relieved when your sister suggested your mother's dress. Perhaps it is too soon after her passing."

Behind Evelyn's back, Ainsley could see Margaret forcing a smile and indicating that he should follow her lead.

"Margaret is right," Ainsley blurted out. "Mother would have wanted you to wear it."

Evelyn's mood perked up immediately. "Perhaps one day your betrothed will wear it for you," she suggested.

Ainsley could not help but laugh. The suggestion was an amusing one.

"Peter is a happy bachelor," Margaret teased, "Perpetually wooing women, never asking more than a few stolen kisses. Isn't that right, Peter?" She looked at him with a mischievous grin.

"I am nothing of the sort," Ainsley answered, knowing full well neither woman believed him.

"I have a feeling about you Peter," Evelyn said as Julia raised her arm out to the side so she could better measure the sleeve. "You will find your match, and she will be just as taken with you as you are with her."

"Or she will run the other way in fear for her reputation," Margaret muttered.

Ainsley laughed.

"How does it look, Julia?" Margaret asked when the maid took a step back to look over the newly pinned and reformed dress.

"All it needs is a little updating and a shorter hem," she answered quietly, keeping her eyes on the skirt.

"Julia, you are a dear," Evelyn said, beaming from her perch. "Margaret, are you sure it's no trouble?"

"You misunderstand my motives," Margaret replied, holding the sewing box open so Julia could place her extra pins and the measuring tape inside. The box was little more than a hatbox upholstered with some leftover dress fabric and trim. "My life is dreadfully dull and it keeps my mind off things." Margaret let out a deep sigh and looked to Ainsley.

"I'll leave you then," Ainsley said, knowing they would need to help Evelyn undress. "It looks beautiful," he said to Evelyn before he turned.

"Peter?" Margaret moved toward the door, closer to Peter and separating herself from Evelyn and Julia.

Ainsley turned at the sound of Margaret's voice. "Yes?"

"What did you want to tell me?" she asked, her voice low.

Ainsley looked over to the beaming bride and realized he could not ruin that moment, especially since he could not verify his suspicions just then. He jerked his head behind him and bid Margaret to follow him into the hall.

"What is it?" she asked in a hushed tone.

"I am in no mood for a wedding," Ainsley muttered.

"Nor am I but Father has reassured me it is to be a tame affair."

Ainsley chuckled slightly. "When has anyone in this family been accused of being tame?"

Margaret smiled but it soon faded. "What did you find out, Peter?" she asked. She swallowed nervously, looking frightened and unprepared for what he might have to say.

"Clara was not Evelyn's cousin." Ainsley answered, his expression plain and his gaze definitive. "They were lovers."

Margaret's breath stopped for a moment and her eyes dropped.

"You know what that means, don't you?" Ainsley asked bending at the knees to look at her face.

"Of course, I know what that means!" Margaret answered harshly, but quietly. "Women talk the same as men."

"They are hurriedly planning this wedding in the hopes that we won't find out about Evelyn and Clara," Ainsley said. "I'm convinced they loved each other even after Evelyn became a Weatherall. I believe that is why Clara was killed. Margaret, I cannot look the other way. A woman was murdered because of some misguided desperation to marry into our family."

"You believe her family would go to such lengths? To murder a young woman?"

"Others have killed for less."

Margaret nodded.

On the carriage ride home Ainsley had decided he could not look the other way. As children, they spent years pretending their Mother's behaviour held no consequences. It had been easier to ignore the problem than face it and deal with any repercussions. He carried a great deal of guilt with him for that, believing he could have saved her if he hadn't been so damned forgiving.

"If they knew Mother, they needn't have worried," Margaret said, partly in jest. "The three of us would be lucky to find matches at all."

Ainsley knew her well enough to smile. It saddened him to think they might never see a time when their lives would not be marred by scandal.

"Do you think she could have done it?" Margaret asked. Her voice had risen and she looked over her shoulder to her bedroom door to check that they were still alone.

Ainsley nodded. "I suppose anything is possible."

A creak in the floorboards behind them caused Ainsley to start. Turning his attention to the door Ainsley saw Evelyn, still wearing his mother's wedding dress, standing on the threshold. Her expression was hardened and she glared at them both.

"You think I could do such a thing?" she asked, her eyes not moving from the ice-cold stare she gave them.

Looking over her shoulder, Margaret inched closer to Ainsley and then stopped, as if suddenly feeling guilty for believing Evelyn capable of such a crime. "Evelyn—" Margaret took a step forward, reaching out a hand but Evelyn gathered her skirt and made for the stairwell.

"Wait!" Ainsley called but Evelyn did not stop.

Julia appeared at the door, sewing box in hand just as Ainsley tore down the hall to pursue Evelyn down the stairs. Her face flushed, Evelyn looked over her shoulder as she tried to get away.

"Don't you come near me!" she yelled as she reached the foyer floor. "I warn you not to lay a hand on me." She turned to face him as he approached her, her hands outstretched.

"It's time for the truth," he said loudly, realizing the commotion would soon attract the others in the house. He knew he only had a short window of time before her father and brother would appear to protect her.

The tears began slipping down her face. "What truth do you want? You want to know if Clara and I were lovers? If I killed her to hide our secret?"

Margaret's footfalls could be heard behind them. She moved slowly down the stairs and stopped a few steps from the foyer. Lingering there, she leaned on the railing. "Peter, tread carefully," she said by way of warning.

It was the last thing Ainsley wished to do. He had been treading so carefully since returning to London it made him ill to think of all the precious time that was lost. For his brother's sake he had been protective of Evelyn instead of asking pointed questions. He wanted to believe Evelyn had nothing to do with Clara's death but the evidence was clear and he could no longer deny her involvement.

"Were you lovers?" he asked.

A distant door could be heard opening and a determined stampede of boots was approaching them from the hall. Lord Weatherall, Lord Marshall, Will, and Daniel spilled into the foyer.

"What is happening here?" Lord Marshall asked brusquely.

Evelyn turned to her father, her tear-stained face causing his features to harden all the more. "What have you done to my daughter?"

"I was simply asking her some questions," Ainsley answered with a forced nonchalance.

"This is not about that woman again, is it?" Daniel asked, walking across the room to confront his brother. Jaw tight, Ainsley did not look at him and in turn refused to answer. Casually, he slipped a hand into his pocket and looked to Margaret.

"Are both my siblings conspiring against this marriage?" Daniel asked, his voice reverberating in the hollowness of the foyer.

"You are not married yet," Ainsley pointed out.

Daniel grabbed Ainsley by his jacket lapels and pushed him back against the wall. Grabbing his brother's wrists, Ainsley tried to push back but the momentum was already in his brother's favour. A loud crack rang out when his back collided with the wall.

"Your bitterness will not ruin me," Daniel shouted, his nose inches from Ainsley's face. "Do you hear me, brother!" He pulled Ainsley back from the wall slightly and then pushed him into it again. "Hold your tongue forevermore on this subject or I will see to it you don't receive a penny of the Marshall fortune."

"I could say the same to you!"

Ainsley snapped his head forward, hitting his brother squarely in the temple. Daniel let go of his grip on Ainsley and doubled back in pain, raising his hand to his wounded head. Stepping away from the wall Ainsley raised his fists, ready to fight should Daniel attack him again.

"Peter." Margaret came down a few steps.

When Ainsley looked to her, Daniel threw a punch, sending him back into the wall.

Ainsley's fists connected with Daniel twice more before they were forced apart by Billis and Lord Marshall. Out of breath and in pain, Ainsley watched as his brother checked his nose for blood.

"I care nothing for your marriage!" Ainsley yelled at him, "I care that a woman was murdered by someone in that family. And as it stands now Evelyn is the most likely suspect."

"How can you say that?" Evelyn asked, looking aghast.

"This is outrageous!" Lord Weatherall boomed. He turned to Lord Marshall. "Your son has some cheek to be making such declarations."

"I would never hurt Clara!" Evelyn yelled against the murmur of the room.

"You wouldn't be the first person to murder their lover!" Ainsley answered.

Daniel's fist met Ainsley's jaw again and he was thrown back into the stairs. His brother would have hit him again had Margaret not placed herself between them.

Ainsley knew his words held spiteful venom but he did not care. He wondered if he would have been better off letting Inspector Simms arrest and interrogate her, rather than confronting her in this way. Despite these second thoughts he pressed on and held some hope that his family could avoid controversy in the newsprint the next day.

"How dare you!" Lord Weatherall bellowed. Will stepped forward as if to challenge Ainsley but Lord Weatherall pushed him back and took his place. "Watch your step, young man! You do not want me as an enemy! I have a mind to challenge you here and now!"

"Enough!" Lord Marshall called. His fingers gripped his cigar loosely. "Peter would never say such things unless he believed them true."

Meeting his father's stern gaze Ainsley touched the side of his mouth and saw blood on his finger as he pulled it away. He glared at Daniel and straightened his coat onto his shoulders. "I met a woman today, Clara's friend."

"Who is this friend?" Lord Weatherall sneered.

Lord Marshall quieted him with a pointed finger. "And?" his father asked.

"She said that Clara and Evelyn thought fondly of each other. Evelyn was Clara's favourite. She alluded to an intimate relationship between them but when Lord Weatherall married Evelyn's mother, Clara was thrown aside. She was forbidden to visit the family, most likely because of the potential scandal. You cast her aside, Lord Weatherall, from the only type of family she had. I have reason to believe Clara was murdered because of Evelyn's desire to marry my brother."

A hush fell over the room, each person digesting the plot

Ainsley had laid out.

Evelyn looked to Daniel, her eyes wide and her lower lip trembling. She began to shake her head but Daniel just turned from her, rubbing his face with one hand, the other placed squarely on his hip. Ainsley watched as she closed her eyes, rejected in front of all of them. When Evelyn turned to him he saw the raw pain his words had caused.

"She was a special friend to me," she stammered. "I... I hadn't realized... I mean, I didn't know she felt more. After my parents married, Father refused to let me see her." Evelyn looked to Lord Weatherall. "Perhaps he saw what I didn't see." She began to pat the folds of the wedding dress she wore, smoothing out the layers around her hips, perhaps using the texture of the lace pattern to calm her shaking hands. "It was true when I told you I hadn't seen her in years. I was forbidden to, even though I thought of her often. It was the announcement in the paper, you see, of our engagement that made her come to see me, but Father would not let Mother or I see her."

"So you went to her?" Ainsley offered.

Evelyn nodded thoughtfully. "Yes. I shouldn't have gone. I had no idea what that area of London was like or that anyone would notice me. I imagine that makes me rather naive. She needed money and I..." she looked to her father and then back to Ainsley. "I gave her some."

"And the mirror?" Margaret asked.

"I had given it to her many Christmases ago, before Father forbid Mother and I to speak to her. I bought two, one for myself as well, as a link, you understand. When I went to see her it was sitting on a table and I was surprised she still had it after all these years. I imagined she had pawned it or something. Given her circumstances." Evelyn swallowed hard and her gaze was locked on the floor. "She asked if it was true, if I was truly getting married. I was so stupid. I laughed and talked of dinnerware designs and crystal goblets. I told her about the beautiful house Daniel had commissioned and then, she smashed it."

She glanced around the room. Daniel had turned to her slightly, as if interested, but kept his gaze trained to the side. Will shook his hands at his side, looking to his father as if at odds with what to do. Lord Weatherall appeared pained and contemplative, seemingly heretofore unaware that his stepdaughter had disobeyed him.

"I had never seen her behave so," Evelyn continued, "I was frightened... I left."

"Truly?" Ainsley asked.

"Yes. When I found out she had died I blamed myself for leaving her there in that horrible place."

"Did anyone know you were going to visit her?" Ainsley asked.

Suddenly there was a metallic click and Ainsley looked over to see Will, his prized duelling pistol now pulled from beneath his coat and held in an outstretched arm.

"That is enough questions," he said. Stepping out from his father's shadows, he held Ainsley in his sight line, one eye closed. "My sister will not be slandered by the likes of that woman or you."

Ainsley thought to turn, to protect Margaret if no one else, but he was too late.

With a bang and a burst of smoke, the gun went off.

"Peter!"

Chapter 29

For even and morn
Ye will never see
Thro' eternity.

The room became hazy with black powder smoke and muffled, almost distant sounds of a woman's screams. Ainsley looked down to his chest and saw nothing. A misfire? His body shook as he tried to make out the chaos that unfolded.

"Peter!"

Through the cloud, he saw Evelyn on the ground, her cream-coloured dress stained red.

"Oh, my God! Evelyn!" Daniel called out.

Ainsley knelt at Evelyn's side, the red stain, at first the size of his fist, expanding rapidly as blood seeped into the satin that made up her garment. Ainsley pressed his hand flat on to her wound in an attempt to stop the bleeding but he could feel it rushing through his tight fingers.

Evelyn moaned, her lips trying to form words as she grabbed Ainsley's arm. Her eyes were wide, as if she knew something was wrong.

"Daniel," she moaned.

"We have to take her to the hospital," Lord Weatherall said frantically from behind Ainsley.

"There's no time," Ainsley answered. "She'll bleed out before we get the carriage hitched." He looked at her wound, easing up his hands and replaced it quickly to stifle the bleeding. He looked up to Will, but he was gone.

"Do something!" his brother growled at him with barred teeth.

Ainsley shook his head. There was not enough time. He could not be quick enough. His slow hands would torture her before he could be of any help. Dr. Lehmann had said it himself, he was a great scientist but a horrible surgeon.

"Peter, save her!" Daniel yelled again, grabbing Ainsley's

lapel as he had done earlier and forcing his brother to look at him. "Damn it, Peter, you will save the woman I love or—"

Ainsley nodded. "Yes," he said, "I'll do my best. Margaret press here, hard."

She placed her hands where her brother indicated.

Ainsley rolled Evelyn on to her side to get a look at her back. The bullet had not gone through. "Help me get her into the dining room," he said, positioning his hands beneath her. He directed them to the dining room. Margaret rushed ahead to pull off the tablecloth and pull the chairs back. Laying her on the table Ainsley used his hand to compress the wound.

"Father, my bag."

Lord Marshall nodded and disappeared.

"Margaret, get me the sewing kit. Light! I need light!"

Julia and Violetta scrambled into the room, pulling oil lamps from all corners of the house and laid them around Evelyn on the table.

"Save her, Peter," Daniel whispered, as he leaned into the table from the opposite side.

Ainsley began to doubt he could. The blood had covered his hands entirely and he was losing his grip. He could not leave her to die, but trying to get her to the hospital was similar to a death sentence. He'd have to get the bullet out and stitch her up.

Lord Marshall returned with his bag, which he placed at Ainsley's side, and a few moments later Margaret rushed in with the sewing box.

He had never thought he would have to perform surgery under such conditions. The hospitals had anesthetics and a team of assistants, and the surgeons all had one thing he didn't have. Speed.

Margaret opened the doctor's bag and looked to Ainsley. "What do you need?"

"Tweezers, scalpel..." Forcing out a deep breath Ainsley rubbed some sweat from his brow with his bloody hands.

You're a good surgeon, Peter, but you are far too slow.

Doctor Lehmann's words resounded in Ainsley's mind as he looked over Evelyn, wondering how best to stop the bleeding. He was too slow, far too slow for the task in front of him. Even if he were able to fish out the bullet and stop the bleeding, she would die of shock, or worse linger for days and succumb to infection.

"Father, take them out," he commanded. He did not look up or indicate whom he meant by 'them' but Lord Marshall knew and escorted Lord Weatherall and Daniel out the door.

"What's he going to do to her?" Lord Weatherall asked in near desperation.

"Everything is going to be fine," Lord Marshall answered as he ushered him out. "My son is a brilliant surgeon."

With the door closed, Ainsley set to work. Margaret and Julia had laid out all his tools, even some he had not requested, arranged them on the tea cart, and wheeled it over beside him.

"Help me with her stays," Ainsley said.

Together they made quick work to remove all the layers of clothing, leaving her in her under shift, which had become so soaked with blood it shone crimson. Ainsley rolled up the sticky fabric and looked at the wound. It was a small hole at the side of her stomach, just above her pelvic bone. It had been shot in at an angle and Ainsley desperately hoped it had missed her vital organs.

"Hold her down," he commanded.

"You think she will be going anywhere?" Margaret asked, hesitantly.

"Hold her down!" His tone must have been determined enough because Margaret and Julia did as he bid without further question.

Scalpel in hand, he made an incision along the entry point, ignoring the tight squirming coming from the patient. It would have hurt worse than the sudden impact of the bullet and her muffled cries drove him to work faster. With the slim forceps, he dug into her flesh and searched for the bullet.

"She's passed out," Julia said.

Ainsley glanced to her face.

"Make sure she keeps breathing. Let me know if she stops."

Margaret nodded, and leaned in closer to Evelyn's face. She held her hand to the side of her throat to locate her pulse. "She's weakening."

Ainsley hurried. He had found the bullet but for some reason could not get the tweezers around it. He moved the tool around and finally he felt the tool become rigid. Slowly he pulled the bullet from her body. The bleeding had slowed but that was scarcely a comforting thought.

"Thread me a needle."

Margaret nodded and went to the sewing box.

"Hurry!"

With trembling fingers, Margaret handed Ainsley the threaded needle. With his fingers, he searched around her wound, seeking any organs or arteries that the bullet may have hit. "It's too dark!"

Julia carefully lowered a lamp toward the wound.

With the needle and thread, he began to stitch Evelyn up. Had he been in the morgue he would have been careful and far more precise but with Evelyn he did not have the time. Within minutes, he had operated, found the bullet, and pieced her back together.

Finally, he turned from the scene and retreated to a table of spirits left from dinner.

"Peter," Margaret began, disparaging of her brother's need for drink.

Ainsley glared at her as he walked back to Evelyn with the bottle and poured it gingerly on her wound. "We need bandages. We need to keep the wound clean."

Margaret nodded and grabbed the tablecloth and began tearing it into strips. She helped him wrap many pieces around Evelyn's midsection, securing the last one with a firm knot.

"What do we do now?" Julia asked.

"We wait."

Chapter 30

All things were born.

A ripped piece of bloodied tablecloth in his hands, Ainsley finally opened the dining room door. Everyone, Lord Weatherall, Daniel, and Lord Marshall all looked up expectantly. Ainsley nodded somberly. "She will need to rest," he said. "We won't know until morning. And we need to move her to a proper bed." Ainsley looked past the three men gathered in front of him. "Where's Billis?" he asked, knowing they'd need his strength.

Lord Marshall spoke up, "He took after Will when he ran off."

Ainsley was not sure how much time had passed. It felt like only a matter of seconds since the chaos ensued but in other respects it felt like an entire lifetime.

Lord Marshall stepped into the dining hall, as did Daniel, and together they transported Evelyn, wrapped in a blanket, upstairs to one of the guest rooms. While checking her pulse, Ainsley received a pat on the back, a gesture of reassurance from his father as he walked by.

"You did well," Ainsley heard him say from behind him, though Ainsley could not bring himself to look.

Hearing his father's footfalls down the hall Ainsley closed his eyes and bowed his head. He had always wanted his father to see what he could do, what his years of schooling had taught him but he had believed he'd never be given the chance. Despite this secret wish, he had never imagined that he would be charged with saving the life of a member of the family.

"How is she doing?" Margaret asked, peering in from the hallway.

Ainsley finally stood, brushing a tear from the crest of his cheek. "Her pulse is still weak," he answered quietly. "We will have to watch for fever."

Margaret came in and stood on the opposite side of the

bed. "Everyone is calling you a hero."

Ainsley shook his head. "I'm not a good surgeon, Margaret," he protested. "I take too long. If she gets an infection—"

"It will be God's will," she answered.

A slight chuckle left his lips. "Dr. Lehmann could have saved her, without question. Or Jonas, or any number of other surgeons. There is a reason they sent me to the morgue. I can't harm anyone who's already dead."

"Peter—" Margaret tried to call after him but Ainsley was already out the door.

☙ ❧

In the foyer, Ainsley saw Billis had returned, a vise-like grip on Will's upper arm. Lord Weatherall greeted Ainsley as he descended, a broad smile on the old man's face. "Bravo, young man," he said in a boisterous tone. He grabbed Ainsley's hand and shook it exuberantly.

Lord Marshall stood to the side, one hand shoved in his pocket, a crystal glass of brandy in the other. Ainsley could taste the liquid on his tongue and salivated for one of his own.

"I imagine having a surgeon in the family has some benefits, eh then?"

Ainsley eyed Lord Weatherall, daring the man to say what he was anticipating.

Lord Weatherall gestured to Will. "See what your man did to my boy?" he asked. Lord Weatherall gripped Will's chin and used it to turn his son's head back and forth.

Ainsley saw the beginnings of a bruised eye and a smear of blood at the corner of a fattening lip.

"There was a scuffle, sir," Billis said. The butler turned his head slightly, revealing a deep gouge on his cheek. "Cutter is prepared to summon the inspectors, sir," he said, gesturing to the footman beside him, "but Lord Weatherall believes there is no need."

Lord Weatherall smiled, somewhat nervously, "We all know my son has a hot temper, but punishing him for that—"

"I have seen men hang for lesser crimes," Ainsley

answered coolly. "Your son is guilty of the murder of one life and an attempt on another. He'd better pray that Evelyn survives or that charge will be upgraded." Ainsley looked from Lord Weatherall to Will, his eyes narrow with disgust. "Forgive me if I misunderstand you, Lord Weatherall, but are you asking me to overlook your son's crimes?"

Evelyn's stepfather began to shake his head profusely, "Of course not. I only ask that we consider the scandal. We wouldn't want Daniel and Evelyn to begin their new life with such a dark cloud—"

"As far as I am concerned there is no dark cloud for Evelyn and Daniel," Ainsley answered forcefully. "But there is one for you. What kind of man raises a murderer?"

"I beg your pardon?"

"I would tread very carefully, Lord Weatherall, because you are starting to look like an accessory."

Ainsley looked to the footman and cocked his head toward the door. "Go and be quick," he said.

"Wait just a minute—" Lord Weatherall tried to step forward to stop the boy but Ainsley placed a hand on his chest. Cameron ran past, opening the door and disappearing into the cold December night.

"Lord Weatherall, let's not create a scene," Ainsley said.

By the time Inspectors Simms and Wright arrived, Ainsley had treated the gouge to Billis' cheek, using some antiseptic and a salve from his medical bag. Each witness had been separated from the rest to relay to the detectives what had happened. Ainsley could not count on Lord Weatherall to give a truthful account but it mattered not. By the time Simms and Wright questioned Ainsley they had already placed Will in handcuffs.

"You are quite the man for attracting trouble, Lord Marshall," Wright said as Ainsley entered his father's study, where they were conducting their interviews.

"Perhaps," Ainsley answered.

"And your sister, she is quite the seamstress," Simms interjected.

Ainsley looked to the inspector, puzzled.

"Your father tells us you fished the bullet out and she stitched the wound," Simms continued.

Ainsley had thought his secret was out the minute he

took charge and tried to save Evelyn's life. It had never occurred to him to continue his charade, and now his father had devised a way to save face and keep his secret.

"Is that true?" Simms asked.

Ainsley smiled. "Yes, that's right," he answered.

"How did you know to take the bullet out?" Wright asked.

"I must have read it in a book, an account of the Crimean, I believe. I can't quite recall."

"And the weapon, a G & J Deane pistol, know where it might be?" Wright asked, looking over his notes.

"Our butler said there was no trace of it by the time he caught up with Will," Ainsley explained.

"Your father has given us permission to search the premises in the morning," Simms said, "I imagine we will find it before long."

Chapter 31

Ye will come never more,

The house fell into an eerie quiet once the detectives left, their quarry secured in the back of the police carriage. Margaret and Daniel kept a vigil at Evelyn's side and Lord Marshall had taken a bottle of scotch to his room. Ainsley was finally able to return to the dining room to reassemble his doctor's bag. He found the room already set to rights, a new gleaming lace tablecloth replaced the one Ainsley and Margaret had shredded for the procedure. The candelabras had been replaced and all evidence of any medical procedure had been erased. Julia was hunched before the small fire, shifting the pieces of burning wood, spreading the embers apart and encouraging the flames to dissipate. She turned and saw Ainsley behind her.

"Oh, beg my pardon, Lord Marshall," she said. "Mr. Billis has asked me to see to the room and take down the fire." She stood, holding the ash-filled metal pail in one of her hands, the iron fire poker in the other.

"No pardon is necessary," Ainsley explained. "I was just looking for my bag."

"Mr. Billis has it, sir," she said hurriedly. "I saw him leave the room with it. Perhaps he wanted it hidden from the inspectors."

Ainsley nodded, the full scope of his conspiracy and the numbers within his circle of trust expanding in his mind. He wondered how long he could keep his profession a secret. "Thank you," he said. He turned to leave but stopped at the door. "Julia, I should thank you."

"Whatever for, my lord?" she asked.

"Today you assisted without question. You could not have known my training as a surgeon."

"You spoke with such authority, sir," she answered, allowing her gaze to drop to the floor.

"You've been such a help to my family these past few

weeks. I know my sister has made your work here rather trying."

"Not at all," Julia answered quickly.

"I am afraid she thought you were a spy hired by our father. She has a tendency to wander from home and it's put her in a few undesirable situations."

"I don't believe it, my lord," Julia said. "Lady Margaret is a fine young woman of modest character."

Ainsley began to smile. "If you say so."

"If you don't mind me saying so, sir, I feel my position will come to an end soon," she said, her tone becoming quiet.

"Why would you say that?"

"With her mistress gone, Violetta could better serve Lady Margaret," Julia spoke slowly. Even in the dim light Ainsley could see her eyes gleam with threatening tears.

Ainsley began to shake his head but, in truth, he had no say in the hiring and firing of family staff. He'd like to see the girl stay. "I shall speak to my father."

"Oh no," Julia said quickly, "please don't."

"Why not? You have served us well."

Julia shook her head emphatically. "In truth, sir, I was not hired to serve the family as much as I was hired for an ulterior purpose."

"What other purpose could there be?"

"Lord Marshall hired me to keep an eye on Lady Marshall." Julia lowered her eyes, ashamed of her confession as she said it. "The late Lady Marshall, I should say."

Margaret's suspicions had not been far off the mark, Ainsley realized. Julia had been hired by Father to supervise, only she was not keeping a close eye on Margaret. "Father hired a spy for Mother?"

Julia swallowed hard and nodded. Perhaps she regretted saying anything about it.

"I have said too much," she answered quickly. She moved to step around him but Ainsley prevented her from reaching the door.

"Tell me," he said softly.

She could not look him in the eye. "He said he could not trust her maid to bring him information. Violetta had been her maid for so long. He wished me to befriend Violetta in the hopes she would give me some household gossip and—"

"And you would relay it to him."

"Yes, sir."

Ainsley's face became hard and tight as the meaning of her words registered in his mind.

"He did it out of love, I assure you. He was worried for her health and," she began to stammer, "her safety."

He could not help but smile. Hiring Julia had been a desperate act by a man worried for the woman he loved.

"I will confess to Lady Margaret this instant," Julia continued. Again, she made a move to bypass him and Ainsley moved slightly to the side as she passed.

It was the pinnacle of loyalty for both Violetta and Julia. His mother's maid had betrayed nothing and yet Julia remained steadfast to her assigned duty. Many English families could not count themselves so lucky and yet the Marshalls had benefited from many such servants, Billis included.

"Julia." Ainsley went to the foyer and saw her halted halfway up the stairs. "Let me speak to Father," he said, "I'd like to see you stay. He will listen to reason."

Julia gave a smile, curtsied slightly, and continued her ascent.

ॐ ॐ

Ainsley headed down the hall to the servant's stairs at the back of the house. Billis' office was across from the kitchen and, as expected, the butler was at his desk a small lamp burning bright on his desk.

"An eventful evening, was it not?" Ainsley asked as a way to announce his presence.

Billis jumped at the sound of Ainsley's voice and it was then that the young surgeon saw his medical bag open on his desk. Billis was applying a wet cloth to a set of parallel scratches running the length of his forearm. The wound appeared red and slightly swollen even in the ambient light.

"Billis?"

"It's just a scratch, sir," the butler answered quickly. He threw the cloth down and began to roll down his shirtsleeve. His gaze found the open medical bag. "I took the liberty of using some supplies. I shall reimburse you."

"I won't hear of it. Did Will give you these?" Ainsley asked, remembering the fight between the butler and Evelyn's brother. "Why did you not say?"

Billis swallowed but said nothing.

"Let me have a look," Ainsley said quickly.

"No." Billis put his hand up to prevent Ainsley from approaching.

"Billis, don't be a fool."

"I shall be fine, my lord," he insisted. "It just needs time."

Ainsley looked to the wound now that he stood closer and saw that there were already signs of an infection around the scratches. When he looked to Billis' face, Ainsley noticed he looked haggard and old.

"Billis, you do not look well."

"Only tired, my lord," the butler explained. He replaced the bottle to Ainsley's bag and clasped the top. Handing it to Ainsley, he let out a deep breath and found his normal composure. "Do you require anything else, my lord?"

Ainsley hesitated, returning Billis' gaze. There was something, Ainsley thought, something that was different about him. In truth, Ainsley had never concerned himself much with his family's servants. He had always had a jovial relationship with them but never much more.

Billis raised an eyebrow at Ainsley's hesitation.

"No, Billis," Ainsley answered at last. He accepted the medical bag Billis offered him and turned from the room. As he walked away, he heard the creak of the hinges and click of the latch behind him.

There was something about Billis' demeanor that unsettled Ainsley, who had always known him to be forthcoming and honest, not protective as he had just been. Ainsley made his way to the stairs that would take him to the main floor of the house. Turning the corner and grabbing the handrail, Ainsley stopped.

Those scratches were not from the fight with Will. The wounds had already completely healed over. Not enough time could have passed to bring the onset of infection and yet Ainsley saw the red, tight skin around his wounds.

Mother.

Ainsley dropped his bag and clung to the railing to remain upright, sure that he would vomit at the thought. Billis had forced his mother under the water. Jonas had suggested that Mother had wounded her murderer, given the evidence of her two broken nails. Ainsley slumped onto one of the steps, bending his knees and using them to hold up his hands as he lowered his face into them. The images swept into his mind, swirling quickly, but each one falling into place like the puzzle he had been constructing with Clara's shattered mirror.

Billis would have known Lady Marshall requested a bath thanks to Violetta's multiple trips to the kitchen for water. He had access to her room, and his sudden arrival would have been surprising but not out of the realm of possibility. But why? Why would he have reason to kill her?

Ainsley put a hand to his mouth.

Father.

Billis' loyalty was unmatched. He would have done anything to save Father from scandal or harm, and Mother had caused both.

Ainsley heard the familiar sound of the door latch followed by the creaking hinges. Slowly, Ainsley inched to peer around the corner and look into the hall. He saw Billis, dressed in his overcoat, hat, and scarf, making his way for the door that would lead him outside and up to the street.

Up the stairs to the main floor Ainsley went, hunting for his coat in a cloak closet in the foyer.

"Peter, what's the matter?" Margaret called from the top of stairs.

Ainsley turned, pressing an erect finger over his lips, telling her to hush. At the front door, he opened it a crack and peered out into the wintery street. Billis' footprints were unmistakable in the fresh snow, and Ainsley could see his silhouette making its way down the street.

Without thought, Ainsley pursued him. He hovered near doorways, ready to take cover should Billis turn to look behind him. The butler never did. Ainsley stalked him for half an hour, feeling the wet snow seeping into his shoes as he walked. He could not stop. No matter how chilled his body became, he could not turn back. Billis must know Ainsley had figured it out, or would soon, and now he was escaping.

Ainsley's mind was awash with all possible scenarios, motives, and opportunity running through each prospect as he shadowed his fresh suspect. Billis had been loyal to the Marshall family since before Ainsley was born, and before his parents were married. His devotion to Lord Marshall was hardly questionable but now Ainsley realized his loyalty stopped there. Billis never spoke kindly of the mistress of the house, Ainsley realized, and servants weren't permitted to speak unfavorably of them either. What had Billis said to Ainsley in his father's study? *"Your mother hardly deserves such a fuss...I have seen the pain she has inflicted on him."* Of anyone, Billis would know Lord Marshall's pain, a pain which Ainsley had been blind to for many years.

Tired of averting scandal, knowing how his master hurt and perhaps being fearful of what the future held, Billis solidified his loyalty and snuffed the fire that smoldered quietly, threatening everything.

He had been a fool, Ainsley realized, to side with his mother so blindly, to conveniently blot out the realities of her existence. He had not recognized her dependence and he had dismissed her immoral behaviour as rebellion against a tyrant of a husband. She had been a lost soul for many years and her death weighed heavily on him, as did his regret for not being able to save her.

The guilt he felt soon turned to thoughts of vengeance as he stalked Billis through the streets of London. The butler, his mother's murderer, walked with purpose and poise, as he always had while serving Ainsley and his family members. He couldn't help but be disgusted at the smugness of this man. He quickened his pace, determined to confront Billis on a street corner if need be.

The night was nearly morning and there were but a handful of people in the streets and no carriages about. The early aura of sunlight began to seep into the dark sky, but between the buildings where Ainsley and Billis trudged it remained night. Finally, Billis paused and raised his face to the gently falling snow and Ainsley stopped suddenly, his early resolve to bash this man's skull in gone when he saw Billis' profile. The man was no murderer. There must be an explanation.

It was then that Ainsley realized they stood in front of the North Western Cemetery, where his mother had been so recently buried. The iron gate was closed but not locked and Ainsley watched from the shadows as Billis pushed in the gate, the telltale drone of the iron bars moaning into the night as he did so. Ainsley slipped in through the opening that Billis unsuspectingly left and followed him into the city of the dead. Gingerly, Ainsley stepped, taking care to remain unseen. It seemed illogical for Billis to come to this place. He had expected the train station, not the gravesite of his newly deceased mother.

Billis stopped at the foot of her plot, the snow-covered mound evidence to its recent creation. Ainsley watched from the safety of a wide tree not ten feet from the butler. Once again, Billis looked to the heavens, and that is when Ainsley saw the glistening tear slipping from Billis' cheek. He was remorseful, Ainsley realized.

After a length of time, Billis pulled his hand from his pocket, Will's missing G & J Deane pistol gleaming in the moonlight as he raised it in the air, turning the mouth of the barrel toward himself.

No.

Ainsley stepped out from his place of hiding and rushed for Billis. "No!" he yelled, his arms outstretched, his feet slipping on the slick wet snow.

The gun fired one shot and Billis fell to the side.

"No, no, no." Ainsley's words slipped from his lips, a mantra of feeble reassurance. He slid into the snow at Billis' side and pulled to turn his body over. He had shot himself in the neck and the blood poured out like a faucet, cascading over Ainsley and the once-pristine white snow on his mother's grave.

Ainsley surveyed the gaping wound and began to cry out, knowing this victim he could not save. "Help!" he called with all the strength he could muster. "Somebody, help!" His voice cracked under the intensity with which he screamed. He began to rock Billis in his arms, as if a child.

Billis' hand left his side and reached for Ainsley's face. Blood slipped from the edge of his mouth and eventually overtook it. Gradually, the flow of blood from his wound slowed, as did the loyal butler's heart. Ainsley held tight, gritting his teeth against the scream of panic that threatened to overtake him. A man was dying in his arms and there was nothing Ainsley could do about it.

No, no, no.....God, no.

Chapter 32

For all things must die.

Eventually, the truth of Billis' guilt came out and the family learned what Ainsley already knew. Each person took the news in his or her own way. Daniel chose to deny the man's existence and focused his attentions on Evelyn's recovery. Margaret wept, not only because of the tragedy behind her mother's death but also the loss of a dear family friend. Lord Marshall, like Ainsley, retreated to his own world, a bottle of alcohol his closest ally.

In time, Evelyn recovered, having missed much of the scandal while sleeping off the pain, thanks to Dr. Lehmann's concoction, and woke to a somber house, the sorrow even more pronounced than prior to her surgery. Ainsley made a point to check on her numerous times a day, and was impressed by his brother's bedside devotion. Daniel had become doting, almost bothersome, in his concern for Evelyn. Perhaps her dance with death was what he needed to show that he cared, though perhaps it was his private escape from grief. Among all the heartache in the house, Evelyn's returning health was reason for joy.

"Doesn't she look less pale?" Daniel asked.

Ainsley pretended not to hear. He knelt at Evelyn's bedside, examining the wound and soiled bandages for signs of infection. Her temperature remained normal but her listlessness worried him.

"Daniel, please, your brother is concentrating," Evelyn answered, straining against some obvious pain.

"What do you see, Peter?" Daniel asked, ignoring Evelyn's warning.

Ainsley sighed as he looked over his hastily administered stitches. He must have shook too much, or perhaps he had pulled the threads too tight; whatever the cause, her wound looked less pleasing than if Dr. Lehmann had operated on her, or even Jonas, for that matter. Ainsley could hardly call himself a surgeon with such handy work attached to his name.

Evelyn must have seen the pensive look on his face. "What's the matter?" she asked.

"Nothing," he answered with a slight shake of his head. His melancholy could not be explained, at least not to the woman he had managed to save. His mother was not so lucky. And despite being present for Billis' death there was nothing he could do. But that did not stop Ainsley from replaying that night over and over again in his mind. He played out scenarios where he confronted Billis before he reached the cemetery, or chased Will himself to retrieve the pistol before Billis could. Such a choice would have come at a steep price though; Evelyn's life, and that Ainsley could not wish away. There was no other outcome to be had and yet that did not alter Ainsley's self-loathing.

After all, he was a good surgeon, just far too slow.

"My brother," Evelyn began, referring to Will for the first time since that night in the foyer, "he must have followed me, you see. Father says he was trying to protect me from scandal. I would never have gone..." Evelyn looked up to Daniel apologetically, "...had I known."

Ainsley placed a hand on hers as it rested on the top of her quilt. "Do not blame yourself," he said. "You will find no reasoning in the trespasses of a desperate man."

Evelyn smiled slightly but Ainsley's heart sank. He did not find comfort in his own words. The opposite was more true. It took all his remaining strength to reassure her troubled heart and yet there would be no relief for his own.

∾ ≍

"He's not himself," Ainsley heard his sister say as he walked down the stairs. The door to the parlour was open and he could see Margaret's silhouette in the doorway. "I don't think—"

Ainsley walked in and Margaret stopped abruptly. She had been speaking with Jonas, who was standing opposite her.

"Jonas came to see you," Margaret said quickly, acting as if they had been caught in a compromising position. "I was just about to send Violetta to fetch you."

Ainsley raised an eyebrow. "Well, now there is no need." He turned to Jonas. "If you have come on the behest of Dr. Crawford you came all this way for nothing." Ainsley walked past them both to the mantel. He pulled a cigar from his brother's box on the shelf and lit a long wood skewer in the fire. "I have no plans to return." He slid into one of the chairs and held his cigar up with an elbow on the arm of the chair and studied it.

"Peter, you don't smoke," Margaret said.

"I suppose it's better late than never," he answered sarcastically. He gave both Margaret and Jonas a sour look while lighting the end.

"Dr. Crawford did not bid me to come," Jonas said stepping forward. "Margaret did."

"It's been weeks," Margaret interjected, her voice more panicked. "You mustn't throw away everything because of..." Her voice trailed off as if unsure what to call it. How did one put into words the tragedies that had plagued them?

"I no longer wish to be a surgeon, Margaret," Ainsley said, avoiding her gaze. "I wish to be left alone."

"So you can drink yourself to death?" she asked, her voice cracking.

Ainsley met her eyes and did not bother to hide his amused smile. "If I so desire." He turned his gaze from them. "I shall be a man of leisure, pissing away my family's fortune, pairing up with innumerable women and all without the faintest care for anyone else but myself." He spoke quietly, suddenly ashamed of his pronounced bitterness.

"Your problem, Peter, is that you still believe you can save them all," Jonas said, "You never learned the necessary art of letting go."

"Why should I?" Ainsley muttered. Putting the cigar to his mouth he glared up at his school chum. "Is that not what makes us human? Our attachment?"

"Human or not, learning to let go helps us keep hold of our sanity."

The room grew quiet as Ainsley pondered this. He could not expect Jonas to understand the root of his malaise or diagnose his depression. Murderer or not, the real Billis, who had always been a part of their family, deserved a better end. Had he been a better surgeon, Ainsley reasoned, he might have done something instead of just watching him bleed out.

"And what if I no longer want to be a surgeon? What care should I have for my sanity then?" Ainsley asked.

Jonas raised an eyebrow, no doubt surprised at Ainsley's unwillingness to forge on as he had. Margaret's face hardened with anger but Jonas pulled at her arm, taking her from the room.

"He needs time," Ainsley heard Jonas say in the hallway.

"He will regret this," Margaret sobbed.

Their conversation continued and eventually Ainsley was able to drown out their voices, concentrating instead on the crackling of the fire and the gentle droning it made as it consumed the wood logs. He heard the doorbell but cared not. The house had been inundated with visitors for many nights, with callers seeking the latest gossip disguised as condolences.

"Where's Dr. Ainsley?"

Ainsley closed his eyes against the sound of the familiar voice, his entire being wishing it were someone else come to call. He thought to leave, dispatching through his father's study and to the back stairs of the house, but as he summoned the energy to lift himself from the chair Inspector Simms walked through the door.

"Simms," Ainsley breathed, cursing his sluggishness. He had only needed a few seconds more.

With his hat in his hands, Simms looked even more wearisome than Ainsley. Jonas and Margaret slipped into the room behind him but said nothing.

"My apologies for calling at your home," Simms began, his voice raspy. "I sent someone to the hospital to fetch you and I was told you hadn't been back since..."

Would he ever have a conversation without a reminder?

"What is it?" Ainsley asked rather shortly.

"We have a body I would like you to look at, well, a number of bodies actually." Simms glanced to Margaret behind him. "Pardon my frankness, Lady Margaret, I need your brother here to help me with this puzzle."

Ainsley began to shake his head but Simms continued.

"At first, we thought it was just a brutal murder, but we found a second victim not far from where the first was found."

"How many days between the first murder and the second?" Jonas asked.

"A week, sir." Simms looked back to Ainsley. "We found another an hour ago. I'd like you to come quickly to help me read the scene."

Ainsley turned and ran his free hand through his hair, rubbing his face in frustration. Was he never going to be allowed peace?

"Dr. Ainsley, I have never seen the likes of this." Simms swallowed. "He's killing children."

All Things Will Die

by Alfred Lord Tennyson (1809-1892)

Clearly the blue river chimes in its flowing
Under my eye;
Warmly and broadly the south winds are blowing
Over the sky.
One after another the white clouds are fleeting;
Every heart this May morning in joyance is beating
Full merrily;
Yet all things must die.
The stream will cease to flow;
The wind will cease to blow;
The clouds will cease to fleet;
The heart will cease to beat;
For all things must die.
All things must die.
Spring will come never more.
O, vanity!
Death waits at the door.
See! our friends are all forsaking
The wine and the merrymaking.
We are call'd–we must go.
Laid low, very low,
In the dark we must lie.
The merry glees are still;
The voice of the bird
Shall no more be heard,
Nor the wind on the hill.
O, misery!
Hark! death is calling
While I speak to ye,
The jaw is falling,

The red cheek paling,
The strong limbs failing;
Ice with the warm blood mixing;
The eyeballs fixing.
Nine times goes the passing bell:
Ye merry souls, farewell.
The old earth
Had a birth,
As all men know,
Long ago.
And the old earth must die.
So let the warm winds range,
And the blue wave beat the shore;
For even and morn
Ye will never see
Thro' eternity.
All things were born.
Ye will come never more,
For all things must die.

About Tracy L. Ward

A former journalist and graduate from Humber College's School for Writers, Tracy L. Ward is the author behind the best-selling Marshall House Mysteries which tells the story of morgue surgeon, Dr. Peter Ainsley, and his highborn sister, Margaret Marshall, as they solve crimes using early forensic science. Currently, Tracy lives on a rural property outside Barrie, Ontario with her husband and their two teenagers.

To find out more about Tracy's books follow her on www.facebook.com/TracyWard.Author or visit her website at www.gothicmysterywriter.blogspot.com